CARNIVAL

A LOU THORNE THRILLER

KORY M. SHRUM

This book is a work of fiction. Any references to historical events, real people, or real places have been used fictitiously. Other names, characters, places, and incidents are the product of the author's imagination. Any resemblance to actual persons, living or dead, business establishments, events, or locales is entirely coincidental.

No part of this book shall be reproduced or transmitted in any form or by any means without prior written permission of the publisher. Although every precaution has been taken in preparation of the book, the publisher and the author assume no responsibility for errors or omissions. Neither is any liability assumed for damages resulting from the use of information contained in this book or its misuse.

Cover design by Christian Bentulan

TIMBERLANE
PRESS

CARNIVAL

AN EXCLUSIVE OFFER FOR YOU

Connecting with my readers is the best part of my job as a writer. One way that I like to connect is by sending 2-3 newsletters a month with a subscribers-only giveaway, free stories from your favorite series, and personal updates (read: pictures of my dog).

When you first sign up for the mailing list, I send you at least three free stories right away.

If giveaways and free stories sound like something you're interested in, please look for the special offer in the back of this book.

Happy reading,

Kory

1

———

Lou sat in the dark of the car, low in the seat so that she could not be seen through the window. She relied on the shadows to conceal her as they always did. Her eyes remained fixed on the front door of 1882 Cherry Lane. It did not open.

She checked her watch again, the face illuminating as she rotated her wrist toward her. It was 9:49.

He was cutting it close. Maybe Jeffrey Fish wouldn't visit the grocery store tonight. Maybe he would stay home and pretend he was a good boy.

Lou knew better.

The front door swung open, momentarily revealing a brightly lit living room decorated in mauve. A boy zoomed a red airplane in the air above his head. Then a man stepped into Lou's line of vision and the boy was gone.

Fish stood on the porch in the cascading light. His mouth moved and Lou could hear the low drum of his voice, though his words were indiscernible across the street. The porchlight haloed his soft brown hair, loaning him a deceptively angelic appearance.

When the woman came to the door, wringing her hands in a checkered dishcloth, Lou sat up. She hadn't seen the wife before and was more than a little curious. The woman was pretty, with a round face and bright eyes. Her full cheeks made her look younger than she was.

Do you know about him? Lou wondered, searching her face. *Do you even suspect, maybe only in the back of your mind, that you're sleeping with a monster?*

Lou didn't think so, as the wife leaned forward and accepted the kiss her husband planted on her cheek.

With a bounce in his step, Jeffrey descended the porch and marched briskly to the waiting black SUV.

The little boy with the red airplane briefly reappeared before his mother closed the door.

Lou slid back down in her seat as the SUV's taillights flicked on.

She watched the vehicle reverse from the driveaway and head east, driving away from Lou's hiding place. The engine was disturbingly quiet—electric maybe? At the end of the road, the car paused at the four-way stop. When she saw the right blinker turn on, she smiled.

"Show me your real face," Lou whispered. *Show me what you* really *are.*

Her bones thrummed with excitement. She sat up and wrung the steering wheel with both hands.

Please.

Instead of turning on the car and following Fish through the moonlit streets of Mount Vernon, Lou took a breath and let the darkness swell around her. She closed her eyes, feeling it envelop her in its totality. When she couldn't hold her place any longer, she slipped.

The world dematerialized. A sensation like cold silk slid over her skin, and then she was through. The frosty interior of the car was replaced by the chilled brick wall under her bare hands. Her nails scraped against the concrete grout.

She pushed away from the wall, leaving the parked car half a mile away. It wasn't her car, after all. She'd only used it as a convenient hiding place while scoping the Fish residence. Boosting a car certainly wouldn't have worked in her favor anyway. Police involvement only complicated things. She'd leave the cops to King.

Lou had her own way—a *better* way—of tracking this man.

Lou surveyed her surroundings. She stood in the deep shadows collected beside the grocery store's western wall.

It protected her from a bitter midwestern wind, but already her skin had begun collecting frost from the air. Her cheeks and mouth grew cold. Water pooled in the corners of her eyes.

The parking lot had only five cars in it. Unsurprising, since the store closed at ten on weeknights. She surveyed the lot and the line of trees encroaching on it.

Her eyes remain focused on the road, searching, waiting, for any sign of Fish.

At 9:54, the black SUV swung into the parking lot, bouncing as it cleared the yellow speed bump, and took the empty space closest to the door. The engine clicked off. The lights died.

Fish jogged across the parking lot, the collar on his jacket slapping lightly against his throat.

I could take him now, Lou thought, her restlessness rising up in her again. *I could step out of this alley right now and just grab him.*

But her curiosity was too great. She wanted to know if she was right.

Fish made it into the store unharmed. Lou sighed and leaned against the brick. Nothing to do now but wait. Not that Fish had actually come for groceries.

Sure, he would pick up whatever menial item his wife had sent him to retrieve, some last-minute necessity like bread for their son's lunch tomorrow.

But if Lou was right, Jeffrey Fish wasn't here to shop. He was here to hunt.

A mother and daughter exited the store four minutes later. The kid blasted music in her headphones so loud that Lou could hear it even from her hiding spot. They drove the red Corolla off the lot, reducing the cars to four. Three guys carrying a case of beer each appeared next. After putting the beer in the trunk, they took possession of the silver Volvo.

Jeffrey Fish returned with a small paper bag tucked into the crook of his arm. He climbed into his SUV, but didn't drive away.

"What's wrong? Did you forget something?" Lou whispered mockingly from the dark.

Six minutes later, she appeared.

A young woman, brunette with an angular face and dark eyes, stepped from the store. She held the green apron that all the grocery employees wore in one hand and had a canvas bag slung over a shoulder.

Well-behaved women rarely make history was printed in block white letters across the canvas tote. She stuffed her apron inside it and rummaged for her keys. The lights of a blue Honda flashed.

Jeffrey Fish visibly tensed in the front seat of his SUV.

"You like that?" Lou whispered. She licked her chilled lips.

And what would you think if you knew you were the one being watched right now?

Lou saw only his chest and a slender white hand on the steering wheel. A shadow cut across his jawline, hiding his face. But Lou knew hunger when she saw it.

It was in the way his hand opened and closed on the

wheel as if aching to reach out and take what it wanted. The way his chest rose too quickly in short, tight breaths.

She knew hunger.

She had her own.

Behind the wheel, the girl turned on her car, adjusted her rearview mirror, and reversed out of the lot.

For a moment the SUV only sat there as the Honda's taillights grew smaller and smaller.

You can go home, Jeffrey, Lou thought. *Take a shower. Brush your teeth. Make your son's lunch. Fuck your wife.*

But when that slender white hand finally turned the key in the ignition, he didn't head in the direction of home.

Instead, he turned right onto the main drag, following the blue Honda's trail.

Lou smiled.

She took a deep breath and pressed her back to the brick wall. The cold seeped through her leather jacket. She enjoyed it, feeling that rough grit brush against the back of her knuckles before letting the darkness overtake her again.

Groundlessness. Weightless freefall. And then the world was made real. Earth formed beneath her feet. The grocery was gone but the night had not changed.

Her hand grasped onto the bark of a thick tree trunk. She lost her footing on the enormous root sloping down into the soil, but regained it, digging her boots into the dirt. Old trees were good cover. The shadows beneath enormous branches were complete.

Lou regarded the house across the street. It was a farmhouse in a cul-de-sac with two big picture windows punched in front. This configuration gave Lou the impression of a worried face. The light was on, illuminating a covered porch and the swing hanging to the left of a turquoise door. The paint looked fresh even if the rest of the house sagged.

After ten minutes Lou checked her internal compass. But there was no pull, no inner wisdom saying she'd gotten it wrong, that she was needed somewhere else. Not that she couldn't imagine all manner of ambush. Maybe Fish decided to rear end the girl. He'd pretend to be a concerned and apologetic citizen, before dragging her off the shoulder into the woods.

Headlights appeared at the end of the road, and Lou's patience was rewarded. The blue Honda swinging into the paved driveway didn't have any dents. The young brunette climbing from the driver's side seat looked unharmed, if tired from her day.

She was already inside the house when the SUV rolled up and parked across from the house on the opposite side of the street.

Lou's side—mere feet from her hiding place beneath the tree.

I'm right about him. I know what he is. That means he's fair game.

She could slip into the dark of his car, wrap her hands around his throat and pull him—well, anywhere. She'd take him to her dumping ground, to the lake half frozen with winter, a place of endless night. She would put a bullet between his eyes and watch the light click off.

Or maybe she would play with him first. Maybe she would let him fight her, just so she could enjoy breaking him.

When it was over, and Jeffrey Fish could no longer prey on the women of this world, she would drag his body into the water and—*no, Louie.*

It was King's words in her head. The bothersome private detective had somehow become one of four voices that now polluted her mind. And it rose, principled and insistent, even now.

We are playing a different game this time, he had said. *This game has rules.*

Lou sighed, her breath fogging white in her face.

They were playing a different game all right. Lou wanted to know how much time they had left on the clock.

How long could Fish go before he *had* to kill? Once Lou herself had taken nearly two months off of killing and it had nearly killed *her.*

She hadn't been able to sleep. She'd eaten only when necessary.

She'd used her body like a punching bag, offering herself up to any half-cocked asshole stupid enough to take a swing.

Was Fish's hunger the same?

Did it make his skin itch the way Lou's sometimes did? Did it feel like cold fingers sliding into his skull, obliterating all thought, replacing all rationality with a single, desperate need? Did it prevent him from sleeping, or sitting still? Did it make him reach for a gun, just to hold it as he paced the floor —or was that only her?

His charade of normalcy worked well enough. Hadn't that been her first thought when she'd seen him in the Huntington Park playground two days ago?

His son had been swinging on the monkey bars while Fish had pretended to read a novel. He'd turned the pages after the appropriate pauses. He'd kept his head tilted down as if carefully regarding each page.

He presented himself as the picture of suburban acceptability in his pressed dress shirt and khakis. He had clean fingernails and a washed, shaven face. The mothers watching their children had regarded him with mild interest. No suspicion had creased their faces. One had asked him about the book.

How well you disguise yourself, Mr. Fish, Lou had thought, knowing Fish couldn't have seen the words on the page.

And what was he thinking now? As he sat in his dark car, watching the house, what was he thinking? Feeling? Deciding?

Inside the house, an upstairs bedroom light clicked on, illuminating a white closet door and the foot of a bed. The girl was in pajamas now, her hair pulled up off her face. It was red and shining, freshly scrubbed. She wore glasses. She bent to plug in her phone, connecting the charger to the small device.

The light clicked off.

The driver's side door of the SUV opened, and Lou dropped into a crouch.

Two shining leather shoes stepped out onto the street. The heels ground into the pavement. She slipped around the side of the tree to get a better view.

Jeffrey was halfway across the street, standing in the moonlight. His shirt shone, wrapping him in a spectral glow. His chest was visibly heaving as he stared up at the dark window. His fists were clenched at his sides. The shirt fluttered in a light breeze.

No, Lou realized, he was *trembling*.

Go in, Lou begged silently. *Go in and try something. Come on.*

Her palms itched. She licked her lips, shifting her weight from one foot to the other.

It was as if she was watching her hunger grow in proportion to his.

With a grimace, Fish grabbed a fistful of his hair and pulled as if yanking his whole body back to the car.

He grunted and changed course. He threw himself behind the wheel. The door slammed loudly.

The SUV hooked a U-turn in the dark street. The tires squealed.

Lou watched the SUV go, the red taillights like hungry eyes in retreat.

The bedroom light clicked on again, showing the young woman framed in the backlit window. She was also watching the taillights fade into the distance.

This is a different game, King had said.

A game that, Lou hoped, didn't get this woman killed.

2
___

R obert King parked his '98 Oldsmobile by the curb outside the row house. Police crawled the lawn and sidewalks like a parade of oversized ants, going in and out of the door with clear plastic bags in their fists.

"Stay here," he told the dog sitting upright in the passenger seat. Lady, a regal Belgian Malinois blinked her brown eyes at him. "I'll whistle if I need ya."

King swung his large body out of the car and crossed the patchy lawn. He waved at the officer guarding the door to get her attention.

"Mr. King, you can't be comin' around here." Clarice McGee's voice was stern, but she gave him a toothy smile, revealing the large gap between her two front teeth. "Do I have to chase you off again? You come to the station and ask your questions. Those are the rules."

"Dick called me in for a consult," King said. He shifted his weight to the hip that wasn't throbbing and pulled his hands out of his pockets. He held them up in surrender. "I wouldn't be here otherwise."

It was true that in the fourteen months since he'd opened his PI office, The Crescent City Detective Agency, he'd crossed paths with the local PD often. Follow up questions and points of clarification could be handled over the phone, but sometimes King needed to see the scene of a crime to make sense of a report. He had to track witnesses to see if he could catch them contradicting their own statements and if he'd seen something for himself, it was easier to note where the witness had gotten it wrong.

The police didn't care much for a meddlesome ex-DEA agent poking around unless they were the ones who'd hired him—and sometimes they did. But mostly it was private clientele, including lawyers and even the DA, who called on him to stick his nose where it doesn't belong.

"Robbie!" a man called. Detective Dick White's voice was deep and robust. "Get in here."

With another apologetic shrug, King angled himself under the yellow tape.

Clarice let him pass, but didn't bother to hide her eyeroll. King would've been hurt had he not seen the smile tugging at the corners of her lips.

King followed Dick down the narrow hallway. Officers turned sideways to pass each other, angling their bodies carefully as to not touch the walls where hidden fingerprints or evidence might remain.

The smell of sweat and cigarettes was strong. Yet neither of these strong scents could mask the putrefaction growing stronger the closer they came to the back of the house.

The hairs in King's nose burned. He knew what he was going to find even before Dick opened the last door on the left. He swung it wide, hearing it bounce off the wall behind it.

King's breath hitched. He reflexively covered his mouth and nose with his hand.

"I should've warned you," Dick agreed. "But you've seen worse with the DEA, right?"

King managed a nod, but he couldn't tear his eyes away from the scene on the bed. It was true that the DEA encountered plenty of murder crime scenes. But since he'd left the DEA, the only dead bodies he'd seen had been those that Louie Thorne—his dead wife's niece—tended to leave in her wake. It was admittedly quite the body count. But Lou was cold, methodical. She killed as a means to an end.

But this...*this*...

A woman was splayed on top of the covers, a stiff and scratchy patchwork of fabric. King wasn't sure what color the blankets had been at the start of their life and it no longer mattered. Now they were soaked in blood.

Her silk negligee was a festoon of crimson splatters from neck to groin, staining the fabric where it had been slit. Her eyes were rolled up into her head, her mouth still partially ajar. Two of her upper teeth were gold and her lower lip had a hoop ring looped through it.

One of her legs had been partially severed, above the knee.

The mangled mass of meat and white bone poked through —King looked away.

The second body was that of a man slumped against the wall. His clothes were mostly clean. But the wall behind his head was splattered with brains and blood from a gun blast.

Dick was chattering away. "He stabbed her thirteen times then shot himself in the mouth. It looks like that happened *after* he tried to cut off her leg."

"Christ," King said. The woman's toes were painted a bright aquamarine. It clashed with the rest of the room and King's eyes just kept coming back to them. "I didn't work homicide. There better be a good reason you called me here."

Because making him look at something like this for no reason would've been a sick joke.

"Oh, right." Dick turned to the closet covering the wall opposite the bed. "At first we thought it was just a domestic dispute. A crime of passion. But then we found this."

Dick opened the closet and King whistled.

Part of the plaster had been cut away to reveal brick after brick of cocaine. They were piled on top of each other like a secret hidden wall within the wall.

King scratched his chin. "That's a lot of dope."

"There's more."

"How much more?"

"It's behind every wall," Dick gestured at the house around them.

"*What*?" King's laughed, unable to believe it.

"*Every* wall." Dick insisted. "Every cut we've made, we've found it piled up from floor to ceiling. It's way too much for a humble couple living a quiet life in the The Big Easy, don't you think?"

"It's too much even for heavy dealers."

"That's what we thought. The knife had the man's prints on it, but now we're wondering if maybe the woman was tortured to get him to talk. It's still possible he offed himself out of guilt for not saving her. Or maybe the mysterious third party hurt the woman, then shot the man before framing him. Either way, we're hoping if we learn more about the drugs, we'll learn about these two. Right now, we don't have anything on the man at all. No name. Not even a wallet with a driver's license in it. The woman is Rita Cross. She owns the house and works as a hairstylist in Treme. But she isn't married and doesn't have this guy's name on even the utility bills. So who the hell is he?"

King whistled. A second later, someone—probably Clarice

—yelped. Then Lady was in the room looking up at King expectantly.

He gave the dog the sign to search the house for evidence. With a delighted yip, she put her nose to the ground and started in on her work.

"Damn smart dog," Dick said.

"Yeah."

"Where'd you get her from?"

"The NYPD. I'm friends with a guy up there. They said that she was perfectly trained as a dual-purpose dog. The department's original plan allowed for the recruitment of six dogs. Then a budget cut revised it down to four. They decided to keep the males and let the two females go. I was able to convince my friend to sign over ownership of Lady in exchange for reimbursing their expenses."

"Budget cuts, man. So, she's from New York?"

"Europe actually. Demand for these dogs is so high right now, nine out of ten of these dogs are imported."

"You're lucky to get her," Dick agreed.

"Damn lucky. Except my French is shit."

Dick snorted. "Excuse me?"

"She learned her commands in French. And my pronunciation is no good. It's why I prefer the hand signals. She listens better to Mel."

"I didn't know Ms. Mel spoke French."

King shifted his weight, trying to abate the ache in his low back. It snuck up on him these days if he stood for too long. "She's got that Creole background."

Dick laughed. "Of course she does. Well, I'll send what we've got about the house, the drugs and these two to your office. Piper's usually quick getting back to me."

"She is," King agreed. "But she'll be in and out for the next two weeks. Carnival."

"We're spread pretty thin ourselves."

King suspected as much. The flood of tourists also meant a flood of police force in the Quarter. Probably another reason why calling in a local PI seemed so attractive, if manpower is thin.

Dick gestured to the hallway and King was relieved for permission to leave the room. It was the painted toes—those damn turquoise toes—that he kept seeing.

Dick closed the door behind them.

Lady barked twice and King looked at the ceiling, tracking the sound.

"She got something?" Dick asked, his hand still on the bedroom doorknob.

"Let's see." Though he had no doubt. Lady really was a damn good dog. He'd only had her for eight months but his affection for the animal was unlike any he'd had for a pet before.

King mounted the stairs, following the sound of Lady's instructive yips.

He found her at the top of the landing, her paws on the base of an open window.

"What have you got?" King asked her, ignoring the worsening ache in his lower back as he crested the stairs.

Lady hopped out the window onto the slopping roof. She scratched at the shingles.

"That isn't going to cave in," Dick said supportively. "If you think you can squeeze out of that thing."

King was able to squeeze through the window with much effort, collapsing onto the shingles with an undignified *harrumph*. His back was definitely talking to him now. He saw a Vicodin and a long nap in his future.

Dick laughed behind him.

"I don't see you coming out after me," King called crossly as he pulled himself up.

Lady's paws framed a splatter of blood about a quarter in size and another beside it, no bigger than a dime.

"Good girl," King said and gave the dog an affectionate scratch behind the ears. He reached into his coat pocket and found one of the treats he kept there now. He never knew when he would need to reward Lady for her work, so it was just easier to keep his pocket stocked.

Lady lapped the treat from his hand.

"What is it?" Dick asked, his head hanging out the window, giving the impression of a guillotine about to come down on the back of the man's neck.

"Blood," King said, seeing his reflection on the drying pool. "Call someone up here to collect it."

3

Melandra had just closed her loft door when the telephone rang. Her hand hovered above the handle.

"No, *nuh uh*," she said aloud, shaking her head. She was supposed to turn over the open sign on the front door of her shop four minutes ago. She wasn't taking calls right now that would put her even further back in her day.

She was late because she'd overslept—and she *never* overslept. But she'd tossed and turned much of the night given the unbearable din of the street outside her window. It was Carnival in New Orleans, a time when an already restless French Quarter fell into a fever pitch of revelry.

Two weeks, Mel reminded herself and her splitting headache. *Two weeks and this will all be over...*

Mel, being the light sleeper she was, found this part of year to be wretched—even if her sales did quadruple as the tourists flooded the Quarter. It seemed everyone wanted their fortunes told and pockets filled with voodoo trinkets.

Money aside, it had still been dawn before the ruckus quieted and she'd finally been able to doze off.

The phone rang again. Melandra turned her key in the lock with a huff.

Nobody called her landline these days anyway, except old friends and telemarketers. If the former, they could leave a message on the answering machine that she'd had since 1999. If they were telemarketers trying to sell her a time-share condo in Florida, they didn't need to bother with the message.

Melandra adjusted her shawl around her shoulders, and backed away from the door despite the small knot forming in her stomach. She descended the metal staircase that bridged the two loft apartments above Melandra's Fortunes and Fixes and the occult shop occupying the first level.

Her bangles clanked noisily against the rail. She surveyed her domain.

The shop was quiet and wrapped in the long gray shadows of morning. She glanced at her watch. 10:05.

Outside the storefront window, with the decal of her business logo printed on its front, a bike messenger whizzed by. He rang his bell twice to alert a woman crossing the street. Otherwise, the area was quiet. No doubt the drunks would be back in the streets by noon, after a late, boozy brunch, taking full advantage of the city's open container law.

God, she hated Carnival.

Head buzzing and eyes burning, she unlocked the front door. She pushed it a little to make sure it would swing. Then she flipped the sign from Closed to Open.

Her bangles continued to jingle on her wrist as she moved about the shop, preparing for a fresh onslaught of shoppers looking to kill the hours until the sun went down and the next round of debauchery began.

She checked that all the candles were forward facing, labels out. She untangled the glittering beads hanging from a hook and straightened the crooked *5 for $1* sign. The Carnival masks were fussed over as well, turning a few toward the window to catch the eyes of passersby.

She checked her appointment book, knowing she would be busy well into the night and guessed where she might squeeze in her food and bathroom breaks.

The back-to-back readings she didn't mind. Using her gifts was one way to channel her own restless energy and gave her a real chance at sleep. For once, exhaustion would work in her favor.

Lastly, once the rest of the shop was ready, she lit incense —deciding on myrrh today—and two candles: one for Mother Mary, another for St. Jude.

She considered these unconscious choices for a moment and wondered if they were a warning. That knot in her stomach hardened a bit more.

Her gaze softened on the candles' flames and the room dimmed around her.

Almost, she thought as she felt the world disappear. *There*. Something was coming through all right. A dark shape. A shadow. Perhaps a woman walking toward her? Or a man...?

The shop phone rang, high and strident. Goosebumps rose on her arms.

She turned from the flickering candle flame, listening to the sound. There was something about its tone she didn't like.

Bad news, she thought. *It's felt in the bones.*

She answered on the fourth ring knowing already it wasn't a customer. She gave the standard greeting anyway in case she was wrong. It wouldn't be the first time, especially on as little sleep as she'd had the night before.

"Melandra's Fortunes and Fixes."

"Mel!" Her name came out in one long sigh of relief. "God above, why are you so hard to get ahold of? I thought you'd done changed your number on me."

"Janie?" Melandra leaned a hip into the glass counter either for support or relief. She couldn't be sure. It wasn't that she wasn't happy to hear from her cousin. It was only that she couldn't shake that feeling nipping at the back of her neck.

This wasn't an expected call. No birthday or holiday today. *So why now?*

"Everything all right up there?" Melandra ventured.

"Oh me and the girls is fine, *yeah*. Not that you'd know. Your ass ain't been back here in what?"

"Six years," Melandra said without hesitating. She wasn't one for guilt trips. "Funny thing is I hear cars travel both ways. Like money."

Melandra had sent money to all her family when they asked for it.

Janice did too. Her tone turned saccharin sweet. "Hey now. I know, I know. It's just so hard with the girls in school. And they got so many *practices*. You wouldn't believe. Band *practice*, cheerleading *practice*, math team *practice* whatever the hell that is."

Melandra felt the knot in her stomach tightening. The longer her cousin prattled on nervously, the more worried she became.

"If everyone is all right, then why you callin' me, Janie?" Without meaning to, she heard her own accent deepening, spreading out. It always happened, when she spoke to her people back home.

There was an audible pause as Janie licked her lips. "Now don't get mad. I didn't have to call you and tell you nothin', but that wouldn't be right. I wanted to call. I *wanted* to. You *remember* that now."

A hard stone dropped somewhere deep inside her. The worrisome turning of Melandra's stomach gave over to full nausea. And then all at once she knew the truth. "Terry is out of jail."

Janice clucked her tongue. "Now how'd you know that? Damn, I swear, you are just like Grandmamie, ain't you?"

Her pulse roared to life in her ears. The room moved on a tilt. She reached out, found the countertop and seized it.

"You there?" Janice asked. "Melandra!"

"I'm here," Mel managed despite her tightening throat and the panic pressing in on her, compressing her vision. All the spit had left her mouth. She licked her lips futilely, finding them parchment dry. "When did he get out?"

"I don't know. But he was here three days ago. He visited his momma out at that home. She don't even know him, got Alzheimer's, and all that. But he went and seen her anyway. He also went to see his girl."

"Alexis?"

"Yeah, his kid, but she didn't want nothing to do with him. She's married with a big house and two little ones. When the hubby flexed on his ass, he left without putting up much of a fight. *Big* surprise. He ain't done nothing for that girl. And she's a good 'un. She got her schoolin' and got a good job. She don't need no dog like him around."

Melandra grabbed hold of the back of her neck. It ached now. It was as if the muscles there were being squeezed by a large, unforgiving hand.

"He came around here too, asking 'bout you."

No, her mind said. *No, no, no.*

Janice kept speaking, unaware of the way Melandra's world spun around her. "I didn't say nothing, mind you. Not a damn word. But Tommy went and opened his big fat mouth like he always do."

Melandra eased herself into the chair before her legs gave out beneath her.

"Tommy got to talking about how everyone was faring these days, you how he likes to shoot the shit. Big ol' lips just flappin' in the wind. He got around saying you were doing well down there in The Big Easy. That you had yourself a nice little shop in the French Quarter and wasn't hurting for no money."

No, no, no, no. Her mind was screaming now.

"I'll have you know that after Terry left, I slapped Tommy upside his damned head. I said, 'Why'd you go and tell him all that for? He don't need to know her business. And he's like, "He's her husband.' And I'm like 'on paper. Not in any of the ways that matter.' I swear he's as smart as a box of rocks, that man."

Mel was on this side of hysteria when a sharp, uncompromising voice cut through her consuming fear.

Get ahold of this. Get ahold of this right now. Don't you lie down when there's a snake in the grass. I raised you better than that.

This was her grandmother's voice. And though Grandmamie had been long in her grave, Mel could've no sooner shut off this voice than cut off her own hand.

She straightened on the stool, adding steel to her spine.

"How did he seem to you?" Melandra said. Her voice wasn't perfectly steady, but that was all right. She was asking the right questions again and that's what mattered.

"Like Terry," Janice said. "He's lean now. Before, ya know, he had a bit to him, but now he looks like one of those dogs that Bubba Rick fights out off Longfellow Road. And he got..."

She faltered.

"Tell me," Melandra said. "You called to tell me, didn't you? So tell me."

"I don't know." Janice sounded sincere. "I don't know what it was but there was something about him. Something about him had changed, you know?"

"Twenty five years in prison will do that to you," Melandra said.

"Yeah, maybe. Maybe that's it. But there was something

about him. It was just a feeling but I don't know. Shit. I just wanted to call you."

"Thank you for that," Melandra managed. She wasn't feeling particularly grateful, truth be told. She felt like the world had just served her a giant pile of shit and demanded she eat it.

"Well, I gotta be gettin' off here but you call me, all right? If you need me. Cars *do* go both ways. I know it."

"Yeah, all right," Melandra said. "Thanks for calling, Janie. I mean that."

And she did.

The moment the call ended, Melandra dropped her phone onto the counter. She put her face into her hands, taking deep, desperate breaths.

Three days. Three days. Her mind repeated it over and over again. *He's been out of prison for three days.*

And it took no time at all to get to New Orleans, did it?

Why didn't he tell me he was getting out? Why—But she knew.

It was just like Terry to sneak up on her like this and she had no doubt he was heading her way. If he could get a car, hitch a ride—and didn't he have enough friends left to manage it—he could be down here...now.

He could be here now.

With shaking hands she searched her robes for her tarot deck. *Grandmamie's* tarot deck. It reminded her of the way she used to search her pockets for cigarettes when her nerves were really bad, back when smoking had been the only way to relieve them.

A ghostly moan circled the shop and the flickering lights startled a scream from Melandra. Another high pitched scream met it, the sounds twining.

"Christ!" Piper exclaimed. Her hand went to her chest. "What the hell? It's just me."

Melandra's hands shook all the harder.

"What are you doing?" Piper crossed to her, letting her backpack slip off her shoulder and hit the floor. Her face pinched with confusion. "Mel, what are you doing?"

"I can't find my damn cards. I can't find them!"

"They're right here." Piper pointed at the wrapped bundle on the glass, a rectangle of black velvet tied neatly with a piece of red ribbon.

Melandra didn't even remember removing them from her pocket, but she must have. She must have reached for them while she was still talking to Janie.

Her hands shook so badly as she unrolled the cards that they spilled from the wrapping.

"Help me," she begged. She offered the cards to Piper with shaking hands. "Help me!"

A calm overtook the girl. It surprised Mel. Usually if someone acted hysterical it induced hysteria in others. Piper seemed to grow calmer, more patient in direct balance to Melandra's outburst.

That's from dealing with her junkie mother, Mel thought distantly with that part of her still in control of itself. *She knows what to do when the world is unraveling.*

Piper held Grandmamie's cards in her hand—something she'd never been allowed to do before—and the look of awe on her face told Melandra she was well aware of it.

"What's happened?" Piper licked her lips. She tucked her blond hair behind her ear with her free hand, the cards grasped in the other. The silver rings in her hand caught the light from the chandelier sparkling. There was a small mole on her right thumb and Mel found herself focusing on that. Right now, she'd take *anything*.

"Mel?" Piper asked gently. "What do you want me to do?"

"A three-card spread."

Piper shuffled the cards without having to be told. Over

and over again they rolled between her nimble fingers while Mel grappled with the terror writhing inside her.

Get on top of this, Grandmamie said. *Get high so you can see that damn snake.*

Piper held out the deck, offering it to Melandra.

Mel closed her eyes and exhaled slowly. She knew that old deck so well she couldn't pick its cards with her eyes open. Every crease, every worn edge—she knew what they were. And if she was going to do this right, she had to blind herself to what she *thought* she knew.

Grandmamie, she prayed. *Help me.*

A feverish chill ran down her spine.

Melandra's fingers traced the cool edges of the cards. The feather-soft grazing of card, after card, after card, until a tremor of electric fire sparked in her fingertips. Then she pulled that card, laying it on the countertop only to begin trailing her fingertips over the cards again.

Tick, tick, tick, tick... Her fingernails caught on the edges.

Another spark, a rush of heat up into her hand, and she pulled that card, too. The heat only deepened when she moved to the next card, so she pulled it as well. Just to be sure, she traced her fingers over the deck once more. But there was no heat on this pass.

The cards were chosen.

Melandra opened her eyes.

Piper gathered up the chosen cards. "You want to flip it or me?"

"You can do it," Melandra said. It didn't matter.

Now that her eyes were open, Mel knew which cards lay before her. Every crease and blemish was recognizable, even when the cards lay face down.

Piper caught the end of the first card—the one representing her past—and flipped it over. A man, half goat, half human stared up at them with soft brown eyes. His head was cocked like a bird's, quizzically with a hint of a mischievous smile playing on his candlelit face.

"The Devil." Piper looked up from its worn image to Mel's face.

"Go on," Mel said. She sounded composed now, far more composed than she felt. Though her lips were still brutally dry, the desiccated skin rasping together as she spoke.

Piper turned over the second card—this one representing her present circumstances—and saw The Wheel of Fortune. "A second major arcana card. This is some fated shit."

"The next one is major arcana too," Mel said calmly. She knew that slight crease on the upper edge, that place where the black background had been worn away to show a bit of the card stock beneath.

Piper flipped it over. Upon seeing the card, she shifted uncomfortably. "Death."

Devil. The Wheel of Fortune. Death.

Sometimes the bills just come due, Grandmamie said. *They just come due.*

She clasped her hands so they would not shake.

"Mel, seriously. What the hell is going on?" Piper tapped the cards, looking from the ominous images up into Melandra's face. "This looks... serious. Like, are you–"

Mel interrupted her speculation. "Don't you worry about it. It's my concern, not yours."

Piper seemed not to hear. She was tapping the Death card. "Is this Lou?"

"No, I don't think so," Melandra said. Then with more certainty. "No, not this time."

Mel was relieved to find that the steel in her spine was holding. At least enough to get her out of this damn store.

"I'm going back to bed," Melandra said, gathering herself up with all the strength she had.

"We just opened."

"My head hurts and I didn't sleep well last night. You run the shop until I come back down, okay?"

If Piper wanted to argue, she swallowed those protests as Mel mounted the stairs to her apartment slowly, aware that Piper's eyes were fixed on her back.

That's why Mel kept her head high and her steps measured.

It wasn't until she closed her apartment door and collapsed against it that she allowed herself to cry.

4

Piper stared at Mel's apartment door for a long time after it snapped closed. She'd never seen Mel so upset before. She considered the woman's personality synonymous with *cool and collected*. Hell, just last year they'd been kidnapped by Russian mobsters and Mel had acted like it was an inconvenience rather than a very possible ending to all their lives. An *inconvenience*.

"What the hell just happened?" she whispered to the empty store.

Piper realized now as she gathered up the cards, she'd built Mel up in her mind. Up until this moment, the woman had been almost godlike. She'd idolized nearly everything about her: her independence, her business savvy, her take-no-prisoners attitude, the way she saddled up and handled whatever arrived on her doorstep like a woman with a pen and a to-do list to obliterate. Given Mel's proximity to King and Louie, this to-do list might include anything from dirty cops to murderous criminals, oh, and let's get another case of Nag Champa in by Wednesday.

She was amazing.

But the woman who had risen from the stool just now had been *shaking*.

Mel—*shaking*.

"What the hell just happened?" she whispered again. She flipped through the cards, trying to make sense of what she saw. She lifted the first closer to her face as if to read it better.

The Devil.

This could be read any number of ways, of course. It could be self-deception. Or it could be a literal person who messed with someone's head or got people into trouble. Either way, it was definitely viewed as a negative force. Piper was pretty sure that Melandra had asked for a past-present-future spread, though she couldn't be sure. There were a lot of ways to throw down a three-card spread. But assuming this was a past-present-future reading, did that mean someone from her past was coming back around? Was this person going to fuck with her?

Piper considered the card beside the Devil—the Wheel of Fortune.

She often thought of the Wheel of Fortune as the karma card.

Change. *What comes around goes around.*

This notion melded with her interpretation of the Devil. A troublesome person coming back around for...what exactly?

It didn't explain the blind fear that she'd seen in Mel's face or the way that she'd practically fled from the shop with all that bullshit about a headache.

Okay, maybe she had a headache, but Piper wasn't stupid. What had scared her? What could stress her out so badly to trigger a migraine? They'd survived shootouts, and what in the world could be worse than a mob boss threatening to kill them all while a gun was pressed to her head?

Piper sighed and lifted the third card.

Death.

Her thumbnail traced the dark hood covering the bleached white skull. In all honesty, this card used to freak Piper out. That was before she'd come to associate the card with Louie. That was a pretty morbid outcome on its own, wasn't it? She wasn't supposed to look at a card and think, *oh hey! I think my good friend Louie is going to get up to some shenanigans again. Better check on that girl.*

She did want to check on Lou. It had been a couple of days since she'd heard from her. Carnival week had sort of washed over them like a tsunami wave, carrying all of them out to a sea of sleepless nights and harried days. King had cut her hours back as much as he could so that Mel could get the extra support in the shop. But this chaos would continue until the first Tuesday of March.

She sighed, regarding that white-washed skull again, noting that the skull resembled a mask. Carnival. Masks. People pretending to be what they aren't...Lies masquerading as truth.

Secrets surfacing.

In essence the Death card was another card about change. Lying beside The Wheel of Fortune and the Devil, it suggested some serious shifts in Mel's life.

If Piper was being honest with herself, it had been a quiet year. Oh, she'd been busy as hell with her two jobs, moving into her new apartment, and resuming classes—all while trying to hold together something that looked like a social life.

But busyness aside, the year had been blessedly free of drama. As long as she ignored the guilt-laden texts from her mother.

Regardless, this spread certainly suggested their momentary peace was coming to an end, because while this hadn't been her spread, Mel was family.

Mel was *family*.

Whatever the hell was about to go down, Piper wasn't going to let her face it alone.

"It was fun while it lasted," Piper murmured, turning the cards over as if the images offended her.

The lights in the shop flickered and the chandelier moaned, but Piper didn't notice either, still engrossed in that terrible memory of Mel shaking as she demanded Piper read her cards.

She was so afraid. So, so afraid. But of what??

"Why can't people just tell me what's going on? God, use your *words*," Piper groaned.

"As a rule, people are poor communicators," a voice said.

Piper's gaze snapped up and her heart dropped. All the air left her in a single *whoosh*.

Dani smiled, pushing her hair behind her ear and flicking her eyes down. "Hey."

"Hey," Piper said, reflexively. "What are you doing here?"

And why do you look so damn good.

Dani was wearing a low-cut white blouse that contrasted against her skin. Her jeans were tight to her hips. Her dark hair was longer than Piper remembered and fell over the front of her gray woolen coat. The diamond solitaire hanging from a thin, almost invisible wire kept drawing Piper's eyes to her chest.

"The sign says open," Dani said with a half-smile. "Have my reading skills deteriorated?"

Piper bristled. *Don't come in here and act cute with me.* "I thought maybe you came by to pretend to be into me again, you know, so you could milk me for another story."

Dani wrinkled her nose. "Yeah, I did that, didn't I?"

Piper settled onto the stool. *Act cool*, she told herself as she tried to affect an indifferent pose. *Just play it cool.*

"So are you here for a story?" Piper asked tapping her fingers on the glass.

"No, I have some information for King." Dani pressed her lips together.

"Do you?"

"He's working on a case for the assistant DA."

"I know—" Piper scoffed. She knew about every case coming across their desks.

Dani shifted her weight. "I'm just delivering the goods he asked for."

Piper felt like someone had punched her in the guts. "What?"

Dani shrugged. "I went by the office to drop it off, but it's locked up. His cell phone is turned off so I thought I'd see if he was here."

Her mind was trying to wrap itself around these details.

Not only was King still in contact with Dani, maybe he'd been in contact with her *all year*. And *how* hadn't Piper known?

"He was called in for a consult with the NOLA PD this morning," Piper managed, feeling a little better that she knew *something* Dani didn't.

Dani extended the envelope toward her. "I can leave the information with you."

"If it's so top secret, how do you know I can be trusted?"

Dani snorted. "Take it."

Piper didn't and Dani put the envelope on the counter with a sigh. Piper looked at it, then up at Dani. "I'm sorry, *how* is this the first time I'm hearing about you working with King?"

"Because I've been avoiding you." Dani pushed her hair behind her ears again.

Piper laughed. "Why would you avoid *me*?"

Because I was the one who visited you in the hospital every day after you got tortured. I was the one that asked Lou not to kill you even though you were going to run your little journalist mouth about her to the press. And I wasn't the one who pretended to fall in love with you just for some stupid information.

"I feel pretty shitty about what I did."

Piper scratched the back of her head. "Well it was a shitty thing to do so..."

Dani's cheeks flushed.

The overhead chandelier moaned, flickering again.

It was the door chime, announcing the arrival of six very hungover-looking women entering the shop. They were bleary-eyed and yawning.

Piper greeted them as her job required before turning her gaze back to Dani.

"Listen, I'm sorry I didn't call you back." Dani spoke softer now that they weren't alone. "I should've but I...I have my reasons."

The pitiful fact was that Dani was as beautiful as ever and Piper was the first to admit that beautiful girls were a personal weakness.

Against her will, something inside Piper softened. "I'll give this to King."

With a huff, she reached out and took the envelope, moving it to her backpack on the floor.

"Thanks. I know it's safe with you." Dani turned, took a few steps toward the door. And Piper thought she was going to leave.

That's it, I guess. Am I just going to let her go?

Before she could decide, Dani whirled back around.

"Do you want to have dinner sometime?"

The words came out of Dani's mouth in a single rush.

Piper snorted. "Dinner?"

I was sucking your face off in that closet last year, we shared a near death experience together, and now you want to act like we've just met?

"I want to talk more about everything that's happened, well, after Dmitri, but you're busy right now and I need to get back to The Herald anyway. We could do a drink if you'd rather—"

"Dinner's fine," Piper said as the chandelier moaned again. Three more customers stumbled across the threshold laughing. And so the rush began.

Dani glanced at the customers. "How about The Praline Connection, tomorrow night? Eight o'clock?"

"Okay."

"Please come," Dani added with a sad smile, backing toward the door.

Before Piper could reply, two of the girls approached the counter, blocking Dani from view.

Piper plastered on a grin that she didn't feel. "Just the skull candles today? And a voodoo doll keychain! Excellent choice."

She glanced at the door one more time as she accepted the customer's credit card, but Dani was already gone.

5

Lou sat up in bed. Only it wasn't her bed. She ran a hand over the coverlet and surveyed the room. Before her was a large window, rounded at the top reaching all the way to the floor. The curtains covering it had been pulled apart, framing the Arno River. Guessing by the light, purple in its iridescence, it was nearly twilight in Florence. Laughter carried up to the room from the streets outside.

There was a small desk against the wall—no note on it— and then the bed she sat in, which was pinned between the stairs leading to the lower level of Konstantine's apartment, and the bathroom on her right. All was quiet except for the noise carrying up from the city itself.

She was alone.

She ran a hand over the covers beside her again as if trying to divine the answer to the question circling her mind. *Had he been here when I slipped into his bed?*

It had happened a lot this year—her tendency to lie down in her bed, in broad daylight, with every fluorescent bulb in her apartment turned on just in case—and still wake up in Konstantine's bed.

Her ability to shift through shadows had always been dependent upon the darkness itself. She couldn't transport herself in daylight. That was a fact. So why hadn't she been able to keep herself in her own bed?

Or maybe it's not about the light at all, a little voice chided. *Maybe it's about being where you want to be.*

Another curiosity, apart from waking in Konstantine's bed four or five times a week, was the way he received her.

He never woke her.

He never wrapped himself around her body or kissed her. He simply let her sleep.

In the fourteen months that this game had been going on, when she had awoken to find him there, he would smile. Only then he would reach out and place a hand on her hip or speak softly to her, but never before she woke.

And she couldn't help but wonder why.

She pulled back the covers and found she was still wearing the clothes she'd worn when scoping Fish the night before. Black cargo pants and a black t-shirt. She crossed to the bathroom, splashed cold water on her face and used his comb to smooth down her hair. Running his comb through her hair felt strangely intimate.

Far more intimate than anything they'd done in the last year.

She placed the comb on the sink and met her gaze in the mirror. Dark hair, dark eyes. Not unlike the grocer girl that Fish had followed home.

I'm your type, Fish, she thought. Not only in her coloring, but also in her jawline.

One step through Konstantine's closet, and she found herself in a cathedral.

It wasn't Padre Leo's cathedral. The old man had named

Konstantine as heir to his dark empire and his exiled son, Nico had blown it to pieces. This church, though not as opulent, was its replacement.

What had Konstantine called it? *Sufficient.*

He'd used this word more than once and Lou simply didn't understand. It was beautiful.

The ceilings rose far above her head, with stained glass filtering the light through the chapel.

The floor, columns, and walls were all old stone. She could spend years tracing each intricate carving with her finger and not take in every detail, every inch of art.

Better still was the silence that hung in the air. Hundreds of years had hollowed out the place, and left it cold, sacrosanct. Just how she liked it.

Sufficient.

Soft voices echoed through the shadows.

Lou traced the exterior of the room, following the familiar sound of Konstantine's voice.

When she stepped around the last column at the end of a long row, Konstantine himself sprang into view. Twilight filtered through a window above him. The way the light hit his dark hair gave the appearance of a halo, reminding Lou instantly of Fish and how he'd looked as he leaned forward to kiss his wife.

Was Konstantine any different than Fish? Lou thought so.

While it was true that the *capo di tutu capi* had his own body count, and had admitted to torturing when necessary, for Konstantine it was never about the kill.

It wasn't about revenge or feeding a hunger. It was about furthering an aim. His actions served an ambition that he wished to see to fruition. And even then, violence was a last resort.

But what about Lou? She had no underworld empire to

secure or grow. She no longer had a family to avenge. All she had was her hunger, the hunt, and the kill.

Surely that made her more like Fish than Konstantine, didn't it?

Lou circled the chapel, watching Konstantine issue orders to the men gathered there. Twelve of them were strewn about the pews. They asked questions—all in Italian, of which Lou knew very little—and Konstantine responded, gesturing as he spoke.

Though she didn't understand the context of the Italian, she liked his voice. Its easy roll rumbled in her chest in a way that reminded her of her father. His voice had also been deep.

Women's voices trailed across the face and ears, but Konstantine's voice rolled through her body. The soft bass vibration of a favorite song.

He turned toward her suddenly, looking in her direction, though Lou was certain he couldn't see her in the shadows.

Still, a smile tugged on his lips and after only a few more minutes of instruction, he sent the men away.

He watched them go, hands in his pockets. His back was to her.

When they were alone, he spoke. "Ciao."

He faced her, still relaxed. He crossed to her with an easy smile on his face. But he stopped just short of where the light became darkness. "How did you sleep?"

"I seem to like your bed better than mine," she said.

His smile deepened. "I am not complaining."

He gestured toward the pews. "Did you understand what I was saying just now?"

He was trying to see her face, she realized. She stepped from the shadows into the edge of the light so he could.

His smile softened.

"No," she said. "Your English is much better than my Italian."

"We are preparing for Carnivale," he said. "We've been invited to visit an associate in Venice. I was giving instructions for our visit and what should be done here in my absence."

Lou's attention pricked with excitement. "Are you expecting to be ambushed in Venice?"

It had been a long time since she'd murdered a bunch of gangsters. Her hunts were one or two at a time these days, a markedly slower pace than what she was used to. She wouldn't have minded the chance to stretch herself.

Konstantine laughed. "Sorry to disappoint you, but no. Vittoria and I have known each other for a long time. I don't expect her to betray me."

"An old friend, huh?"

Konstantine reached for her. She stepped forward, allowing him to touch her.

"If only that were jealousy in your voice," he lamented. "I would be thrilled."

It was her turn to laugh. "Why?"

"Jealousy means possessiveness. It means you consider me *yours*. Nothing would make me happier."

Here they were again, skirting the unspoken. They'd done this dance for fourteen months. Konstantine would circle around this issue, clearly trying to discern what she wanted from him—how much she wanted—and Lou would duck away from the questions. Or she would make a joke.

As she was about to do now. "I came to collect you from Nico, didn't I?"

"You came to kill me yourself."

She looked away, aware that his hands were still on her forearms, his thumbs running over her skin.

"And how long will you be in Venice with *Vittoria*?"

He pulled her closer until their bodies touched, hip to hip. When he spoke, she felt his breath on her hair. "A few days. We have contracts to negotiate and she's very stubborn. I suspect that she won't make it easy."

Lou was tall enough that her chin was at his neck and collarbone. She placed a sudden kiss there, already inhaling the scent of him before she realized she was doing it.

His arms wrapped around her instantly, reflexively, holding her against him.

And she returned the embrace. Had they done this before? Simply stood there and held each other? She didn't think so.

Her heart began to speed up in her chest.

Lou pulled her gun.

She pointed it at the man crossing the cathedral. He froze, mid-step.

Konstantine didn't release her when he spoke. "I would never *creep* up on her if I were you, Stefano. That's how you get a bullet in the head."

Lou was certain Konstantine spoke English for her benefit.

If Stefano was worried about being shot, he hid it well. He was the picture of composure now with his shoulders relaxed, and head slightly cocked.

"*Buonasera.*" He slid his gaze from Louie to Konstantine. "*Hai una telefonata, signore. È molto importante.*"

"You've got a call," Lou said, catching the gist of it.

Konstantine squeezed her once more before reluctantly letting her go. "Will I see you later?"

Konstantine's unbridled hopefulness made her smile. She shrugged. After all, it wasn't that she was consciously choosing to come to Konstantine's bed. "Maybe."

He bent and placed a kiss on her throat, almost the same place where she'd kissed him.

"Until then."

With a stiff nod to Louie, Stefano turned and followed on his master's heels.

Lou lowered her gun, watching them disappear into the bowels of the church.

KONSTANTINE WAITED UNTIL THEY WERE ALONE IN THE long hallway that led out of the church before he voiced his concern to Stefano. "You enjoy interrupting us."

"*Quella cagna ti distrae*," Stefano said beside him. *That bitch distracts you.*

The words sent red hot fury through Konstantine's body. He whirled and seized Stefano by the collar. He threw a punch into the man's jaw, feeling the bone creak under his knuckles.

Stefano's head rocked back, his shoulder hitting the wall hard. The breath left his lungs in a *whoosh* felt across Konstantine's neck.

"Never call her that again or I will put a bullet between your eyes. Do you understand me?" Konstantine's hand burned and his chest heaved with anger. "*Dimmi che capisci?* Speak of her as if she were *my wife*."

When Stefano didn't answer, Konstantine slammed him against the wall again.

Stefano rolled his eyes up to meet Konstantine's. "*Capisco.*"

Konstantine released him with a shove.

"But it's true." Stefano touched his jaw with a grimace. "She distracts you and you don't even care. It should have been you to pull a gun on me. Admit it. You didn't even hear me."

Konstantine hadn't. He'd been thinking of his body against Lou's, and marveling at how natural it had become to hold her after so many years of longing for it. They hadn't consummated their relationship—and he hadn't pressed her because there was a terrible certainty in his heart that the moment they did, she would leave him.

"I'm in my own house. What do I have to be afraid of?" Konstantine asked, rolling his neck.

Stefano pushed off the wall. "Did you learn nothing from Nico? Nothing at all?"

Konstantine remembered the ambush. The alarm raised as his own men were slaughtered from within. Mutiny had been part of Nico's strategy. He'd turned half their gang against Konstantine. But Konstantine had methodically culled all traitors from his ranks since that night.

Of course, that meant bringing new men into the Ravengers, men who did not share a history with Padre Leo, or Konstantine himself. Men who might be more loyal to the money he put in their pockets than to himself. For that reason alone, it didn't pay to be lazy with his own security, did it?

Stefano was not one of these men, which was why Konstantine listened. Stefano was like a brother. A tempestuous little brother who often touched a nerve, true. But his loyalty could not be questioned.

"You didn't even hear me," Stefano repeated, cursing.

"I have a lot on my mind," Konstantine said, straightening.

"Of Carnivale?" Stefano asked with an arched brow.

It was a generous offer because they both knew he hadn't been thinking of Carnivale. Konstantine remembered the way Lou looked the night before, when she'd appeared in his bed.

He'd gotten home late. Preparing to leave Florence for even a few days proved to be a monumental task. Coordinating crews, supplies, procuring a suitable gift for Vittoria, all while overseeing the day-to-day operations of his gang had kept him up until well past midnight. It was nearly one in the morning when he'd arrived and stumbled up to his bedroom, too footsore to change into his bed clothes.

His bed had been empty when he'd stripped down and put on loose pants, leaving his chest bare. Then as he was brushing his teeth, a peculiar feeling had overcome him, like a change in pressure between his ears.

He stepped from the bathroom, toothbrush still in his mouth and there she was, curled into his pillows as if she'd been there all along.

She hadn't even awoken when he bent to pull the covers over her.

He was careful not to disturb her when she slept for fear she might disappear like a mirage. It was enough for him that she was beside him—that whether she was willing to admit it to herself yet or not—she was choosing him, slowly, night after night. It was the surest sign of progress he had.

He wanted that to continue.

And just now, in the cathedral, she'd openly walked into his arms.

His heart hitched.

"You must admit she has made things much safer for us," Konstantine said. "After Nico and then Dmitri, our rivals won't even look at us crossly."

"Because they think she's a devil you've sold your soul to in exchange for all the power you have, and that if they hurt you, she will hunt them down and eat their children."

Konstantine smiled. "I don't care why they are afraid, the result is the same. No one wants to challenge me."

And it was true. They had already feared her before Konstantine had crossed her path—whispers of a woman who killed criminals in the night. It frightened them how she could appear, disappear without a trace. But then they'd believed she was a curse on the Martinelli family. It was his father's men, shipments, and sons she was murdering—

mostly. But that shifted with Nico, with his complete and utter obliteration and now no one understood whose side this mysterious woman was on. Only that if they came for her, or for Konstantine, they would die. They need only look to Nico and Dmitri's mistakes to see the truth of that.

It had helped that the underworld had already greatly feared Nico and Dmitri. How much worse Lou must seem to them, when she can destroy their nightmares so easily.

"It doesn't matter what they believe. I'm safe with her," Konstantine insisted.

Stefano sighed. "That you think this, scares me."

"I cannot spare you that burden," Konstantine said, stopping Stefano with one hand. He inspected his friend's jaw. He wiped away a smudge of blood with his thumb before lightly slapping Stefano's cheek.

Stefano resigned himself to this affection. "At least *she* is paying attention. And I don't think she'll let anyone else kill you."

Konstantine shook his head and smiled. "No, I believe she wants that honor for herself."

"And what about the times when you're not with her?" Stefano asked, stepping from the shadowed hallway into the courtyard leading to Konstantine's private offices.

Konstantine spared him an affectionate smile. "That's what you're for."

6

The chime above the agency's door dinged and King lowered his copy of The Herald to see who had entered.

"Okay!" Piper called out, tossing her red backpack on the floor. "You've got some explaining to do, *sir*."

King reached for his coffee mug. He tilted it to his lips and found the coffee cold. He grimaced.

Lady's tail thumped on the floor upon seeing Piper. Piper acknowledged this with an affectionate pat on the dog's head, but didn't take her eyes off King.

"Seriously, you better fess up."

"It would help," King began, pushing back his chair and crossing to the coffeemaker. "If you gave me an idea of what you want me to confess to."

Piper threw an envelope down on his desk. King recognized it as one of Dani's assembled info packets. "Confess to the fact you've been working with one *Daniella Allendale* behind my back!"

He topped off his coffee, the carafe clattering back onto the burner. "I wasn't doing it behind your back."

Her mouth fell open as she gazed up at him from the floor where she squatted beside the dog. "How could you?"

"By telephone. Though sometimes we meet in person."

"Be serious!"

King laughed. "She's an investigative reporter. It's what she does."

Her hands went to her hips. "*I* get you the details you ask for."

King took a long sip on his coffee, trying to cool it with his inhale alone. Sensing that there was an accusation in this somewhere, King placed his bet. "It's not like I think she's better than you at the job. But sometimes we need extra hands. You *know* this."

And it was true. King couldn't comfortably take on any more cases if he'd wanted to. He'd turned down three spouses seeking to confirm infidelity this week alone. With his aching back, he couldn't imagine hiding in bushes, climbing trees, or hobbling after husbands and wives in this cold weather anyway. But that wasn't the point.

Piper threw up her hands, her face getting redder with every word. "I don't understand how I didn't know. I'm involved in *every* case that comes through here. You've never *once* mentioned her. You never asked me to call her to confirm something. You never sent me to pick something up or mention where your source info came from. *Why?*"

"I didn't realize I was supposed to," he said. Frankly, he was doing his best to keep his nose out of Piper's business. "Lou has been working with her too. Hasn't she said anything?"

"What?" Piper's outrage spiked. She collapsed to her knees on the floor. "*Are you kidding me?*"

Lady saw this dramatic display as an opportunity. She rolled onto her side, offering her tawny belly.

The door at the end of the office opened and Lou stepped out, closing it behind her.

The room was nothing more than a storage closet, pitch black, and empty, but Piper had jokingly put a name plate on it that read Ms. Thorne as if it were an actual office.

Lou froze as soon as she took in the scene. "What's wrong?"

"Traitors!" Piper said, pointing at Lou and then King. "Both of you."

Lady pawed Piper's hand, reminding her about the belly offer. Piper began to absentmindedly rub the dog's stomach.

King sipped his coffee again. "Piper wants to know why we didn't tell her Dani has been part of our investigations."

Piper scoffed. "Damn right I want to know."

"I thought you didn't want to talk about her," Lou said.

Piper placed a hand on her chest. "When did I say that?"

Lou pushed her mirrored sunglasses up onto her head and frowned. "I asked if you've seen Dani and you said, 'I don't want to talk about her.'"

"I was *joking*."

Lou arched a brow, bending down to give Lady a good scratch behind the ears.

Piper sighed and folded her arms across her chest. "So what have you guys been doing with her exactly?"

"It isn't like we've been having secret sleepovers and not inviting you," King said. The urge to add cream and sugar to his coffee rose but he batted the temptation away. He was trying to keep his diet clean until Fat Tuesday. He'd promised himself a box of paczkis if he could manage it.

"Okay. Fine. But I don't like it when you guys don't tell me things." Piper openly pouted now. "It makes me feel like I'm not part of the team."

King laughed. "What are you talking about? Of course you're part of the team."

Lou was watching the girl with a curious expression. Then she said, "She asked me about you."

Piper visibly perked up. "Really? What did she say?"

"How's Piper."

Piper inched forward. "And what did you say?"

Lou shrugged in her leather jacket. "I said you were fine."

King didn't understand the look of disappointment crossing Piper's face.

Lou's frown suggested she didn't understand either. "Was I supposed to say something else?"

King crossed the office, skirting around the puppy pile and took his seat behind his desk once more. "Honestly, we just ask her to make phone calls or fact check for us."

Piper stood from the floor, brushing invisible dirt off her knees. "Speaking of phone calls, Planned Parenthood called me back to let me know my STD tests were clean."

She scowled at Lou.

"Why did you give them this number?" King folded the paper again and placed it on the corner of his desk, out of the way. He was searching for a coaster for his coffee. Maybe he would find it faster if he weren't trying to sip his coffee at the same time.

Lou shrugged inside her leather jacket. "I used Piper's name to get an STD test."

King choked on his coffee. Neither of the women seemed to notice.

"It was smart going to the Baton Rouge clinic. They would've recognized you here." Piper clasped her hands behind her head. "And I'm all for protecting your anonymity, babe, but now my sex history is all messed up. Do you know how long it took me to convince them I don't need birth control?"

"Why don't you need birth control?" Lou asked, deadpan.

"Do you know how lesbians have sex, Louie? Do you need a diagram?"

Lou's lips twitched. "Maybe."

"Why are you worried about being clean?" King asked, then as if realizing the words that just came out of his mouth. "None of my business, is it?"

He found a coaster from Richard's Crab Shack and put his mug on it.

"It's not a sex thing," Piper said. "I convinced her to get the tests because she's always fighting these guys with open wounds. They bleed. She bleeds. It's just cross contamination. Don't make that face. This is a good thing! It took me two months to convince her to get these tests."

"Congrats on your bill of health." For some reason King was relieved.

"Yeah," Piper agreed. "But that doesn't exonerate you from keeping Dani a secret. I feel like you've been cheating on me."

Lou reached out and placed a hand on the back of Piper's neck. Piper's face reddened by three shades, but her shoulders visibly relaxed.

"Okay," Piper said finally, as if Lou had spoken. "Yeah, I'm being dumb."

King watched them smile at each other. Lou slowly took her hand off the back of Piper's neck and it gave him the distinct impression he'd missed something.

A strange warmth spread through his chest. *Lucy would love this*, he thought. Lou with a friend her own age would've made her happy beyond belief. Not that she'd believed her niece incapable of friendship. But how often had Lucy expressed in those last months of her life, that she'd worried about Lou being alone?

If she isn't connected to anyone, what will she do once I'm dead, Robert? She'll only have her revenge. I don't want that for her.

King had done his best to assure his wife that he would look out for Louie after she was gone. But watching Piper and Lou together now, both playfully rubbing down the dog on the floor, King knew he'd had no part of this, not really.

King turned over his watch and realized what time it was. "Aren't you supposed to be at the shop?"

Piper quit baby-talking the dog and shrugged. "Mel told me to go home."

"Wasn't it busy?"

"Yeah and she spent the morning in bed with a headache. But when she got up she told me she had it covered and sent me home."

Interesting. "She seem okay to you?"

She shrugged. "Don't you need me to do something around here?"

King saw hesitation flutter across her face. He could press harder about Mel or he could drop it. Maybe it was nothing but her lingering insecurity about Dani. He made a mental note to check in on Mel later just to be sure. To Piper he said, "You got homework?"

"That's the thing about asynchronous online courses, man. I can do my work whenever I want and no, I'm caught up for this week. I worked ahead thinking I was going to be too busy during Carnival."

King pointed at the empty desk across from him. "I'll send you the witness reports for the Henderson stalking case. Can you get them organized by timeline for me?"

"*Can I?*" she huffed.

King let this slide, understanding that he could expect more of such comments until Piper forgave him for this Dani blunder. "And then I'll have you make some phone calls."

"Sure you don't want *Dani* to make the calls?"

King tilted his head.

"All right, all right." Piper gave Lady one last pat, retrieved her bag from the floor, and crossed to the desk.

Lou stood, tugging at the end of her leather jacket as if it had ridden up. She met King's gaze. "Any updates for me?"

He gave her a quick once-over, hoping he wasn't being obvious.

But she looked good. Her face had more color these days and the bags under her eyes were gone. He suspected that she was finally getting some sleep after months of insomnia.

Not that he could judge. Lucy's death had laid him to waste too.

For a month after her passing, he'd slipped back into his drinking habit, his shitty eating, and deep depression. It had taken him months to get back on the horse of clean living.

Melandra had taken such good care of him in the wake of Lucy's death. He wasn't exactly sure what he would've done without her insisting that he eat, sleep, and take a goddamn shower.

He hoped he could repay her one day.

The detective agency had also helped. Work had always been his preferred form of escapism. Between work and a renewed mission to look after Lou—the last piece of Lucy left on this planet—King had managed to cobble together a decent reason for living, as old and tired as he was.

King opened his desk drawer and grabbed the napkinned bundle resting in the top drawer, between a stapler and a wad of rubber bands. He unwrapped the bologna and cheese sandwich he'd packed that morning and leaned back in his chair.

"Both the video tapes and the witnesses you delivered were crucial to closing the Wilkins case. It was pivotal. We won it."

Lou didn't even acknowledge the praise.

King took a big bite of his sandwich. He spoke around the lettuce filling his cheeks. "How'd you get Sholanda to talk?"

Lou did smile now, a gentle tug on the right side of her lips. "Trade secret."

"The jury lapped up her story. The guy's going to jail for at least twenty years and that's with parole and good behavior."

"They should kill him," Piper said without looking away from her laptop. "Eighteen little girls walled up in his basement. Christ. But *no*. Just because the judge thought he was a 'good Christian man', they let his ass go. So freaking gross."

"I might pay him a visit," Lou said with a sinister smile. This one reached her eyes.

King imagined her stepping from the shadows and wrapping her fingers around Devaroe's throat. A squat, middle-aged man with a hooked, warty nose, no doubt he would squeal like a pig at the sight of her.

"Speaking of crazy bastards, did you get rid of Miller?" Piper asked.

Lou answered without turning around. Her eyes remained on King. "Two days ago."

Piper shuddered, making her chair creak. "Good. I can sleep better knowing that guy isn't out there doing God-only-knows-what."

"Bothered you, did he?" King asked, between bites.

Piper gave him a disgusted look. "He hunted blond women—" She paused in typing long enough to point at her own blond hair. "Tortured them for days in his sound-proof apartment and then when they died from the torture, he fucked their corpses. Sometimes for *weeks*. Hell yeah I'm glad he's dead. I just don't understand how he was allowed to go free in the first place."

"Hung jury," King said, sucking mayo off his thumb.

"Because of his girlfriend's testimony. How could she lie like that?"

"Maybe she loved him."

Piper scoffed. "If I found out my partner was sexing up corpses, that would be a hard pass for me. Thank you, *next*."

"He had a corpse in his apartment when I took him," Lou said, sliding her shades back down on her eyes.

King started. "Did he?"

"*No way*." Piper gaped over the top of the computer.

"I left the front door open so it would be noticed. The smell should annoy someone."

King opened his web browser and did a preliminary search. "The story hasn't broken yet. You should tell Dani. She'd love to be the one to drop that bomb."

Piper made a sound behind them that sounded suspiciously like a repressed scream.

Lou pivoted away from Piper, and mouthed *I already did* for King's eyes alone.

Aloud she said, "I found a new target."

King glanced up from his computer. "Really? Using your compass thingy?" He made a circular motion over his chest.

King would be the first to admit he didn't fully understand what Lou called her compass, only that it was somehow connected to her ability to travel through the dark. In a way, it made sense to him that if Lou can't see where she was going, she would *feel* places instead. But it wasn't only limited to places, was it? She could also target people or even ideas, including *where is a serial murderer?*

"I've been following him for a few days. He's good at hiding in plain sight, but he's definitely a target."

"What do you know so far?"

"His name is Jeffrey Fish. He lives in Mount Vernon, Ohio with a wife and son."

"How'd you get his name?"

"I went through the mail in his mailbox."

"That's a federal offense," King said, but he was impressed. "Anything else?"

Lou stood and slipped two fingers into the back pockets of her jeans. She pulled out a folded square piece of paper and handed it over to King, who leaned forward to retrieve it.

He sank back into the office chair, brushing crumbs off his lips. He unfolded the piece of paper and first read the plate number and address for Fish off the upper corner. But below that was a photocopy of a driver's license.

He read aloud, "Jennifer McGrath."

"She works at a grocery store near his house," Lou explained.

"And he's stalking her?" Piper asked. She came around the desk to look at the photo. "She's pretty."

King frowned at the photocopy in his hands. "How did you get a photocopy of her driver's license?"

"I took it from her purse while she was sleeping."

"And just hop-skip-jumped to a Kinko's or something?" Piper marveled. "Damn, you're cool."

The corner of Lou's lips tilted up.

"I told you no contact," King said. Realizing that he sounded like the petulant father he most certainly was not, he sighed. "If she knows she's being followed she could panic. Or at the very least, she could tip him off by acting differently. Or Fish could see you."

Lou wasn't smiling now. Her hard stare made the hairs on his arms rise.

"Women aren't stupid," Lou said. "Most of them."

"Yeah," Piper added companionably. "We are actually much better at staying alive than men are, thank you very much."

"We're talking about human behavior, and we talked about this..."

Boy had they talked about this. King had tried every line of reasoning his mind could conjure to control Lou's happy-go-lucky trigger finger. True, it had been her idea to hunt serial killers who'd escaped the system. She wanted to bring retribution to the men who thought themselves apex predators above the law.

And Lou had been damn good at it with that unnatural gift of hers, combined with an unshakable aim. She'd already picked through six killers before he'd had a chance to explain *due process* to her.

Yes, you can simply appear and murder these men where they stand and who could stop you? But think of the families. They want closure. They need it the same way you needed closure for your dad.

That had slowed her down.

But catching her prey alive wasn't Lou's natural inclination and they both knew it. It just wasn't how she liked to do things. And the learning curve had been steep.

She crossed her arms, King's first real sign of trouble. "Fish is alive and he hasn't seen me."

King shifted in his seat, trying to ease the pressure in his hip. "We just need him to fuck up. That's all. And this will help get a better sense of what's going on and develop a connection between them." He held up the photocopy of the woman's driver's license. "Thank you."

He and Lou had begun a dangerous game—two games, actually. One hunt was tailored for men like Jeffrey Fish. These men could still be prosecuted. They could be convicted of their crimes and those convictions could let parents and spouses and children rest easier knowing justice was served.

But then there was the other hunt. When a monster didn't qualify for the prosecute file, King considered him for the *execute* file.

He'd grappled with that a lot at first. Who was he to sentence men to death? Who decided who deserved a one-way trip to La Loon—Louie's dumping ground?

He convinced himself that his candidates were only men like Miller—who had a high chance of reoffending and had somehow escaped retribution. By taking care of the men the system had freed, they were saving lives.

Weren't they?

"Guys like Devaroe and Miller have beat the system. There's no way to make them pay for what they've done. So they're fair game. But someone like Fish—there's still a chance to make it right," he said aloud. He sounded defensive to his own ears. "Who knows how many women he's killed and families he's destroyed. We're doing this for them."

Lou sighed. "Miller was the last one from the list you gave me. Who else have you got?"

You need something to hold you over, he thought. *Fine*.

He opened his desk drawer and removed the insert. His fingers searched the bare metal bottom beneath. After a moment of groping he found a folded up piece of paper.

He pulled it out—and feeling a little like a drug dealer—extended it toward her across the desk. She took it, opened it up, read the names. She said nothing. She only slipped the sheet of paper into her back pocket, where the photocopy of McGrath's license had been moments before.

Then she lifted the slate gray urn from the edge of his desk and smiled.

"I miss her," King said, falling back against the chair. "So shoot me."

He brought Lucy to work with him every day.

"Don't tempt me," Lou said. Without the smile, King couldn't tell if she was joking.

"I think it's sweet," Piper said, typing away. "Nothing wrong with wanting to keep Lucy close. I like to think she watches over us."

Lou turned the urn in her hand as if reading something. But King had inspected that container enough to know there were no words on it.

She returned it to the desk without comment.

"Be careful out there," King said, sensing the imminent goodbye.

But Lou lingered.

She turned to face him, squaring her body. "If Fish makes a move before we get this so-called evidence, I won't hesitate. I'm not going to let her body be the evidence we need for a case."

King opened his mouth to protest, but stopped.

Lou was already opening the storage closet marked Ms. Thorne, and stepping inside. The door shut with a ringing finality

Piper caught his eye across the room. "Don't look at me, man. You know she does whatever the hell she wants."

A feeling of unease grew in King's stomach. "Yeah, she does."

Mel turned counterclockwise in the storeroom again, glancing from her makeshift list to the shelves. The closet smelled like old cardboard and incense. At the back of the room was a black safe with silver embellishments. It stood as tall as she did.

She lifted a box from the shelves and counted the remaining sugar skulls. She scribbled on the list. They were burning through their inventory—not that Mel was complaining. It was good that sales were high. It only meant that she would have to place another order today and pray it arrived in time. Slipping the pen and paper into the folds of her skirt—they had hidden pockets that she'd sewn in herself —she flicked off the light and exited the storeroom.

The store had a few more patrons than when she'd entered. Piper was showing two men the selection of Fortunes and Fixes hoodies, holding one against the taller man's chest.

Several girls crowded around the incense stand, slipping long sticks into their plastic bags. Another couple were fingering the beads, chatting excitedly to each other about having survived Bourbon Street the night before.

Oh my god, she walked four blocks before she realized her skirt was tucked into her panties!

He puked for three hours. I swear to God, I thought he was dying.

There's a reason they call them hurricanes.

Mel was about to circle the shop, saying the perfunctory *finding everything all right,* when the two young men shifted, revealing someone else.

This man was browsing the t-shirts in a lazy, languid way. The way he held his body caused a knot to form in Mel's gut. Her heart dropped like a stone in a well.

It's my imagination, she begged.

But she watched the man, lean and wiry, move across the shop, watched the girls with their cache of incense part so he could cross to an adjacent shelf.

Mel absorbed everything about him. The light denim button-up shirt, the acid-washed jeans. The tan belt and matching, scuffed shoes. His curling dark hair hanging under his leather cowboy hat. A crow feather protruding from that hat. The fishhook earring in one ear and the bone choker with turquoise accents encircling his throat.

All of it was familiar, but it was the way he stood, the way he held himself that she knew best.

Her heart kicked against her ribs painfully, fear rising high in her throat.

Run! Her mind screamed. *Run up to your apartment, lock the door, call the police. And then what?*

Then what?

"Terrence." She meant it to be a cold acknowledgment. But her voice came out in a desperate rasp. "What are you doing here?"

His fingers froze on the Papa Legba statue, the smile already pulling into place before he turned to face her.

"Melandra," he said and tapped the brim of his hat. His eyes raked down her body lasciviously. "Nice place you got here."

She drew her shawl around her body. "Get out."

It was hard to put the full force of her anger—and her fear —into her voice while trying to keep her voice low. She glanced nervously at the patrons around her. Piper held a hanger in one hand while one of the men tried on a hoodie. They were turned at such an angle that Piper wouldn't be able to see Melandra in her periphery.

"Is that any way to talk to your husband?" Terry drawled softly. His voice rasped like sandpaper. "Not that you've treated me like a husband for some time now."

Fresh horror chilled her bones. The last sliver of her hope, of her wishful thinking that somehow this was all a horrible, terrible dream, slipped through her hands like sand.

"I haven't gotten a visit in, what? Twelve? Fourteen years? And you stopped sending money two years ago. Thought I'd just up and die without it, I reckon."

She'd clung to the wish that he wouldn't seek her out at all. After all, maybe prison really could change a man. He certainly *looked* changed. He was leaner now. A wolf-thin shape of his former self, but far more muscular. He'd been a scrawny terror of a boy when they'd met and had grown into a wiry man. Now it looked like the lanky man—all elbows and knees—had put on about fifty pounds of muscle.

"Did you forget about me in there? Did you forget about your own husband?" Terry licked his lips and hooked his thumbs into the waistband of his jeans. "Or did you think we were all paid up?"

"I don't owe you shit!" she hissed. Her bangles jiggled as she jabbed her finger at him.

She caught the stare of a young woman coming around the candle display. *Damn*, she thought. *I'm being too loud.*

Or not loud enough, her thoughts countered.

"Come on," Terry said. His smile hadn't faltered. "We had an agreement. You write the checks. I keep my mouth shut."

"In hell," Melandra groaned, forcing a smile at the woman lifting a candle from the shelf.

The register dinged behind her. Mel glanced over her shoulder and saw that the men were committing to the hoodies after all and a fistful of lighters.

A cool hand wrapped around hers.

Reflexively, she jerked back, yanking away.

The hand only clamped down harder. Closing on the wrist until pain shot up Melandra's arm. "Easy now."

"*Don't* touch me." She tried again to free her wrist but he held fast.

"Now, now," he said, pulling her close. "Don't want to cause a scene, now do we? That's bad for business."

She could smell his aftershave, splashed generously along his neck and collarbone. The heady scent made her stomach turn.

Don't panic, she told herself. *You are in control here.*

"From what I can tell by this lovely establishment you've got here, that you haven't been paying me nearly enough for the burden of keeping your secret. But that's all right. We're going to make up for lost time, aren't we?"

Mel couldn't quite get enough air into her lungs. The room was darkening at the edges. It felt like he was leeching all her strength from her body with his grip alone.

"There we go," he said, softly into her hair. "There's the girl I know."

"Mel?" a voice called out. It was strong enough to pull Mel back from the edge of hysteria.

The hand around her wrist released her immediately. Mel stumbled back as if pushed.

Piper placed a hand on Mel's shoulder, turning her. "Hey, are you okay?"

"I'm fine."

Piper regarded the man in the leather cowboy hat. "Can I help you with something?"

"He was leaving," Mel said, meeting his gaze.

"Was I?"

Piper was already squaring off as if preparing to fight this man. Melandra was certain her bravery and scrappy attitude were due to the fact that she had no idea how dangerous Terrence Williams was.

The chandelier moaned overhead and the enormity of Robert King crossed the threshold. A second later, a cool snout was pressing itself into Melandra's palm.

"Security is here." To Terrence, she said, "See yourself out, buddy. Or he'll help you out."

Terrence drew himself up and took King's measure.

A low grumble echoed through the shop. Melandra had a moment of wondering if the heat had kicked on before realizing Lady was growling.

This stopped King in his tracks, glancing down at the dog. "What is it?"

"Some jackoff here is being—*hey*," Piper cut off mid-speech. "Where did he go?"

Melandra's eyes searched the aisles. She pulled back the curtain on her reading room and found it empty. Out on the street, she thought she glimpsed an oil-black crow feather sticking out of a leather cowboy hat. But she blinked and it was gone.

The cold snout pressed into her palm again. "*Bonne fille.*"

The Belgian Malinois leaned her weight into Mel's legs.

"What did I miss?" King asked, his face pinched with confusion.

"Some asshole was messing with her," Piper said.

"Language," Melandra said. She was trying not to tremble all over. "We have customers."

She pointed at the counter where the women were waiting to buy their incense and candles. Piper slinked away.

"You okay?" King asked. His gaze was heavy and assessing.

"I'm fine."

"You don't look fine," King said. "Who was the guy?"

"No one."

King arched a brow.

"Someone I used to know," she said. "Please drop it."

"Okay."

"I'm just stressed." She wasn't sure why she felt like she had to defend herself.

King looked around the shop. "Let me take care of things down here. Take a break. Go lie down or something. Take Lady with you. She loves a good nap."

Mel looked to the window once more, expecting to see Terrence framed in the glass, watching her like a tiger through its bars.

But the sidewalk was full of tourists, walking, laughing, gearing up for the oncoming night.

And a headache was forming behind her eyes again. "Just for a couple hours."

To the dog she said, "*Allons-y*."

She mounted the stairs to her apartment with only one wish in her heart—that this was the end of it. That Terrence had had his say and would leave her be now.

She knew better.

8

Lou stood in front of the ramshackle bar on the outskirts of Colcord, Oklahoma. There was only a blinking yellow light at the four-way stop regulating the town's non-existent traffic. A lone building, the bar itself, was surrounded by a gravel lot on all sides. Apart from the dark and sloping landscape behind it, there was nothing else on which to fix the eye for as far as Lou could see. Only two cars sat in the lot. A black Ford pickup and an old white station wagon that had a ring of rust outlining the wheel well.

Lou unfolded the piece of worn paper from her back pocket and read it once more in the moonlight.

The name on it. *Ricky Walker.*

Lou smiled at the period punctuating the name, as if King had made it a point to seal the man's fate with that small punctuation mark.

Is this what you are now? a small voice asked as she folded up the paper and slipped it into her pocket. *A hitman?*

It wasn't Aunt Lucy's voice or her father's. It was that new cold voice, an unforgiving version of her own.

She suppressed a bitter laugh. She wasn't hunting and

killing these men for King. She wasn't fulfilling some old grudge for him. Likely King had never even met these men. He'd heard of their stories secondhand, done his research, and earmarked them for death because his beloved justice system had failed to do so. And she knew King well enough to know his conscience weighed on him far more than hers ever could. He would not have signed anyone's name to a letter of execution unless he was certain of their crimes.

Ricky Walker, for example, had raped and murdered four boys. DNA evidence submitted at his trial proved he'd committed the crime. There were even eyewitnesses to the abductions of the last two kids. Still he'd been let go.

No. Lou wasn't doing this for King. He was handing over these names the way a zookeeper fed meat through the bars of the tiger cage. He was trying to placate her, domesticate her, and she knew it.

And how do you feel about that? the cold voice asked. *Do you want to be domesticated? Here, kitty kitty.*

It's not like that, she thought crossly. After all, wasn't King only doing what Lucy had asked of him? Lucy, her benevolent Buddhist aunt got her way even in death.

Lou's ease with death, with killing, had never set well with Lucy.

Lou understood that some creatures of this world were simply predators and she was one of them. She was part of an ecosystem, an elaborate dance of checks and balances. A tiger would never feel guilty for the meat it ate. Lou felt no guilt for the lives she took.

At the very end, Lucy understood that. If killing only very bad men helped King sleep at night, and feel as though he was upholding a promise to his dead wife, then fine.

Lou could play along—within reason—though she'd learned not so long ago, *bad* and *good* were relative. A system built for justice and equity could be polluted with cutthroats.

An underground network built upon rule-breaking and exploitation could offer liberation.

And who taught you that? Konstantine?

Rolling her shoulders as if to relieve them of some unseen burden, she crossed the parking lot and stepped into the bar. Some whining country music played. At first, Lou thought the bar was empty. But then she saw the bartender perched on the stool looking up at a television mounted above the bar. It played a boxing match between two fighters Lou didn't recognize.

The man watching the television sat hunched on the stool, his paunch of a stomach hanging over his belt. His t-shirt had ridden up on his stomach, revealing the hairy flesh beneath.

"Ricky Walker?" Lou asked.

The bartender didn't even look at her. He just pointed a thumb over his shoulder. "He's back there. Three sheets to the wind."

Walker sat in the last booth on the right. His head was down on his arm. He snored softly. A glass full of half-melted ice sweated in his grip. His short, gnarled nails had black grime beneath them. His stubble was mostly gray.

She slid into the booth and regarded the man. The smell wafting off of him was acrid, like a mixture of piss and sweat.

He's sick, she thought. *He's sick as hell.*

She wondered if she could smell it because of her time with Lucy. Her aunt's illness had had a stench too. It was like Lou could smell the body souring, going bad like old meat.

"Ricky Walker?"

No answer.

She kicked his leg under the table.

He harrumphed and drew himself up, fixing his bleary eyes on her. He squinted in low light before pinching the bridge of his nose. "Hi. How you doing?"

"Are you Ricky Walker?" she again.

"Yeah, that's me." He lifted the glass to his lips mechanically and then frowned when only ice hit his lips. "Do I know you?"

"No," she said.

He shook the glass, rattling the ice. "Chuck!"

Chuck slid off the bar stool with a grumble and brought a bottle with him. He took Ricky's empty glass and filled it to the rim. "Another Walker for the Walker. A drink for your lady friend?"

"No," Lou said.

It was no matter to Chuck. With a shrug, he slinked away taking the bottle of Johnny Walker with him. He had eyes only for the boxing match.

"How long?" Lou asked.

"Seven inches," Rick said and snorted. It echoed in the glass. "But it's what you do with it that counts."

Lou smiled. It was a promising answer. She liked it when they were mean. "Cirrhosis?"

He drew long and deep on his drink. He sat it on the table with a *humph*. "Alcoholic cardio- my—cardio my..."

"Alcoholic cardiomyopathy?" Lou offered.

"My heart's failing. It's swollen or shit like that. Hey, are you from the clinic? Come out here to tell me to stop drinking again? It won't work. I told y'all it's all I've got. That and the dreams. I ain't getting my heart rate up or whatever you said. I'm chilled, all right? *Chilled* as ice."

He shook the glass at her, the ice clinking against the sides as if to emphasize his point. Whiskey sloshed over the rim onto his thumb. He brought it to his mouth and sucked it.

Lou said nothing as he tipped the glass back and drank the remainder in one go. When there was only ice left, he groaned. "Chuck!"

Chuck didn't come. He was cursing at the television.

"It's all I've got," Ricky said again. His slurred murmuring seemed for his ears only. "And the dreams. I got the dreams too."

That's more than some, Lou thought. "Do you want to dance, Ricky?"

The man lowered the glass and sucked his lips. He smirked at Lou, which could have been interpreted as unabashed lust if the gaze had not been so unfocused. Lou doubted he could see her at all.

"You're not really my type," he said with a low laugh. "But you'll do."

He slid from the booth as she did and followed her to the dance floor—if that's what this space could be called. In reality, it was the simple open space between two sections of tables, with the jukebox resting against the wall.

The fluorescent lights from its frame warped and spread like a prism across the surface of Lou's sunglasses and Ricky squinted. The ice tinkled in his glass as he sauntered toward Lou, a leer on his lips.

"Yeah, you're mighty pretty," he said, sucking his teeth.

"For a female?" Lou returned as Ricky slid one arm around her waist.

He stiffened.

"Or for an adult?" She clamped onto him, pinning his arm against her leather jacket, letting it rest where the top of her pants and belt met.

She didn't need to get him into a corner. The bar was already dark enough.

A STRANGE PRESSURE POPPED BETWEEN THE BARTENDER'S ears the moment before the sound of glass breaking rang out. He turned away from the match on the suspended television.

Ice and glass fragments spread across the middle of the floor. It sparkled in the jukebox's shifting lights.

"Goddamn it, Ricky," he said, climbing off the stool and grabbing a white towel. "You're paying for that glass."

Chuck stooped over the mess and began to gather up the shattered pieces. He turned to the adjacent booth, expecting to see the couple there, but it was empty.

Maybe they went to the bathroom. Or maybe they snuck out the back for a blowjob.

Just as well. Chuck was tired of the old man's shit anyway. So what about the booze and the glass? If Walker thought he could dine and dash, he was mistaken.

The joke's on you, Chuck thought. Ricky had left his credit card behind with his tab.

THE WARM REPRIEVE OF THE BAR WAS SACRIFICED ON THE altar of total night. Lou's boots shifted, adjusting to the hard-packed earth forming beneath her. A chorus of toad song sprang up around them. Something in the tree above spread its wings and took flight. Its considerable wingspan kicked up the air around them, blowing the air back from her face.

Ricky seemed totally unaware that the bar was gone and he stood in unadulterated darkness.

Lou could pull her gun now, put a bullet between Walker's eyes and be done with it. He would never know what hit him.

That would be too easy, she thought. *Merciful.*

No. Let Ricky Walker see the horror of La Loon with his own eyes. Let him see what waited for men like him.

"Can you swim?" Lou asked.

"Yeah, I can fucking swim." Ricky's hands were trying to get under her leather jacket, searching for her tits. But he was having trouble with the unyielding material. His breath fogged white in her vision, fogging the mirrored sunglasses she wore even at night.

"Good," she said, stepping backwards into cold water. It sloshed over the rim of her boots wetting her socks. No matter. How many times had she done this? Walked fully clothed into this lake, a body—sometimes living, sometimes dead—in tow?

She continued into deeper water and like a puppy Walker followed her, planting a sloppy kiss on her throat as he moved forward. With a wave of revulsion, she fisted his hair and yanked it back.

The water had reached halfway up her thighs, inching toward her pelvis when his fingers finally managed to get under her leather jacket.

His eyes widened the moment he found the guns in their holsters.

"What the fu—"

Lou latched onto the man, grabbing him hard enough to pull him off his feet.

Then she fell. Straight back into the cold water, slapping its surface hard. Walker coughed in surprise as the water hit his face. But they were already sinking into its dark depths, already passing from his world into Lou's. There was no going back.

Like the shadows, the water gave for Lou.

It seemed to wrap itself around her, entwine itself with her body until the shadowed depth gave way to red waters. The cold to warmth.

The moment Lou knew the transfer was completed, she pushed for the surface, bringing Walker with her.

She released him and started up the clumsy embankment until she was on the barren shore.

Walker stood in waist-deep water, stunned. He regarded violet twilight sky with its twin moons. The abnormal mountains in the distance, so monumental as to look like a water-color backdrop spread for decoration only. The strange yellow hue they projected on the red waters of the lake surrounding him.

"I don't understand," he said, turning full circle in the shallows. "Am I having a flashback or something?"

"Highly doubt it."

He waded to the water's edge where the black foliage met the patina of Blood Lake—named so, unimaginatively, Lou admitted—because of the blood-red color of the water.

He grabbed a palm-sized leaf and began to inspect it. "I ain't never seen anything like this."

"You want to die in the water?" Lou asked calmly. She was trying to shake the water out of her boots. She'd never gotten used to the awful way her saturated socks squished between her toes. "Or on land?"

"No," he said.

A roar echoed through the valley. The rumble was so deep it shook Lou's core.

Lou smiled.

Walker on the other hand, had most certainly pissed himself. "The fuck was that?"

"I call her Jabbers," Lou said, plainly. She opened her leather jacket, trying to flap some of the water off its surface. She'd treated it twice to protect the material from her bouts to La Loon. But that didn't mean she wanted to let the water set in.

"Jabbers?" Walker asked, wiping the water from his face nervously.

"Like the Jabberwocky," she said. "Have you read Alice in Wonderland?"

"I don't read."

"No," Lou said companionably. "I suspect you were too busy raping children."

"What?" The first real note of terror seized Ricky's features.

Then Jabbers emerged from the forest and turned his terror complete.

"My god," he said. He staggered back as the beast drew herself to her full height. Lou thought she was at least nine feet tall, maybe twelve. "Oh my god, no. I'm sorry. I'm so sorry."

Lou snorted. "Sorry for what?"

"For what I did to those boys. For what I did to my momma. For—for that money I stole and—and anything else I can't think of right now. I'm sorry for everything. Please take me back. Take me back and I'll make up for it with every minute of my life. Give me more time. Please. *Please*."

His begging confused her. What did Ricky believe? That she was some Angel of Death? Some demon who brought him to hell for his punishment, and if he only repented, confessed, he could be delivered from evil?

The serpentine creature cast a cursory glance at Lou as if also confused by the man's pleas.

"He's all yours," Lou said, waving her on.

The scream hadn't even fully formed in Walker's throat before Jabbers was on him. One foxlike pounce and her widening jaw snapped shut over his neck, severing the head from the body cleanly.

Then she had the leg, dragging the rest of him onto shore.

The beast purred affectionately, rolling its eyes up to meet Lou's over its dinner.

"Yes," Lou cooed, patting it on the head in much the same manner that she'd scratched the Belgian Malinois earlier in the day. "I missed you, too."

9

Piper read the address off her phone again as if she hadn't eaten at this soul food place a hundred times before. Recognizing this for the nervous tick it was, she sighed and forcibly put her phone on the counter. She had twenty minutes to get to the restaurant where she and Dani were meeting for dinner.

Dani. Dinner.

It's just dinner. It's not like you're proposing to the girl who totally ghosted you.

Against her will, her mind replayed last January, when Dani had walked into their lives.

All the make-out sessions in Mel's storage closet. The way Dani's eyes had shone in the light the night they watched Henry's drag show in a Bourbon Street bar.

The way she'd looked in the hospital bed, black and blue after surviving Dmitri's quest for information about Lou. The way she'd laughed when she'd shown Piper her finger reattached to her hand.

She'd been so sure that Dani was into her, and she'd never

misread a girl before. The fact that she'd been so off the mark with Dani had shaken her confidence.

What the hell am I going to say?

Piper exhaled slowly, aware that her arms and chest were buzzing with nervous energy. She stared at the laptop on her kitchen counter in front of her. She shifted her weight on the stool as if this would alleviate some tension. It didn't.

"It's dinner. Just a meal. Maybe a drink," she told herself again. "Calm down."

She bit her lip for focus and reread the discussion board post in her Intro to Policing class. It was due at midnight, so she had better finish it before going to dinner. She reminded herself how important salvaging her GPA was. It had dropped from 3.5 to 2.8 in the semester when her mother had been at her worst. Piper had to get a 4.0 in this class—and every class from now until graduation to pull it up again.

The sharp image of her mother in the dark, dingy room, smoke hanging in the air as track marks ran up the interior of her pallid arm sparked in her mind.

She blinked, pushing the thoughts away.

Not my circus, not my monkeys, she reminded herself. *I'm building my future now. Come on. Focus.*

If Lou could have her whole family slaughtered when she was a kid and grow up to be this badass that the whole criminal world fears, you can write a freaking discussion board post. The teacher doesn't even read them. Just post something already!

She opened her textbook and reread a section before referencing it in her post. She added the citation at the end and—*send.*

She checked the clock on her phone. Fourteen minutes.

She slid off the stool and snatched her puffy black coat off the hook by the door. It took a minute to find her keys and wallet, before stuffing them into her pockets along with her phone.

The stairs leading from her loft down to King's office were dark, so she moved carefully, one hand on the wall until she reached the bottom.

The agency was awash in moonlight along the bare wooden floors. The ruckus of the tourists laughing on Royal Street echoed softly through the room, sliding over the bare desks and empty chairs. After double checking that she'd locked her apartment doors, she locked the office door behind her as well. If someone tried to break in—a disgruntled client or someone looking to sabotage evidence—there was no guarantee they wouldn't ransack Piper's apartment, too.

People were assholes. Better safe than sorry.

Pulling her coat around her against the chilly night, she stepped into the throng of partygoers. The scent of alcohol and weed hung in the air. A woman's robust laughter broke open around her.

Piper did her best to push on. The crush of bodies flooding the Quarter slowed her progress. What should've been a quick twelve minute walk took her twenty minutes. When she arrived, she was late.

"I'm looking for someone. She might be here already," she said to the hostess, holding the collar of her coat down to be better heard. She caught herself licking her lips, yet another nervous tick, and refrained.

"That her?" the hostess asked, pulling the pen from her hair and pointing it at a table a couple of rows back.

Dani sat alone. She looked elegant with her hair swept up off her face and a wine glass in hand. She gazed wistfully out the window beside her, watching the people pass. If Piper didn't know better, it looked like Dani was going to cry.

Piper tapped the hostess stand. "Yeah, thanks."

Gathering the last of her bravery, she crossed the restaurant and pulled out the wooden chair opposite Dani's.

Visible relief washed over the girl's face the moment her chair screeched across the floor. Dani sat up straighter. "I was starting to think you weren't going to come."

"Sorry." Piper shrugged out of her coat. She hung it off the back of her chair. "I remembered a homework assignment at the last minute, so I wanted to turn it in. Then the crowds slowed me down."

"You're back in school?" Dani asked, her hands wrapping around the stem of her wine glass.

Piper spread her hands on the table. "Yeah. I'm taking classes at Delgado. Once I get my GPA up, I'll transfer somewhere."

"How in the world do you have two jobs, go to school, and still sleep?"

Piper snorted. "Who said I sleep?"

They shared nervous laughter.

When it died away, Piper said, "I take my classes online. At this rate, it'll take me about three years just to get the Criminal Justice associates."

"That's still great!" Dani's enthusiasm seemed forced. "I mean, you're so busy. You can only do so much."

Piper nodded. She was glad to be back in school and knew she was doing her best, but she was keenly aware that Dani already had her degree and years of work experience. It was hard not to feel like she was behind.

"So, criminal justice." Dani had been watching Piper's face as she talked. When their eyes met, Dani flicked hers away. "You want to be a cop?"

"I was thinking law, actually. You can do a lot with a law degree. Even join the FBI."

Dani nodded, reaching for the wine bottle in the center of the table. Piper noted it was out of her reach and nudged it forward. When their fingers brushed, a blush spread across Dani's cheeks.

Noticing, Piper clasped the back of her neck, rubbing it. "I don't want to be in a courtroom or anything. But I really enjoy the investigation part. Due process. All that. I'm learning a lot working with King at the agency."

"What about tarot reading?"

"That's fun too," Piper said. "But it's not a career. No health insurance, you know?"

Piper snorted at her own joke. She also noticed that Dani did not. She seemed a million miles away as she tipped the bottle over to refill her glass. Piper didn't miss that she'd filled it to the rim. So much for a six-ounce serving.

"What about you?" Piper asked, hoping to shift the focus away from her. "You still at The Herald?"

Piper felt stupid as soon as she asked. They both knew she knew Dani was at The Herald.

Dani drank deep from her glass, making a sound that could be taken as a *yes*.

"I mean, are you happy there?"

"I like the promotion," Dani said.

"Right. I saw—" Piper cut herself off from saying *I've been reading The Herald all year, following your stories and looking for your picture.* That seemed too desperate. "You were promoted to Assistant Editor, right?"

"They offered me a permanent column, but I really like investigative reporting. I don't want to do lifestyle pieces or give advice. Who am I to give advice?"

A nervous laugh escaped her.

Piper noted all this distantly. Her attention was on Dani's hands, trying to see the scar where Dmitri had cut it, taking it as a trophy. But the candlelit room didn't offer much light.

Dani caught her staring. "There's not much of a scar. I got lucky. Well, kind of. PT was a bitch."

She bent her finger to demonstrate that its mobility was

still restricted. It could only fold down half as far as her other fingers.

"I've learned how to type without it." Dani who'd been sliding down in her chair, straightened again. "It slows me down when it stiffens up."

The waitress appeared in her white and black ensemble, apron tied around her waist. "What can I get y'all tonight?"

"Fried chicken with mustard greens," Dani said reflexively.

"Same," Piper parroted. "And cornbread."

"Anything else to drink, hon?" she looked up from her notepad.

"Can I get a wine glass?" She flicked her eyes up to meet Dani's. "Assuming you don't mind sharing."

"Another bottle then?" the waitress asked.

Dani nodded. "Thank you."

The waitress left them alone, initiating another stretch of awkward silence.

Piper watched her gaze out the window for a longtime. She saw the dark circles under her eyes and the sunken look of her cheeks.

She's lost weight. Too much weight.

"How's the shop?" Dani asked.

"It's crazy during Carnival. But staying busy is good. Mel gets stressed when there's not enough money coming in." It was Piper's turn to feign enthusiasm. When the bottle of wine and fresh glass appeared, she was able to busy herself with that.

"I bet. And probably no shortage of drunks. And assholes."

Piper thought of the man who'd harassed Melandra. Despite the stupid feather in his hat and bone choker tied around his throat—both of which Piper thought were pretty cool—Piper hadn't liked the look of him.

"There's always assholes. Assholes come cheap."

Dani laughed suddenly. Her voice echoing in the wine glass.

"What?"

"Cheap."

Piper half-smiled. "Are you drunk?"

"I had a bottle of wine before you got here," she admitted, sliding her glass onto the table as if realizing holding it might be a bad idea.

"You drank a whole bottle of wine in eight minutes?"

Dani pulled up her sleeve to reveal a silver watch. "I've been here since seven."

"Why did you come so early?"

"I thought sitting here would help my nerves." Dani pressed her lips together, searching Piper's face as if unsure of what else she should say.

"Why were you nervous?" *Oh yeah, let's pretend I wasn't freaking out too. Not one bit.*

Dani dragged her hands down her face. "I wanted to apologize to you for ghosting you last year. I should've at least called or sent a letter or something. What I did was wrong—on so many levels."

A letter, Piper smirked. *What is this World War Two?*

"I realize I never explained what happened, so it must've seemed especially shitty to you."

"I'm just...confused. One minute we were hot and heavy. The next I'm at your bedside in the hospital every day and when you're released, I can't get you to even return a text."

Dani chewed her lip. "I didn't want you to think I stopped talking to you just because the case was over—"

"You were doing your job." Piper shrugged and hoped it looked nonchalant because she felt anything but. The ache in her chest was building. "I get it. I'm also a workaholic."

"No, see. *Ughhh*." Dani pulled at her face again. "You weren't just a job."

"Look, you don't have to say that—" Piper's voice broke off the moment she met Dani's eyes.

They were bright with unshed tears. Her lower lip trembled and she broke the gaze first, looking away to the big picture window beside them and the street beyond it.

"You weren't just a job," she said again, looking apologetic. "At least not by the end of it."

Piper reached for the wine bottle. "Then it's even more confusing why you'd stop talking to me. It seems like you talked to everyone *but* me. I mean, *Lou?*" Piper clicked her tongue. "Lou was going to kill you and dump your body... wherever she dumps bodies. How was it easier to talk to *her* than me?"

Dani laughed. It was a choked, miserable sound.

A couple at the adjacent table glanced over, curious.

"Come on. Don't cry," Piper said, shifting in her seat. "People are going to think I'm being mean to you."

Dani brought her fingers to her eyes, delicately dabbing at her lashes. Mascara came off on her fingers. "I'm sorry."

"Don't be sorry, just tell me what happened." Piper took another long drink of wine. In case whatever Dani said next turned out to be horrible. That was the thing about asking for the truth. You couldn't be mad if someone gave it to you.

Dani was clearly mustering up the courage to speak. She licked her wine-stained lips, staring down at her clasped hands on the white linen tablecloth.

"I don't know where to start," she admitted, sniffling. "And it just sucked that I was super into you and then I fucked it up. You've got no reason to trust me."

"I might if you told me what happened. Start with when you left the hospital." It was the last time Piper had seen her.

The waitress appeared with two plates. "Here you go,

honey." She set a plate of steaming fried chicken down in front of Dani. "And one for you too, sugar. Everything look all right?"

Piper made a show of looking the plate over. "It looks amazing, thank you. Can I get some butter for the cornbread?"

"Sure. And hot sauce for the chicken, sweetheart?"

"Yes, ma'am." Piper accepted the bottle of hot sauce pulled from the waitress's apron.

"And you, baby?"

"It's perfect, thanks." Dani spoke without looking up.

As if sensing the mood of the conversation the waitress excused herself.

"When I left the hospital, I didn't sleep for twelve days."

Piper paused in unwrapping her fork. "What?"

"It took me a while to figure out that it was the apartment keeping me up. That's where they got me—Dmitri and his guys." Dani flicked her eyes up as if to gauge Piper's reaction. "That's where they...that's where they started in on me."

She lifted a fork but seemed unable to take a bite yet. It hung loosely in her grip.

"After two weeks, I had a breakdown because apparently not sleeping makes you crazy. They tried putting me on sleeping pills but I started sleepwalking, so I quit that. I used all my vacation time and moved back home for a while until I could find a new place to live. I couldn't be in the apartment anymore."

"Of course not." Piper couldn't even live in the same house as her stoned mother and dope-dealing boyfriend. She understood the way the walls of a place could close in on someone, hang like an atmosphere, pressing against her chest until she couldn't breathe.

"I couldn't tell my parents what happened because they would've made me quit the paper. But the longer I tried to ignore the trauma, the worse I got. It was almost a month after I left the hospital that I went into therapy and was diagnosed with PTSD."

Of course you were, Piper thought. *How the hell could you not have PTSD?*

"My therapist advised that I slowly try to reconnect with the people involved, to get a better sense of my triggers. We started by going back to the places where it happened together and walking through these mental exercises. It was... *awful*. It took me five months before I got up the courage to reach out to King and let him know I was still interested in working cases for him if he needed the help. It was seven months before I managed to say a word to Lou."

Piper cut into her chicken. She had questions, of course she did. But Dani wasn't even looking at her. She had a million-yard stare, replaying the story in her head and Piper knew better than to interrupt the momentum now. Her questions could wait.

"Every time I heard their voices, I *knew* the pain was about to come."

"King and Lou?" Piper asked around a mouthful of chicken.

She put her fork down. "You have to understand that your voices were the ones I heard that night. In the garage. After Dmitri...after he did the worst of it. Then I blacked out and you were there. I was scared and in pain and it was your voice in my head."

My voice triggers your PTSD. Ouch.

"I think my brain got confused. It began to associate all of you—King, Lou, Mel, everyone involved that night—with danger. Even a text message from you or King would trigger a panic attack."

"So it's somehow worse with *me* than with King, Lou, or Mel?"

Dani's face crumpled. "I know. I know and I'm *so* sorry. I think it's because I cared about you the most and because I was already feeling so shitty about trying to use you to get the story. Whatever it was about you, I couldn't see you. Seeing you, talking to you, any contact at all would've reminded me that it was real. That shit had really happened. It wasn't a dream I could just put behind me. And I was more than a little embarrassed that you'd seen me that way. I mean, I'd pissed myself—"

"You were *tortured*." Piper whispered. "Of course you pissed yourself."

Dani help up her hand. "Don't. I don't want to go into details, okay?"

"Okay."

"I just wanted to apologize for my shitty communication skills," Dani said, meeting her gaze for the first time since she'd begun to cry. "And I need you to know that I didn't stay away because I didn't like you."

Piper sat back against her chair. "That's what it felt like. You got the story you wanted and then you disappeared."

"I know," Dani said. "I know and I'm sorry."

Piper looked at the steaming chicken on the plate and tried to muster her appetite.

"Why did you reach out to King first?"

"My therapist told me that sometimes working can help with PTSD. She thought focusing on the job I love would be one way to get back in the game. She asked me, 'Are you going to let one asshole destroy your dream of being the best damn investigative reporter you can be?' And I was like, 'No. No, I'm not.' Because I love it. It's all I want to do. So I finally returned King's texts and started helping him on cases."

Piper thought, *But you had no reason to reach out to me.*

Piper arched her brows. "And Lou can give you the 'big break' case of your career, sooner or later."

"I like you, Piper," she said, softly. "Every time I walk through Jackson Square I'm hoping that I'll spot you there at your table. I'm also terrified that you'll be there."

Piper's heart seemed to swell in size, pushing against the base of her throat.

"I've given up on the idea that we could be something more. Good relationships are built on trust and you have no reason to trust me after what I did. And I'm still so messed up, I couldn't offer you a decent relationship anyway." Dani searched her face. "But I'd be *so* grateful if we could just learn how to be friends."

Piper stared into the wine glass as if she could use it to divine her future.

Dani fidgeted in her seat, drawing her arms across her chest. "Say something. Please."

"*Only* friends?" Piper smiled, twirling the glass on the table. "I never pegged you for a quitter, Daniella Allendale."

And for the first time that night Dani truly laughed.

Waterlogged and dripping, Lou pulled herself from the cold water. She stood on the embankment, trying to catch her breath. The night sang to her. Night jars trilled. A fox yipped in the distance. Something splashed in the lake. A fish? She wasn't sure. She saw only the ripples spreading across the moonlit surface.

Her skin and hair itched. She remembered the affectionate way Jabbers had dragged her thick white tongue over bloody knuckles and up the side of her neck. She could smell the monster's breath in her hair. She was filthy and longed for a hot shower.

But before she could do that, she wanted to check on Fish. The situation with Jeffrey could turn at any time. No point in showering prematurely in case she needed to take care of him tonight.

Lou hated washing her hair too much.

She stood in the dark, shaking the water off her leather jacket. She flapped her harness, checking to make sure the guns were fine.

Her chilled hands pushed away the strands sticking to her

face and lips. She wrung out her hair and sighed, inwardly willing her compass to life.

Fish, she thought. *Where is he tonight?*

She wondered if she would find him on the prowl. Maybe he'd be loitering around the grocery store again, but to no avail. The girl wasn't working tonight. Lou knew this because she'd slipped into the manager's office herself and checked the posted schedule. Now that she had the woman's name, it was easier to do such things.

And Lou trusted her compass. How many times had it whirled to life inside her, screaming the alarms, *Lucy! King! Piper* when it was time to act. This didn't mean that Jeffrey wasn't up to no good. After all, Lou noted the feeling of unease settling within her. Like a coil of snakes, it slithered in her guts, somewhere deep and unseen.

Locking in on Jeffrey's location, she said goodbye to her nighttime paradise, and shifted through the shadows once more.

The cacophony of a thriving nature was replaced by silence.

Lou felt the cold cement under her hands and realized she was against a concrete wall. There in front of her, spotlighted as if on stage, was Jeffrey.

Too close, she thought. *I'm too close.*

But this was the last pocket of shadow in Jeffrey's garage. Against one wall was a long craftsman worktable, tools, and the small lamp responsible for spotlighting Jeffrey's shoulders.

He wore his pajamas. A bizarrely mundane matching set, both the top and bottoms composed of soft blue and white stripes.

Your wife buy you those? Lou found herself marveling at the strange regularities of suburbia. *Here was a killer. Here he was working in his two-car garage, on a quiet Midwestern street, in his soft pajamas.*

She almost laughed at the sight of him bent over the table in concentration.

At least Lou never tried to hide what she was.

Then she saw the blood.

It dripped from his right forearm onto the concrete floor. Lou shifted, trying to get a better look and her shoes squeaked on the concrete.

Jeffrey whirled. His eyes frantically searched the dark. But he could not find her in the shadows. With his back angled in the light, Lou had a better sense of the situation. In his left hand was a straight-edge razor. Around his right arm, above the bend of the elbow, was a leather strap tied. On the forearm itself were six vertical lines. The first three were crusted black with dried blood. The three above it, as if he'd moved up the arm toward the fold, were bright crimson and oozed along the curve of his forearm, dripping onto the table.

The utility lamp illuminating his pale arm added a theatrical quality to the scene. His lower jaw jutted forward and his chest heaved with his labored breath. The whites of his eyes shimmered as he stood there, listening. Waiting.

Is this what you do to quell your hunger? Lou remained still in her pocket of shadow. *Does it bring you back from the edge?*

She knew the pain couldn't fulfill him.

Lou herself had tried that trick in barroom brawls and petty fights. She'd invited any man willing to take a swing to have a go at her. But even the best of split lips or scuffed cheeks hadn't scratched that itch within her.

Nothing short of the actual kill would do.

An unexpected swell of pity washed over her. She had never in all her years of hunting felt pity for a target before.

Was it his wounded expression?

Was it the way he cowered to his desires, clearly owned by them?

He ripped the strip of leather off his arm and threw it

back into the case on his wooden work bench. He wiped the blade and spilled blood with a navy blue mechanic's rag before tossing both into the box as well.

His back was to her as he rummaged for something. When he produced a thin roll of gauze and began to wrap his wounds tight, she realized this must be a longstanding ritual for him, these nighttime cuttings.

And what do you tell the wife and kid, Jeff? Kids ask questions. How do you explain the gauze? Is his daddy clumsy in the garage?

He slammed the lid down on his box. He reached overhead and drew the utility light close. The combination lock on a safe sat illuminated in the light. Lou watched him twirl the dial left and right, enjoying the *tick, tick, tick* of the spinning dial.

He placed the toolbox inside the safe and pushed the door closed. He tugged the handle and spun the dial.

Can't be too careful, can we?

Fish didn't seem to think so as he threw one more nervous look over his shoulder, then crossed the garage, past the parked cars, and into the house.

For several minutes Lou stayed where she was. She was no fool. Fish could throw on the lights, trapping her in the garage. He could only have pretended to go up to his bed, waiting to lure her from her hiding place.

But when she heard water running through the pipes above, she suspected Fish was washing up for bed.

Lou crossed the garage silently, stooping down beneath the wooden work bench just as Fish had done minutes before. She brought the utility light down with her and illuminated the lock. The combination had been easy to see and memorize.

Inside the safe, she found not only the plastic bin containing his *toys*, but a stack of photographs beneath it.

Lou flipped through the photographs one after another.

They began innocently enough. A woman tied to a chair. A woman naked, blindfolded and crying. These could be mistaken for light BDSM photographs, just a bit of couples play.

But then the blood came and the anguished expressions on the women's faces—at least eleven by Lou's count—told Lou these were not consensual sex games.

Anger sparked along her spine.

It seemed that it wasn't enough for Fish to stalk, hurt, and murder the women he wanted. He clearly enjoyed documenting the experience as well. More than one photograph immortalized his dick buried to the hilt, but he'd photographed the rest of his process as well, from the time he took them, while he was hurting them, until their deaths. Most of the photographs were of the deaths.

Do you have a favorite moment, Fish? Let me guess. I bet the police could guess too. Maybe I should show them these photographs. Would you like that?

King's strident, angry voice overrode her pulsating anger. *Don't take anything! Even if it's proof, you can't take it. It would be inadmissible in a court of law if it's obtained without a warrant. Put it back.*

All the pity she'd felt for Fish while watching him self-harm was gone.

She wanted to have a nice, long, and uninterrupted session of her own. See how much of this she could reenact.

Boots shifted gravel on the other side of Fish's closed garage door.

Lou froze at the sound. She waited, holding her breath until she heard it again—rocks shifting under someone's weight.

Lou did her best to wipe down the photographs and put them back under the toolbox. Then she shut the safe and gave the lock a spin.

She regarded the two tracks of boot prints on the garage floor left by her soggy steps.

They'll dry before morning, she told herself, hoping she was right.

The gravel shifted again and this time so did Lou. The cement wall at her back gave and opened onto the cold night. Lou was across the street now, not far from the parked car she'd used as sanctuary earlier that week.

She bent beneath the hedgerow framing an adjacent property and searched the Fish family's driveway.

There, where the rock retainer wall gave way to the open drive, someone stood. Lou moved to the left, trying to get a better view despite the hedge's jutting branches. A gap appeared and Lou leaned in.

It was hard to tell if the person was a man or a woman. The form was slight which suggested female to Lou's eye initially. But then she thought of the dock full of Hong Kong heroin dealers she'd dispatched seven months ago. They had been as short—or shorter—and their bodies even leaner.

This observer took photographs of the Fish residence with a large lens camera. He—or she—wore black gloves, black jeans, black boots, and a hoodie was pulled up over the head.

Then as suddenly as they came, they started down the walkway again, casting glances at the house as they passed.

Who are you? Lou wondered, watching the person go. *Who are you?*

Lou watched their staccato steps cut up the sidewalk, around the corner and then they were gone.

LOU WAS MORE THAN READY FOR A SHOWER. THE GRIT IN her hair only intensified the itching and her feet had grown so cold in her boots that she could barely feel them. Cold, wet socks were the bane of her existence. She pressed open the closet door, expecting to find her warm and welcoming St. Louis apartment awaiting her. Only it wasn't her apartment on the other side of the door.

Konstantine's bed was neatly made with his sweats thrown over the covers. The shutters on the arched window were closed, but moonlight filtered through the cracks, giving the bedroom a ghostly glow.

This is getting ridiculous, she thought. She chided her inward compass. *Do you even know where I live anymore?*

She was about to step into the closet again, redirecting herself home when a sound caught her attention.

Water splashed against tile and the low melodic tone of a sultry tenor reached her.

She stepped from the closet and to the bathroom's open door. Steam hung in the air like low clouds, but it wasn't thick enough to obscure the view of the naked man in the shower.

Konstantine's back was to her. It was stained red from the assault of the shower. His right arm was covered in tattoos from shoulder to elbow. The black ink was beaded with hot droplets.

I wanted a shower. A shower is what I'll get.

She checked her GPS watch synced with her new location. It was after four in the morning. She wasn't sure if Konstantine was starting his day or ending it.

It didn't matter. Lou unlaced her boots, and worked her wet, clinging clothes off her body. When she opened the shower door, a hand shot out. She ducked, snatching the wrist.

"Does this mean I can't join you?" she asked, rolling her eyes up to meet his.

His gaze raked over her naked body. Goosebumps rose on his skin.

The tension in his body vanished. "I didn't realize it was you."

Obviously, she thought. "If you don't want me to join you—"

He reached out for her, seizing her with both hands, and pulled her into the hot stream.

"Late night or early morning?" she asked.

"I'm just getting home. But preparations for Venice are complete and we leave in two days."

"I don't think you want me to touch you yet," she said, adding distance between them even as he moved in.

"I can always wash again." He leaned into her, tucking his lips under her jawline and caressing the skin where the neck and jaw met. Lou tipped her head back to allow it.

He pulled back and frowned at the pink water swirling down the drain. "Are you bleeding?"

"It isn't blood," she said. She didn't have any of Walker's gore on her. "I call it Blood Lake for a reason. The waters are red."

He gathered a handful of her wet hair into his hands and brought it to his nose. "You smell like sulfur."

"That's La Loon too," she said, letting her hands rest at last on his hip bones. She squeezed him, loving their hard edges.

"Perhaps it *is* hell then," Konstantine said, giving her a devilish smile to match. Lou had noticed, in the passing months, that this smile always came to his lips the moment she put her hands on him. "Doesn't Hell smell like sulfur?"

Lou tilted her head back again, letting the hot water assault her scalp. "You're the good Catholic boy. You tell me."

"May I?" he asked. She opened her eyes to see him closing the lid on the shampoo bottle.

She redirected the shower head so that the water hit her upper back instead of her hair. When Konstantine's fingers touched her scalp, delicious warmth ran through her. She wasn't entirely sure if it was the hot water or the massage. He paused to pick something out of her strands. Seaweed? Algae? She had no idea.

She found herself leaning her body against his.

"You're like a *gatta*." He laughed softly. "*Meow*."

So domesticated, the cold voice whispered.

It was gone the moment he put his hands on her stomach, walking her back into the water's stream. His fingers moved clean water through her strands. His torso brushed hers. Their hips slid against one another, the tops of their thighs brushed.

Lou relished every point of contact.

"What do you do next?" His breath was on her ear and it tightened muscles low in her stomach.

"Conditioner?"

He surveyed the bottles on the ledge.

"You know," she said, smiling up at him. He had only a few inches on her. "I *do* know how to bathe myself."

He didn't hide his smirk. "Why would you when I am here? I'm always at your service."

She saw the gooseflesh rise on his arms and chest.

"You're cold," she said.

He rubbed conditioner between his palms before pushing his fingers through her hair. "It's worth it to share the shower with you."

"Come here."

"Don't you want to rinse?"

She pulled him into the hot water. Her hand trailed down the front of his body, over his abdomen. Her finger rested on the small divot beneath his navel.

"I let my conditioner set. What should I do in the meantime?" She rolled her eyes up to meet his, still tracing his Adonis belt.

"You're my guest," he began, his voice notably dropping an octave. "I should entertain you."

She didn't miss the tight set of his shoulders or the way he slid his gaze away.

He's already preparing for rejection, Lou thought. *And why shouldn't he? I've turned down every advance for over a year.*

It wasn't that she hadn't reciprocated attention. She'd ground her body against his. She'd given him blowjobs, hand jobs, and let him see her naked more times than she could count, but she hadn't let him between her legs.

Part of her was curious how long she could get away with it. Another part simply hadn't cared. She'd always been able to gain pleasure from topping her partners, often more pleasure than from the sex itself.

But this resignation in his hazel eyes now, this anticipation of defeat—

No. That won't do.

Lou kicked the bottles off the wet ledge and propped her foot there. The bottles clattered to the slick floor.

She leaned her weight back against the wall, giving Konstantine a look to match the blatant invitation.

He gulped visibly. He looked down as if unable to control himself. Then he met her gaze again. "Are you sure?"

She arched a brow.

He didn't make the mistake of asking her twice.

When his fingers brushed her wet sex, she slid her arms around his neck, trapping him against her. Part of it was to help her balance, part of it was simply to ensure the compression she desired.

Konstantine didn't mind providing it.

He began with the clitoris, letting the slow heat build until her mind lost track of its thoughts. It was if the steam around them filled her head, suppressing and obscuring everything except the feel of his chest against hers, his lips on her throat, his hand between her legs.

She gave herself over to it.

KONSTANTINE PULLED BACK, SEARCHING HER FACE. HE wanted to look into her eyes the moment he slid inside her.

Her eyes were closed in concentration. A delicious blush had spread across her cheeks.

When her brown eyes finally opened, meeting his, he relinquished her clit and plunged into the hot center of her. Her eyelashes fluttered. Her mouth opened in a soft pant.

The moan that slipped between her lips vibrated through him.

It was as if a cord was cut inside him. His limbs felt heavy and weak, all the tension leaving the line. Yet he built a steady rhythm.

He noticed every shift in her body, every response to his tender probing. When she moaned into his ear his desire exploded. His erection grew so hard it hurt.

He wanted to lay her down somehow. He wanted to taste her. But the shower wasn't big enough.

He knelt instead, his back and heels pressed against the shower door. He was too large to be in the bottom of the shower, but that didn't stop him from nosing his way between her legs and finding her clitoris with his tongue. She trapped his hand in place, making her request for dual stimulation clear. Once he returned his hand to its original task, she released him and cupped either side of his head encouragingly.

He continued like this, with his mouth and his hand in synchronicity, despite the fact the water was turning cold against his back.

She fisted his hair the second before her whole body

tightened. The sounds coming from her throat were more of a whimper than a moan.

Her legs shook when she released his head and for a moment she stood there trembling against the wall.

"Are you—"

"Shut up," she said.

Konstantine obeyed and after a minute or two, she took his hand and slipped it between her legs again.

11

Mel moved the brown grocery sack from one arm to another, trying to alleviate the weight in her arms. Her mind was trying to puzzle out dinner. *Takeout or a nice and easy chicken salad?*

It was hard to focus. It wasn't the chilly air, which she usually attributed to clearer thinking. It was that gnawing feeling that hadn't left her since the day Terrence walked into her shop.

She'd hoped King had scared him away, or even Lady—as Terrence had always hated dogs.

But she knew that she hadn't seen the end of him and that was what weighed on her.

She felt eyes on her back and turned.

A man stepped out of the adjacent corner market with a pack of cigarettes in one hand and a lighter with the price tag still on its plastic casing in the other.

Speak of the devil.

She stopped dead on the corner, facing him.

Better than having him at my back.

"Melly," he said in mock affection. His thin smile appeared. "Fancy seeing you here."

"This is my shop," she said, gesturing at the Madame Melandra's Fortunes and Fixes sign. "As you damn well know."

"I think you mean *our* shop," he said with a wicked smile. He tapped the soft pack of Marlboro's against the heel of his hand.

"*Our* shop," she spat. She almost threw her groceries down on the sidewalk.

"We're married. According to God and the State of Louisiana, what's yours—"

"I'm about to give you what's *yours*," she said and here she did stoop and lean the grocery bag against the storefront.

Don't let no man undo you. Grandmamie's voice rose like a tidal wave. *You're better than this.*

That sharp rebuke diffused her anger.

"You can't loiter here," she said. "Pick any other convenience store in the Quarter or in all of New Orleans for all I care. But you can't hang around here."

He cupped his hands around the end of the cigarette, letting his gaze hold her own. They stood like that, opposite sides of the street, staring for almost a full minute, as Terrence drew on his cigarette. He broke the gaze first, tipping his chin up and blowing thin gray smoke into the sky.

"You wouldn't believe the things people would do for a cigarette in prison. But not me because I had a good little wife who sent me money when she was asked. Do you know *why* she sent me money? Because she didn't want to be in prison either. And why might I *protect* her? Because not only was she my wife, but she was more use to me on the outside."

A sly grin spread across his face. He slid his hands into the front pockets of his jeans and crossed the street to her.

"But if she's no use to me, maybe I shouldn't keep her secrets no more. What do you think?"

Mel tried to steady her breath, shifting the groceries in her hands. "I swear if you—"

He shoved her into the front of her shop, his hand at the base of her throat. The groceries slid from her grip to the street.

And there he was, the Terry she knew and remembered.

"You'll *what*?" he growled. "*What* could you possibly do to me? You can't tell me where I can and can't go. I'm free now. No thanks to you."

As if realizing his position, he released her. He stood back, tugging at the bottom of his white t-shirt. He touched his bone choker self-consciously, as if *he* had just been the one with a hand on his throat.

He bent, lifted her grocery sack off the ground and thrust it into her chest. She wrapped her arms around it reflexively.

"I asked around about your friend, *Mr. King*. I know you're not together, and I know he's a cop. Why you makin' friends with the po-po, Melly? Does your po-po friend know what you did?"

Mel's heart knocked in her throat.

Terrence smiled. "I didn't think so. Or you'd be in jail ya self right now." He flicked the ash off his cigarette. "I'm glad the two of you aren't together. I wouldn't take too kindly to another man touching my wife."

"I'm not your wife," she said. She wanted to throw the sack in his face.

Pull yourself together. Come on. Pull yourself together. He knows how to get a rise out of you. That's all he wants, to get a rise out of you. Push back or he'll just take more ground.

"I don't remember signing no divorce papers," Terry said, sucking his teeth. "I wonder why that was?"

Because I was hoping you'd rot in that place. That if I just forgot about you, you'd disappear like the damn nightmare you are.

"Get the fuck out of New Orleans, Terry. This is the last time I'm telling you."

He laughed, opening his mouth to pinch the tip of his tongue. He removed a piece of tobacco stuck there. "I ain't leaving unless you give me my due. You don't want me around, fine. But a new life costs money and you're already several years behind in your checks."

She unclenched her jaw, trying not to grind the enamel to a pulp.

"Don't you remember your promise?" he said, feigning a pout. "Or do promises not mean anything to you now you're a big time bitch?"

Mel saw the courtroom the way it had looked decades ago, how Terry himself had looked in his orange county jumpsuit, his hair inside its black du-rag. The look he'd given her when the officers pulled him from his seat and dragged him through the doors out of her life.

Why had she even gone to the damn trial? More importantly, why had she gone to see him on that first visitation? If she'd stayed away, if she'd never seen him at all, maybe she'd be free—truly free—now.

But she'd gone because of the photographs.

Across from her, sitting with his shackled wrists on the table, she'd told him about the search warrant. How, the day after Terry was slammed onto the floor of their trailer so hard the dishes rattled in the cupboards, the police had returned with a warrant. They'd torn the house apart, taking no care to replace cushions removed or fix the rugs lifted.

Mel could do nothing but stand in the middle of the living room, one hand clasping her opposite elbow and wait until they were done.

Her heart had quickened when she'd seen the uniformed officer marching toward her.

"Do you know what these are?" he'd asked, thrusting the photographs into her hands.

She'd hoped he hadn't noticed the tremble in her hands as she'd taken them.

The first photograph was of the red Firebird. A dent—a very *human*-shaped dent—curved the grill of the car. Across the paint was something drying—blood? Brain? She couldn't be sure. The other photographs were the same. Every conceivable angle documented the damage to the car. Why had Terry taken them? It couldn't be for an insurance claim because they didn't have car insurance. They couldn't afford it. That's when she'd known it was evidence.

"Well?" the officer had asked, impatiently. He ran a hand through his buzzed blond hair.

She'd licked her lips. "I don't know what they are."

"You don't know what they are?" He snorted, derisively.

"Photographs," she said.

"Is that all they are?" he pressed.

It took everything Mel had had to look up from the photographs, tearing her eyes away from the blood-crusted dent, and meet the officer's eyes.

"I don't know," she'd forced out.

He'd snatched the photographs from her hand and marched away with them. On her front porch, he'd slipped the photographs into a clear plastic bag.

"So they have the evidence now," Mel had told him during that first visitation.

Terry had grinned at that. "They won't know what happened unless *I* tell them."

Horror had rocketed through her then.

"You don't want me to tell nobody, do you?"

"No," she said.

"Good." He'd leaned back in his seat and sucked his teeth.

"You're a good girl and here's what my good girl is going to do for me."

She was going to stay married to him and she was going to send him money. In exchange, he was going to keep her secret.

What had happened when she'd protested? When she'd insisted that she didn't have that kind of money to send him every week?

You'd better find it, he'd said. *Find it or I'm going to tell them what you did. I'm going to tell them you killed somebody and they'll put you in here right next to me.*

It wasn't until four or five years into her payments that Mel realized her mistake. If only she'd never visited, or if only she'd walked away and had never sent her first payout—then it would've just been her word against his.

But she'd paid and she'd kept paying—and only a guilty person would do that.

I can tell them I paid because he's my husband, she said.

And wasn't that why she'd let the marriage stand? It was all she could do to keep that fail safe in place should he turn on her and bite the hand that feeds.

But she was tired of it. She was tired of the lying, tired of the stress, of handing over the money she worked so hard to make to this asshole who didn't deserve a dime of it.

Most of all, she was tired of the guilt eating her from the inside out.

"You remember," he said. Sly confidence filled his face again. "You remember what really happened that night on the old town road outside Baton Rouge. And you remember your promise to me and to God."

Mel heard the sudden squeal of brakes and smelled the burning rubber. She recalled the splatter of rain on the car's windshield and hood. And the unmistakable sound of crying.

"Don't you want to make up for what you did? For all this

freedom you've got out here?" Terrence considered the burning cherry of his cigarette carefully. "I'm thinking a hundred grand will set me up just fine. Get me out of your hair...for a while."

"There's no way in hell," she said with a bitter laugh. "Even if I had that kind of money I wouldn't give it to you."

He sucked his teeth, drawing himself up to his full height. "Sell the shop if you have to, call in favors, I don't care how you get it. Give me the money or get used to seeing my pretty face right here, day and night for the rest of your life—if you're lucky. If you're not lucky, maybe I'll stroll on down to the po-*leece* station and make a report. I'm a good reformed citizen now. Maybe I've got something to say."

He flicked his cigarette onto the sidewalk and ground it out with the heel of his boots.

"Since I'm a nice guy, I'll give you a day to think about it." With a wink and a tap of his hat, he started off down the sidewalk toward Royal Street.

For a moment, Mel could only stand there with her sack of groceries in her hand.

A hundred grand. she thought. *No way in Heaven—or Hell*.

But even as she said it, she heard the rain falling on a windshield and a woman crying softly.

12

Piper knew it would be a busy night the moment she unfolded the card table and twin metal chairs in Jackson Square. There was no shortage of fellow palmists and tarot card readers, so she hoped bathroom breaks weren't out of the question.

Just a couple hundred bucks, she told herself, as she opened the backpack between her feet and dug out her cards and donation box. *Then I'll pack up and get some sleep.*

A desperate shiver ran through her body at the idea of falling into her warm bed for a good night's rest. She'd only managed five or six hours the last few nights and it was catching up to her.

But she also knew better. Piper had never been able to walk away from the chance to make money. It was true that King was letting her rent the apartment above the agency for a pittance and that her wages between her two official jobs with King and Mel had allowed her to put back more money than she'd ever had.

It also helped that she wasn't trying to pay her mother's bills anymore.

A pang of regret shot through her at this thought. That happened whenever she imagined her in that dark and dingy house off the canal with her druggie boyfriend and a coffee table covered in dope, needles, and god only knew what else.

That's not your problem, she thought. *It never was your problem.*

Yet sometimes she shot up in her bed in the dark, heart pounding with an all-consuming belief that it had happened. That her mother was finally dead. But she wasn't and Piper was finding a way to live with that—in the limbo of loving someone she couldn't help.

It wasn't like she didn't have plenty to be getting on with.

She had herself to feed, tuition to cover, her own rent and utilities. Now that she was back in school, she also had her grades to worry about.

It's going to be okay, she told herself. *If only you'd get more sleep.*

Piper unwrapped the cards, feeling the cold cardstock slide out of the black silk into her dry palm. She returned the scarf to her backpack and moved the donation box to one side, propping it open with a little sign.

Tarot and palm readings, by donation only.

She hadn't even gotten comfortable in her chair when her first customer—a forty-year-old woman with thick black eyeliner and a streak of grey through her box-red hair sat down.

"Can you do me?" she asked.

How much? Piper thought, but had the good sense not to make the joke aloud.

"Tarot or palm?" Piper asked and just like that she was off.

She was six readings in before she had a chance to count the money—$103—and bring out the water bottle from her bag. She drank half the bottle in one go.

Two teenage girls with perfect white teeth and ripped

jeans came to the table. The blonde placed two fingers on the table's edge and opened her mouth to speak, but a husky masculine voice came out instead. "This bitch is closed."

Piper lowered the water bottle and found a glorious drag queen standing on the other side of her card table.

Henry, a longtime friend, stood in six-inch stilettos and a golden brassiere. His ass was—as her mother would have put it—tight enough to bounce a quarter off of, and expertly framed by the fishnet hose pulled over it.

The hand on his hip had been recently manicured and the long nails gleamed like honey in the square's streetlights. His other hand was wrapped possessively over the back of the metal chair, preventing either of the girls from sitting down.

"But—" One of the girls began to object, a deep crease forming between her eyes.

Yet one look from Henry sent them both scurrying deeper into the square.

Piper grinned. "Don't frighten the children, H."

"I didn't come all the way down here in my Louboutins to be stopped by some teenage horndogs."

Piper laughed. "Splurging for :ouboutins now? Wow, your dances at Wild Cat must be paying well these days."

He settled down into the folding chair and crossed one leg over the other. "I thought I'd find your skinny ass here. I was starting to think you were avoiding me."

He pushed out his rouged lower lip.

Piper offered her hands across the card table. "Sorry, man. I've been so busy."

He clasped them briefly, giving them a squeeze. His nails grazed her wrist. "I know. So I thought I would come and see you for once. You're always coming to see me, aren't you? I'm sure I owe you."

Piper withdrew, settling back against the chair. In truth, a short mental break wasn't totally unwelcome. "It's good to see you."

Henry tilted his head and batted his enormous eyelashes. "I know." He flashed her a roguish smile. "Now tell me what the hell have you've been up to."

Piper gave him the condensed version of her life—investigation, case building, criminal justice classes, day-to-day at the shop, and the status of her apartment, finishing up with the special hell that was Carnival.

"God, don't I know it," Henry said, gesturing at the rambunctious crowd of drunks around them, covered in beads and plastic masks and ridiculous hats. "Let's hole up in your apartment until it's over."

"You have an open invitation," she promised.

She hadn't made the invitation earlier because one Miss Louie Thorne had a tendency to pop out of dark corners unannounced whenever she pleased, and Piper hadn't been ready to explain that phenomenon to anyone.

"At least you aren't ignoring me because you're shacking up with some girl."

Piper took the money out of her donation box, wrapped it up, and tucked it into the bottom of her backpack. "There's no girl."

"No one on your radar at all?" Henry asked, arching a painted brow. "You haven't seen a girl for days? *Months?*"

Piper noticed his shift in tone and frowned at him. "I had dinner with Dani last night. First time I'd seen her in over a year."

She searched his face when she said it, confirming her suspicions.

"But you knew that, didn't you?"

"I'm friends with Tyriqua." When Piper didn't seem to register the significance of the name he said, "The hostess who seated you told me she'd seen you come in."

"You've got spies in the Quarter," Piper snorted, shuffling the cards absentmindedly. "Why am I not surprised?"

Henry, like Piper, had lived in New Orleans all his life.

"I haven't seen you, is all. I needed to know you weren't dead in a ditch or had fallen into prostitution."

Piper grinned. "Since when do you have a problem with prostitution?"

"I don't. I love prostitutes." He clasped his hands around his knees, glancing around the square. "It's kind of cold out here. You just sit out here all night?"

"Not all night. Just until I make my personal quota."

He's pretending not to care much about Dani, but in a second he's going to ask—

"So what's going on with Dani anyway?" he asked.

Piper smiled. "Who?"

Henry rolled his bedazzled eyes. "The journalist who used you for a story and then decided she likes you—probably because you laid her better than she'd ever been laid in her life—and now wants to kiss and make up."

Piper felt the heat rise in her face. "We didn't have sex."

Henry arched his brows again. "Well that speaks volumes all on its own, doesn't it? Piper, heart-slayer, *didn't* bed a gorgeous woman who wanted it. *Damn.* The world must be ending."

"You're reading too much into it." Yet Piper wondered why her heart was knocking strangely in her chest.

"Hmmm," he said, unconvinced, and let his gaze slide out over the square again. Piper followed his lead, noting the lit lamps, the crowds chattering. People standing around with their cups of booze or hot drinks. A brass band was tuning up to begin their set. The square echoed with laughter and the chatter of dozens of overlapping conversations. One girl holding a hurricane glass looked ready to puke in the shrub beside her.

Henry pointed at the other tables clustered around. All of them were full with a few hosting lines.

"You ever get your own cards read?" he asked.

"No. I don't have time for that."

He checked the clock on his phone, then seemingly satisfied, reached across the table. He waved his manicured nails. "Hand them over."

Piper laughed. "What?"

"The cards. Give them to me. I'm going to tell your fortune."

She drew them back instinctively. "You don't know how to read cards."

"No, but you do. You pick them and I'll turn them over and you can read them for yourself."

She wanted to argue that wasn't actually him reading the cards, but his face was so determined she laughed and gave up the deck.

It was incredibly difficult to read one's own fortune, even if someone else volunteered to do the flipping and shuffling. Everyone had a self-view and self-beliefs always got in the way of seeing a situation objectively. That's why it was better to get someone else's interpretation.

"This should be interesting," she said, unaware that she'd folded her arms over her chest.

Henry watched her with a devilish grin as he shuffled the deck. "Do you have a question?" he asked in a mock fortune-teller voice. It was over the top, dramatic, and actually went well with his drag queen persona. The wide eyes helped.

Piper giggled. "Let's just do a Celtic cross."

"Ah, yes," he said, remaining in character.

Piper laughed, her knee accidentally bumping the table. It rocked. "You can stop shuffling. Spread them out for me so I can pick ten."

Henry did as he was told and Piper took her time

thumbing through the deck. She only picked the cards that made her hesitate, the ones she kept coming back to.

When she had all ten cards removed from the deck, she moved the pile over to one side and handed the ten cards to Henry.

"Keep them in order, like that," Piper instructed. "Just flip one at a time."

He nodded, gravely. Piper wondered if maybe he would do a fortune teller skit of some kind for his next drag show. Surely there was a song that would work for it. Didn't The Rolling Stones also have a song about a fortune teller?

Despite his long, elegant nails, Henry flipped the cards easily, one at a time, putting them down where Piper instructed him to.

"Look at all these cups," he said, batting his eyes at her. "I wonder what they mean?"

She refrained from rolling her eyes. "The cups suit usually has to do with love and relationships."

"Oh," he said in mock surprise. "Imagine that."

"I thought you didn't know anything about tarot."

"I know a little. Enough to know this is all about *love*." He tapped the Ace of Cups. Then he plucked one card off the table and held it up at her accusingly. "The Lovers? Come on now."

He tapped the Queen of Wands.

"What about this one?" he asked.

That's Dani, she thought. "A strong, independent and passionate woman."

Henry arched a brow. "A reporter perhaps."

And Piper couldn't argue. The cards she saw spread before her had every indication of a new and promising love. One that, given enough time, could bloom into complete fulfillment. A soulmate connection. But it wasn't a straight shot to happily ever after. There were obstacles—big ones—that would slow down progress.

A shiver ran down Piper's arms.

He laid another card down and then frowned. "This one looks less cheerful."

It was the Five of Swords. Ill-gotten gains. Victory through deceit.

"It's a card about double-crossing someone," Piper told him.

"She did double-cross you." He pulled the card close to better see the artistic detail.

"Yeah," Piper agreed. But the positions of the cards also mattered. This betrayal was in the future, not the past. In fact, it was just on the horizon.

Henry threw down the cards, giving Piper a minute to look them over.

There was the promise of romance, but on the fringe cards something darker lurked. *Keep your eyes open*, her intuition said. *Keep your eyes open for what's going on around you. Something is happening right under your nose.*

But she couldn't be sure if that was about Lou, about hunting killers, or her work at the agency. Or if maybe it was about her mother. Or maybe Mel, who she'd been thinking about on and off all day. The way her hands had shook. That man in the bone choker...

Pay attention to what? she wondered.

"Just talk to her," Henry said at last, misreading her troubled expression. "I'm sure she's sorry. So she got a little short-sighted in the face of her ambition, but I think an ambitious woman is exactly what you need in your life. You should give her another chance."

"Why?"

"Because I can tell you're super into her and I can't let you walk away over something as stupid as her doing her job."

Piper gathered up the cards, unable to shake the worry knotting in her guts.

Pay attention...to what...

"Earth to Piper." He clapped his hands.

"Okay, okay. I'll text her," she agreed, shuffling the cards to clear them of her own energy.

"Good," Henry said, loving when he wins.

He reached into his golden brassiere and fished out a folded $20 bill. He threw it into Piper's donation box and leaned forward coquettishly.

He placed his chin in the palm of his hand. "Now, do me."

13

Lou dreamed. A white t-shirt. Red blooming through cotton as she was lifted by strong, sure hands, and thrown into waiting waters. The ghostly face of retribution emerged from the dark like a carnival mask. A gun turning its black eye on her.

Pop! Pop! Pop!

With a gasp she sat up in bed. Her heart knocked against the base of her throat, making it difficult to breathe. The back of her neck was soaked with sweat. When she wiped at her forehead, she found it wet too.

She slowed her breath. She counted the green and gold fleur-de-lis emblems embroidered in the blanket stretched over her legs.

Green and gold.

Konstantine's bed. She turned and saw him sleeping on his back, chest bare. The sheet cut across his abdomen as his chest rose and fell slowly. One hand was tucked under his head, the other in the waistband of his pants.

She clasped her hands behind her neck and squeezed. It

had been a long time since she'd dreamed of her father's murder.

What had triggered it now? Why should the terror of that night—a decade and a half behind her—rise up now?

She slid from the bed as quietly as she could, looking for her clothes. They were still soaked from her time with Ricky Walker, but she didn't need to wear them. Konstantine had given her a pair of gray sweats and a large white t-shirt that hung off one of her shoulders.

You're dry. You're safe. So why the dream?

She didn't want to leave the clothes behind. She grabbed them in both fists and turned to the bed once more.

Konstantine continued to sleep, but Lou had a sneaking suspicion that he was pretending.

Why? So she could sneak off without explanation?

The shadows softened and stretched around her. It thinned for her as it always had, offering her passage.

Say something. Anything, she thought. *Tell him goodbye. Give him a kiss.*

Konstantine's apartment fell away and in its place her own apartment formed around her.

The old world charm and sounds of a languid canal were exchanged with the bright city lights of downtown St. Louis. The Gateway Arch, illuminated at night, stood guard over the Mississippi River. Lamp posts and skyscrapers twinkled like trapped fallen stars.

Her bed was as she'd left it, unmade. Its downy comforter was rumpled and bathed in moonlight. Lou admired the skyline for a moment longer before crossing to a laundry basket and tossing in her soaked clothes.

Gauging by the color of the skyline, she'd only slept a couple hours after falling into bed with Konstantine. Her GPS watch said it was just past three in the morning here.

It was too early to pester King or check on Fish

again. She could hunt. But she was tired. Her head buzzed and her eyes felt like they had sand in them. She fell onto her mattress and pulled her comforter over her body.

You're going to bed? Then why did you leave Konstantine at all? You could've slept in his bed as well as yours. Hell, his bed is more comfortable.

That much was true.

Lou suspected it was because Konstantine had a proper frame, headboard and all, whereas she had only a mattress on the floor.

But that didn't explain the restlessness that filled her.

It made her legs itch and palms ache. She turned onto one pillow, fluffing it. When that provided no relief, she turned onto the other. She removed the comforter, then added it again.

She slid her hand into her pillowcase, searching for... *there*. She retrieved the 5x8 photo from the pillowcase's cotton folds and held the photo up to the moonlight.

Her father smiled down at her. His hair was wet with ocean water, his eyes bright with his laughter. Lou, no more than eight at the time, was tucked under one of his muscular arms.

She wondered if she would have forgotten his face—as she had her mother's—if not for this photo.

Jack Thorne. He was young when he was murdered by the mafia—by Konstantine's family.

The dream pressed in on her again, a white shirt soaking through with blood. The *pop-pop-pop* of gunfire. Angelo's phantom face.

"Stop it," she whispered to the dark. *You didn't even see him get shot.*

The moment that Angelo had burst through the back gate one late summer night in June, her father had lifted and thrown her into their pool knowing the waters would save her.

How often had Lou wondered if maybe he had simply jumped into the water with her—if only to shield her body with his own—how he might have survived. Perhaps she would've been able to take them both away.

But Lou hadn't been able to successfully carry anything through the dark with her until she was older. That was probably why these fantasies of saving her father were so few and far between these days. No matter how she turned the memory—and hadn't she turned it every way imaginable?—it always came out the same.

Jack Thorne had made his choices. And Louie had been left to live with them.

So why the dreams? she wondered, looking at the swirled patterns in her ceiling.

Lou knew her mind well enough to know when it was signaling something to her. It was trying to bring something up from its murky depths into the light of Lou's awareness.

But the message wasn't yet clear to her and forcing it wouldn't make the revelation come any faster.

Finding the pillows flat and comforter suffocating, Lou stood and stretched. She checked the time again.

4:08.

She got a drink of water. She placed the empty glass on the counter.

Without consciously deciding to, she let her apartment dissolve around her once more. The granite countertops and water-stained glass faded from her view. In its place a shadowed bedroom rose to meet her.

Coarse carpet formed under her feet. In front of her, a queen bed sat center stage in a small bedroom. Beneath a purple comforter, a blonde head poked out. Lou traced the outline of the bed, vaguely noting the closed laptop and text-books covering one side.

Lou moved these to the floor, lifted the comforter, and slid in.

The girl woke immediately.

"Lou?" Piper raised her head. She blinked and wiped her eyes.

"Yeah."

"What's wrong? Did—"

"Everything's fine," Lou said to counter the girl's rising alarm.

"Oh." Piper's frown deepened. "You okay?"

"I couldn't sleep."

Piper lifted the sheets, frowning. "Whose clothes are you wearing? No, don't tell me. You smell like *man*."

Lou snorted.

But Piper's humor didn't hold. "Seriously, are you okay?"

"I'm fine." Lou tucked the pillow under her head. "Why are you looking at me like that?"

Piper propped her head in her hand. "I don't know. It's dark in here so I can't see your face really well, but you look...weird."

"Thanks."

"I mean, your face is fine but you look upset. Did you have a bad hunt or something?"

Lou thought of Walker's last pitiful screams before Jabber's milk-white maw wrapped around his throat.

"No," she said.

Piper finally lowered her head to the pillow, fluffing it for added height. "So there's nothing you want to talk about? No feelings you're dealing with? No explanation why you smell like some Italian dude and are clearly wearing his clothes, but you just climbed in bed with a lesbian in the dead of night? *No*? Everything is *perfectly* fine, is it?"

"I'm fine," Lou said, noting her own defensiveness.

Piper snorted. "I'm not sure if you're aware, but you *do* have emotions, Lou-blue. Like everyone else. Maybe you want to check in on them once in a while."

Lou thought of the dream again. Of her father's startled cry before he threw her away—even if it was to save her life. "I had a bad dream. That's all."

As soon as she said it, she felt stupid.

Piper's face softened. "What kind of bad dream?"

"The night my parents were killed."

Piper sat up, exhaling. "Why are you dreaming about the night you lost everything? Did something scare you?"

"No."

Piper was undeterred. She lowered her voice conspiratorially. "Are you sure? What did you do tonight?"

"I went to the bar and got Walker—"

Piper clucked her tongue. "*No.* What did you do with *Konstantine*? Did you have sex?"

"No."

"No, I guess having sex wouldn't send you running to my bed in the middle of the night." She broke into a huge grin. "*Or would it?* Was it *bad* sex?"

"No." Lou gave her a dangerous look.

Piper only laughed. "Oh man. You're killing me. Listen, you just need to listen to yourself. Figure out how you feel. That's what I'm trying to do."

Lou frowned. "With who?"

Piper put one hand under her head and snorted. "Freaking Dani. I mean why does she have to be so beautiful and intelligent. And have you seen her hands? They're so pretty and she kisses like—"

Lou sat up in bed. "Do you want me to leave? It sounds like you need to be alone. Or I could go get her."

Piper elbowed her under the covers. "Don't even joke

about that. Besides you're the one who *didn't* have sex and then decided to come sleep with a lesbian."

Lou elbowed her.

Piper folded, protecting her ribs. "Don't worry. I'm not going to let you do what I do in these situations."

"What do you do?"

"Run off and sleep with someone else. That's how I roll."

Lou only frowned harder.

"Seriously, ever since Dani showed up, I've been thinking about calling my ex about twenty times a day. I know, I know. It's not healthy. Unless you're here for some distraction too, because if you *are*—"

Piper puckered up and leaned in for a kiss.

Lou pushed her off, smiling.

Piper continued making dramatic kissy faces until Lou had the pillow pressed firmly over her face. After a momentary struggle, Piper tapped out.

Once the laughter died and they'd settled back down to their own sides of the bed, Piper spoke up once more.

"Listen. We are smart, capable women. We'll conquer this bullshit. At least we aren't psychopaths."

"I murder people."

"Yeah, but you've also got some empathy. Lady loves you and dogs are never wrong." Piper adjusted her head on her pillow. "You're worlds apart from trash humans like Jeffrey fucking Fish. Oh, do you want to know what I found out about him today?"

Lou turned on her side to face her. "Yes."

"In high school he worked part time in a cemetery. Two cemeteries actually that were side by side. One for people, one for pets. It looks like he was there for about a year before he got fired."

Lou's compass stretched out through space and time, locking on Fish. But there was no immediate thrum of danger. No doubt he would make his move soon, but at least for tonight, the beast was still caged.

"Can you guess why he got fired?" Piper asked, rolling on her side to face Lou.

Lou thought of the photographs again. The glossy sheen capturing the pain and fear on the women's faces. Their tear-stained faces. The spit drying on their lips and chins from so much screaming.

"No," Lou said.

"He was caught digging up the graves. Digging them up so he could look at the decomposing bodies. What a freak!"

Lou thought of the grocer standing in her bedroom window, face scrubbed for the night. Lou didn't want her to become another photograph in Fish's collection.

She couldn't let that happen.

Piper placed a hand on Lou's arm. "We'll stop him before he hurts that girl. You're amazing and I'm going to help you get the evidence you need. We've got this. But first, we have to sleep."

Sleep, Lou thought and worried she wouldn't be able to manage it in this bed either.

But she was wrong.

14

King reached into his fridge and grabbed the cold neck of the soda bottle. He twisted the cap off with the end of his shirt and threw it into the sink. The first deep gulps were delicious, even if they did burn his throat.

He'd left the office for a mid-day lunch. It was a perk he enjoyed as the boss with the added convenience of living around the corner from the agency.

With a satisfied sigh, he put the soda down and unwrapped two leftover steak enchiladas. He peeled back the aluminum foil before popping them into the microwave.

That's when he caught Lady's steady gaze. She was too proud—or well trained—to outright beg, but King was no fool.

"Oh, all right." He reached into the cabinet beside his stove. He drew out a long rawhide bone and held it in front of her snout. "Will this do?"

She closed her jaws around the bone, her tail swishing gleefully behind her as she took her prize over to the rug. She stretched long, her hind legs thrown out behind her.

With seconds left on his lunch, King's phone rang. There was no number, which was enough to tell King exactly who was calling. "King here."

"Good evening," a man said. The lilting Italian accent gave the man's words a melodic quality. "I have the information you asked for."

"That was quick." King's enchiladas beeped. He grabbed a plate from the cabinet and dumped them from their wax carton onto the plate before fishing through a drawer for a fork.

"What's for lunch?" Konstantine asked, obviously hearing the microwave ding.

"Mexican." King found his fork and shut the drawer. "So what can you tell me about those drugs?"

"They were mine," Konstantine said plainly.

King's fork hovered above the enchiladas. "Really?"

"Yes," he said with a hint of amusement in his voice. "But I didn't make the kill personally, if that is your next question."

King saw Rita Cross's slack jaw and one gold tooth. His stomach soured.

He'd never be so bold as to outright accuse the Ravengers' kingpin of murder, but King also wasn't stupid. There was no doubt in his mind that he had blood on his hands. Perhaps not as much as Lou personally, but enough.

"Why were they killed?"

"He was stealing the drugs and she was in the home when they came for him."

He says it so matter of factly.

"And where is the man responsible? Do you know?"

"I'm afraid that if you go looking for him, you will not find him," Konstantine said.

King sank onto his sofa, placing his plate on the coffee table in front of him. He placed his soda on a Margarita

Shake coaster and threw his fork onto the plate. The anger building inside him made the enchiladas less appealing

"Convenient." He consciously unclenched his jaw. "Did you see the handiwork yourself?"

"No."

"It was brutal. The woman..." He lifted his fork and put it on the plate again. "It was bad. Did you tell them to kill her?"

"No. I do not condone violence against women. And daily operations aren't my responsibility."

Daily operations. Christ. King dragged his hand down his face, trying to clear the image of the fly landing on Cross's toe.

"When a man steals from our organization, as Shawn Mince did, there are consequences, Mr. King. If the consequences aren't severe, more people would steal, don't you agree?"

King marveled that a world as lawless as the drug trade relied so heavily on order, but it made a certain amount of sense. In the Ravengers, Konstantine might be CEO. His managers aren't going to ask him to discipline an employee who's stolen a stapler. King supposed he had bigger problems to contend with.

"So his name was Shawn Mince and he was stealing the drugs from the Ravengers?"

"Given the quantity found, it seems that he was taking them for a long time."

"Why did he keep them rather than sell them?"

"There was likely no opportunity for him to sell without being discovered. He tried and was caught."

"So your manager handled the problem?"

"Manager?"

"Drug mule. Lackey. Local boss. Whoever is in charge here in New Orleans. This guy discovered that Mince was stealing and he made an example of him."

"Yes."

King patted his pocket looking for his notebook and pen. "Any chance I can get a name of the guy who cut up Rita Cross? He deserves to be taken in, don't you think?"

Konstantine's voice crackled across the line.

"You there?" King checked the bar strength on his phone. Damn dead spots. "Hold on. You're breaking up."

King stood, glancing at the urn.

"Keep an eye on that, would you?" He motioned toward his lunch.

King opened the French doors and stepped out onto his balcony. The cold February nipped his cheeks and ears. He flipped up the collar on his coat, realizing now that he'd never taken it off, and checked the phone again.

"You still there?"

"I'm here," Konstantine replied, his voice clear as a bell.

"I want his name."

"I cannot give you a name."

King wrapped a hand around the balcony. Red pressed in the corner of his vision. "I suppose this is about the drugs. It's a lot of drugs to lose."

"Did I lose them?" Konstantine asked.

King heard the smile in his voice.

Then he realized with clarity this wasn't about the drugs or the murder.

King leaned a hip into the balcony. "Do you own the *entire* NOLA PD or just a few of the officers?"

"You are confusing me with Dmitri Petrov, Mr. King. I am not in the business of owning anyone."

"So the cops just take all the drugs out of the house, pack them up and what, ship them to your local supplier?"

Konstantine said nothing.

King opened his mouth to dig deeper—he wanted the

name of Rita Cross's killer damn it—but a man on the street below caught his eye.

He was tall, lean with a bone choker tight across his throat. His leather hat had a crow feather protruding from its left side.

King first noted the lack of coat. True it was warmer in New Orleans than say, Chicago, but one didn't walk around bare armed even in the crowded Quarter. Not in February.

In the light from the convenience store window King thought he could make out the hazy outline of a prison tattoo. But it wasn't clear from where he stood.

The man watched Melandra's Fortunes and Fixes with a hungry expression that King didn't like one bit. As if sensing eyes on him, the man looked up suddenly and met King's gaze.

The smile that spread across his face, a scarecrow's smile, made the hair on the back of King's neck rise.

"The fact remains that a woman was killed. Brutally," King said, but the anger in his voice had cooled. "Forget about the drugs for a second and think about her."

"I assure you that the man responsible for her murder will be handled. I cannot control the actions of every man I employ. I can only make my *sentiments* known."

So your guy makes an example of Shawn Mince and then you make an example of your guy, King thought. It was a stark reminder, should King have made the mistake of thinking Konstantine was only a diplomat.

A low growl made King look down. Lady's nose was stuck between the balcony's slats. If King didn't know better, she was following the man with her gaze.

"Yeah, he looks like trouble," King agreed, giving the dog a pat on the head.

"Excuse me?"

King turned back to the conversation. "If you can't give me names, I guess we're done here."

"I regret that I cannot help you in your investigation. But I assure you the man has been punished."

Tell that to Rita Cross.

"Is there anything else I can do for you, Mr. King?" Konstantine said.

King searched the swelling crowd for the man with a crow feather in his hat. "Actually, there is one more thing you could do."

S omeone knocked on the door. Lou turned toward the sound, toothbrush in hand. Her foaming mouth frowned. This was the second time in twice as many years that someone had knocked on her apartment door. Her instinctual response was to run. Simply step into her converted linen closet, close the door, and disappear.

Instead she crept toward the front door.

The last time someone had come, it had been a law firm courier, delivering letters from her dead aunt. But Aunt Lucy was in her grave—or urn, so to speak—along with her parents. There wasn't anyone left to send letters. And Lou had never given her address to anyone else.

Lou looked through the peephole. A woman with a bouquet of flowers and a blue denim hat stood on the other side of the door. *ABC Florists* was stitched into the cap's bill with red thread.

Tired of waiting, the woman put the vase on the floor, wedged the card into the door's frame and left. Lou waited until she heard the door to the stairwell clank closed before she opened the door.

The card fell onto the floor, face down. Lou plucked it from the carpet along with the vase.

Her first emotion: *annoyance*.

Lou carried the flowers inside and shut the door behind her, compulsively turning the lock even though the top floor of her apartment building was now empty.

Why would he bother?

Lou appraised the gift. It was a strange vase. Large and wooden with intricate carvings on its sides. The explosion of garden roses, carnations, pink lilies, alstroemeria, baby's breath, greenery and a few flowers Lou didn't recognize on sight.

Then a phone began to ring.

Lou cocked her head, locating the sound before lifting the vase. Taped to the bottom of the vase was a burner flip phone. She let it ring while she rinsed her mouth in the kitchen sink.

Lou answered it on the sixth ring, certain she knew who was calling. "How did you figure out my address?"

"Do you like the flowers?" Konstantine countered.

"*How* did you get my address?" Because Lou had been careful, long before Konstantine had taken it upon himself to scour the world on her behalf, to keep her whereabouts untraceable.

"The law firm who manages your father's estate and trust have a list of properties. Five are located in your area. I used internet maps to figure out which one was you. Only one fit."

When she'd let him heal in her bed after Nico's assassination attempt, he would've seen the skyline for himself. Who else had been in this apartment? Lucy, King. She should've known the skyline was a liability

"You don't know what I like," she said plainly, even as she leaned in to smell a gorgeous peach garden rose.

"No?" He voice was full of amusement. "Did I get the flowers or the colors wrong?"

She didn't humor him with a reply, but inwardly she thought *color*. These blooms were too soft and feminine. She preferred deep reds and purples.

"Perhaps you'll like what's in the box better? Can you figure out how to open it?"

She frowned at the arrangement. "There's no box."

"The vase," he said after some hesitation.

She traced the whirls etched into the wood, feeling for any loose seams. One small node, and another shifted slightly under her fingertips as she passed over it. She went back and pressed them again. One then the other and when that did not work, both at the same time.

Something clicked. The wooden panel slid away.

Lou removed the Browning pistol. It was a standard hi-power Browning. She palmed the walnut grip and noted the adjustable sights.

"They discontinued these," Lou said. "How did you find a new one?"

"Almost new," Konstantine corrected. "Very gently used."

Lou was certain that guns were never *gently* used but didn't argue. She appreciated the weight of the Browning in her hand.

"There are two," Konstantine said. "The hammers have been replaced to prevent them from biting your hand."

"Do you think I don't know how to hold it?" Lou inspected the wooden vase again and discovered the second secret panel.

"No," he said. Then after a short pause, he added, "What do you think?"

That I guess you do know what I like.

Lou heard something in his voice then. But he'd covered it so quickly she couldn't be sure.

"I think...I'd love to see what you can fit in a chocolate box."

He laughed at her joke, but it was too tight. It wasn't the easy vibrato that she enjoyed.

When the laughter died away and the silence stretched itself long, Konstantine said, "When will I see you again?"

Was that what this gift was about?

She hadn't returned to his bed since the night in the shower. She hadn't slipped there by accident—at least not that she was aware—not even to say hello.

Maybe that was what she heard in his voice.

"When do you go to Venice?" she asked instead.

"Tonight," he said. "For three nights at most. Vittoria..."

The hair rose on the back of Lou's neck at the way he said her name.

"She's *very* challenging," he said with a tender laugh.

"Have a good trip." She regarded the beautiful pistols in her grip, preparing to end the call.

"Wait, Lou."

Lou put the phone to her ear again. When she thought he wasn't going to answer he finally said, "I hope I see you in Venice."

Lou decided to take the Browning pistols with her to check on Fish. She crossed to her kitchen island and unhooked a small latch tucked beneath the lip of the counter.

The side sprang free and Lou descended the steps into its darkness. Even years after building this room, it still smelled of sawdust and soft pine. She breathed deeply, loving the scent.

She found the string overhead on the first try and pulled, illuminating her hidden storeroom.

Guns lined the shelves neatly. A belt of grenades hung

from a hook on the wall, as well as her father's service vest. She touched it tenderly, without realizing she'd done so, as she reached out for a box of 9mm bullets. She loaded both Brownings.

She considered the weaponry lining the shelves but decided the guns would do.

It was early in the day, which made it harder for her to move around and less chance of serious trouble. A flamethrower, grenades, or heavy artillery of any kind simply wouldn't be feasible.

Night was easier.

Upstairs with the island sealed again, Lou put the Brownings in her shoulder holster. She placed one on each side. It was true she was ambidextrous when it came to shooting. She'd trained hard on both sides of her body, but she favored her right. She slid the leather jacket on, covering the guns and added her mirrored sunglasses as a finishing touch.

Stepping into her dark linen closet, she breathed a nervous sigh. Even after all this time, after more than fifteen years of hunting men, she still got excited. It didn't even have to be the killing moment. The stalking, the watching—all parts of the chase were enough.

No one else would notice the electricity in her fingertips, or the way her heart sped slightly in her chest. But she did.

She was most herself when in search of something. There was no denying it.

She leaned against the bare wall, smelling the cedar sachet she'd thrown in the bottom of the converted closet. She reached out and touched the rough wall, feeling wood grain pull at her fingertips. Her nails caught on the end of a brace, one of the four that used to hold up shelves before Lou removed them.

She closed her eyes, focusing on that compass inside her. She willed it to hone in on Fish. After a moment of cool darkness, a sense of floating in black waters, the tug came. A pin was dropped in the map of her mind and she felt the currents of those waters shift direction like rounding a river bend.

She let go of her hold on the world, parting the shadows around her, and slipped through. When Lou found herself in the solid world again, her little closet had expanded by three or four times its size.

The only light in the room came from beneath the crack in the door. Lou stepped toward it groping the wall on the side of the door until she found a light switch.

A bathroom sprang into view. A single toilet beside a safety bar was in the left corner behind her. Adjacent to that sat a white sink beneath a mirror. Smeared soap creased its corners.

Lou pushed the door open a crack.

It was a hallway full of shuffling bodies. Teenagers opened and slammed lockers. Books were shoved roughly into backpacks.

In the sea of bodies, Lou spotted Fish. He stood a head taller than most of the teens. They parted around him like water around a boulder.

Surveying him there, shoulder to shoulder with a brunette girl, pointing out something in the textbook she held open in her palms, Lou understood why her compass had selected this bathroom.

Light from the hall's windows struck him in all directions. It sprang from open classrooms and the fluorescents beating down from above. There was no way she could've gotten closer to him.

Fish reached forward to turn the textbook's page. Lou didn't miss the way his shoulder brushed the girl's. Nor did she miss the nervous smile that reflexively crossed the student's lips.

Even from where she hid in the bathroom, Lou saw the gauze peeking out from under his light purple dress shirt.

What do you tell them, Fish? She wondered. *Oh that? It's nothing. I cut myself working in the garage.* Or perhaps to his little wife, *I've been pretending to make your kitchen island for six months so that I have an excuse to stare at my precious photographs. It's better than slitting this pretty girl's throat, isn't it?*

How many monsters simply walked the world as this man did? Hidden in plain sight, in classrooms or offices or marital beds.

Fish licked his lips, laughing at something the girl said. Lou understood the look in his eye and was certain that she was one of the few people in the world who knew it for what it was.

You're playing with your food, Fish.

Lou's head throbbed. Her fingers itched to pull her gun. She became hyperaware of a thunderous pulse in her throat and her own gnawing hunger in her guts.

She wanted him. She wanted to take him right here and now to her own special place. She wanted to hurt him, watch him cry, watch him beg.

We're playing a different game, King had said.

Lou hoped Fish was about to lose.

There were signs he might. His polished edges were wearing away, as she noticed the deepening dark circles beneath his eyes. His once clean and clipped nails had been recently chewed. The thumb in particular looked savaged, the cuticle red and pulled back.

Does anyone else see these things? Or is it only me? And then, *He's trying. He's trying to hold himself back.*

And who was she to judge? Hadn't she been pacing her apartment just an hour before?

Do you think his craving is stronger or weaker than yours? a voice asked. It sounded suspiciously like Aunt Lucy's voice of reason. Aunt Lucy's kind patience was enough to tug at her heart. It was enough to stunt the hunger building inside her. And it was typical of Lucy to bring compassion to any moment like this. *Do you like how it feels when you're that restless?*

The crack through which Lou surveyed Fish's world suddenly widened.

A teenager in hot pink pants stepped back surprised.

"God, lock the door!" a girl huffed. Her bright eyeshadow creased with her scowl. As her eyes roved Lou's body the scowl only deepened. "This is the *handicap* bathroom, lady. Are you even—"

Lou pulled the door shut but didn't lock it. Instead, she hit the light switch and was gone.

16

A sharp voice pulled Mel from her thoughts. "Mr. Rushdie can see you now."

A receptionist with bushy eyebrows regarded Mel over his computer. His gelled hair was slicked back from his face and his gaze was indifferent at best. Mel wondered how long this one would last, as it seemed that Rushdie had a new receptionist every time she visited the cramped little office downtown.

Mel rose from her seat in the waiting area and threw a nervous glance at the three fake plants against the far wall before reaching the mahogany door at the end of the room. It opened before her hand could clasp the handle.

"Ms. Durand." The balding man extended his liver-spotted hand toward her. "Come on in now."

"Thank you for making the time to see me." Melandra sidestepped through the narrow doorway into the cramped office so that the lawyer could close the door behind her.

The desk sagged with stacks of file folders one on top of the other. Some stacks looked quite precarious, nearly on the verge of tumbling into the floor. The filing cabinets behind the desk, all as tall as she was, looked no better. Some of the drawers didn't even close. Tabs protruded from them at unkempt angles like crooked teeth.

"I understand you want some legal advice about your business and husband." Rushdie shuffled past her, his head half-tucked like a turtle. One of his shoulders hunched up, giving him an uneven walk just short of hunchback.

"Please sit down," he said, when he came around the desk and found her still standing awkwardly in the middle of the room, wringing her hands. "We're all friends here."

Mel forced a smile and obediently perched on the edge of one of the stiff chairs.

Rushdie seemed to sense that further encouragement was needed. "Why don't you tell me what's on your mind?"

She licked her lips. "My husband—" *God* she loathed to say the word. "—just got out of prison and now he's here in New Orleans."

"Is this a happy reunion?"

"No," Mel freely admitted. "No, not at all."

"You've seen him?" Rushdie was searching the papers on his desk, looking for something.

"A few times. He's been trying to...harass me into giving him money and says he is entitled to part of my business because we're married."

Rushdie settled on a piece of paper, lifting it closer to his bespectacled eyes. "Is this the gentleman you came to me about in '99?"

"Yes," Melandra said. Though she thought the word *gentleman* was a gross and inaccurate description for Terry.

"He was already in prison then?" He eyed Melandra over his thick spectacles. Her mouth hung open in a heavy pant.

"Correct."

"And your little shop is something you built while he was in prison."

Mel tried not to stiffen at the patronizing *little shop* comment. Maybe it wasn't much to this guy, but she'd worked hard to get her business off the ground and keep it off the ground.

Rushdie leaned back in his chair. "I remember you cancelling the divorce proceedings in '99, but if you've changed your mind and want to pursue divorce, we can certainly begin those proceedings now. And we can make the case in court that you're a good, hardworking woman who doesn't deserve to give half her livelihood to such a man. It helps that he was in jail for so long. It will be easier to paint the picture of why you shouldn't have to share. But Ms. Durand, they're going to ask why you didn't divorce him sooner."

Of course they'll ask and what the hell am I supposed to say?

Rushdie arched his brows. "Did you still love him perhaps?"

The attorney's slow, southern drawl gave the impression of mock sympathy.

Mel straightened. "No."

Rushdie nodded as if he'd expected this. "All right. Did he threaten or coerce you into staying? He has the history of violence against you, does he not? And let me be honest here. Even if that's not the story, we might want to embellish, if you know what I'm saying."

Mel wasn't sure how much Rushdie remembered from the murder trial that eventually led to Terrence's incarceration. So she briefly retold him the story.

She began with the affair, with the hickeys on his neck and finding his parked car outside Sholanda's trailer on many a night when Terry said he'd gone to the bar.

What she *didn't* say was how she'd gone to the trailer herself one morning. After sitting in the gravel for fifteen minutes working up the courage to knock on the door, how

Sholanda had opened the door before she even knocked. The woman had known perfectly well who Mel was. She'd offered Mel sweet tea in a plastic tumbler and waited until Mel managed to ask in perfect calm, *Do you love him?*

Sholanda said that she did.

Even though he did that to you? Mel had pointed at the black bruise spreading across Sholanda's right cheek.

Even so, the girl had said. And Mel felt like she'd never understood another person so deeply in her life than she had in that moment.

And Melandra—god forgive her—didn't mind the affair.

For one, she was no longer the target of Terry's drunken assaults. Years of being forced onto the mattress or struck across the face, shoulders, and back had slowed from every day, to weekly, to monthly, until nothing at all. He still took her money. He still pawned anything of value that she didn't carefully hide away. But that felt like such a minor insult after everything else.

Mel left Sholanda's trailer that day without having drunk the tea and it was the last time Mel had seen the woman alive.

A year later, Terry beat the girl to death. She'd been four months pregnant with his child.

To all this, Rushdie only shrugged. "Has he hurt you since he's got out of prison?"

Mel shook her head. Though she thought of the snarl on his face as he'd thrown her into the wall outside her shop and the way he'd grabbed her wrist before that.

Rushdie sucked his teeth. "Too bad. But we can still make all the arguments. It's really just a matter of how well we prove your virtue and his indecency. The good news is that he's got quite the track record of indecency. We only have to hope that he doesn't try and play the *reformed* card."

He reached for the cigarettes on his desk.

He paused, rolling his hound-dog eyes up to Mel's. "Do you mind?"

"Not if you give me one." Mel's bangles clanked on her wrist as she reached forward.

Rushdie grinned. "Why yes, of course. I think my office might be the last public place in the whole state of Louisiana where smoking is allowed."

Mel smiled, accepting the cigarette offered.

"Here now," he said, coming out of his seat with the lighter in one hand.

Mel leaned forward, letting him light the end of her cigarette.

Something about the scene reminded her of Grandmamie's porch. Of some hot summer day, or at least, it seemed like all her days in the parish bayou were hot summer days.

She'd just finished collecting the chicken eggs as she was told to do, dumping them carefully from a faded apron into a basket by the front door.

"You missed one," Grandmamie had said from her place on the porch step. She'd pointed a crooked finger at a patch of high grass in the yard. "There."

Of course her grandmother was right. Grandmamie was always right.

"After supper you make sure those chickens end up back in the coop now. Latch that door tight." She'd flicked her ash. "I've seen them racoons running around here. And a fox too. Can't have them eating our girls, now can we?"

Mel had been watching the thin gray smoke rise from the cigarette between the old woman's fingers. "What are them like?"

"What are what like?" Grandmamie had asked. Her dark eyes narrowed. She glanced at the cigarette. "This?"

"Yeah. You're always smokin' them. Do they taste good?"

Grandmamie had laughed. It had been a dry, cracked sound, like leather left out too long in the sun. "No, they don't taste good."

"Then why you smoke 'em?"

"Because I'm stupid. And stupid people do stupid things."

"Can I try it?" Mel had said.

"You want to be a stupid person too, I suppose?" Grandmamie cackled. Her eyes regarded Mel in that steady, sure way of theirs. "If I let you take a puff, will you promise not to smoke them ever again?"

"What if I like them?"

"Do you *promise*?" Grandmamie grinned. "Yes or no, girl?"

"All right," Mel had said, already sensing some sly trick to the promise. Grandmamie had had a way of running her crooked fingers through her short gray curls when she was up to mischief.

Mel had come forward, leaning to take her promised puff on the cigarette.

Grandmamie had clucked, snatching the cigarette back. "Don't wrap your whole damn mouth around it like that. Just a bit of lips. Heaven."

Frowning, Mel had tried again, feeling her braids slide over her shoulder as she leaned forward. The plastic beads clinked together.

She'd inhaled and felt the white-hot burn of the smoke hit her throat. It spasmed, giving over to ragged coughs.

Grandmamie had smiled her slyest smile yet.

"That's....*awful*." Mel had managed to speak between choked gasps.

"Remember that next time you want one. They'll kill you. Turn your insides black. Make you cough until you hurt. Stain those pretty teeth yellow."

Mel had tried to nod, to say she understood but she hadn't

been able to stop coughing. Tears had streamed from her eyes.

Finally she had realized the sound stinging her ears was her grandmother's laughter.

"You knew it would hurt me." Mel wiped at her eyes and spat on the ground. "So why you'd let me do it?"

"Ain't no use telling you something once you get it in your head. You're just like me that way."

Mel remembered the regret and weariness in Grandmamie's eyes when she'd said that. But there had also been tenderness Mel didn't understand until she was much, much older. Years after Grandmamie had died, and Terry had gone to prison.

"You're doing that thing you do," Mel had said, straightening. She pushed her braids back from her face and glared at her grandmama. She spit on the ground again, hoping that would get the taste out of her mouth. It'd been like eating dirt.

"What's that thing I do?" Grandmamie had paused to pluck a piece of stray tobacco off her tongue. Mel had mimicked her, thinking maybe that was how she got rid of the taste.

This had only made her grandmother laugh harder. "You ain't got no tobacco in your mouth. Show some sense."

"You're the one letting fourteen year olds smoke!"

Grandmamie had given her a warning look. While her grandmother had always been kind and patient, backtalk was not tolerated. "What's *that thing I do*?"

"Where you is tellin' me somethin' and not tellin' me somethin' at the same time."

"I suppose I am." She flicked her ash again, watching it fall onto the porch step before wiping it away with her sandal. "Come over here and hear the truth then. You're old enough."

Whenever Grandmamie had treated her like an adult,

Melandra had never been able to resist it. Now, looking back, Melandra suspected that Grandmamie was well aware of this fact.

Grandmamie had rummaged in her black purse, the one they'd gotten from the $1 bin at The Salvation Army. She'd pulled out a slick deck of cards wrapped in black cloth.

"You know my cards will be your cards one day," Grandmamie had said, holding her cigarette between her lips. It bobbed as she spoke. "I'm going to leave them to you when I die."

Mel hadn't been able to imagine a world in which her grandmother, as battle-worn as any general, could *die*. Yet Grandmamie was dead three years later.

"Why me?" Mel had dared to ask. Grandmamie had despised compliment-seeking all her life, and in a way Mel knew that this question could be mistaken for such.

But Grandmamie only arched a clever brow. "Why not your aunties Simone or Adele? Or your cousins? Maybe you think I favor your mother over my other children?"

It was true that Melandra had been the only child of Grandmamie's eldest, Melva. But Melandra didn't think that made her a favorite. In fact, Melandra would've bet a great deal of money—had she had any—that the only thing Grandmamie carried in her heart for Melva was heartache. And all five of her cousins were little. The closest to her in age—Janie —was only seven.

"I want to give you these because you're the only one like me." Grandmamie had snuffed out her cigarette in a glass ashtray resting on the top step and gave her a hard look. "I think you know what I mean by that."

Of course Melandra knew.

"But let me tell you a secret," Grandmamie had said, leaning close and leveling Mel with her a stare that straightened any spine. "We may have a lot of vision, we may see a lot of what other folks don't, but we've also got a big ol' blind spot right here, you hear me?"

Grandmamie had touched her heart.

"Shuffle them."

Grandmamie had handed over the cards then. Mel had been impressed by how big they were in her hands and how heavy. Melandra had done as she was told.

"Now flip over the top three."

Again Mel had obeyed.

Grandmamie had clucked her tongue. "The Devil. Justice. Death."

"You go in deep with a bad man when you're young. Not even twenty by the looks of it. And you stay in deep with him for most of your life. Only death gonna get you out."

"No I won't. I won't *fall* for nobody."

Grandmamie had spared her a sad smile.

Mel stood up. "You said the tarot is a guide, not a sentence."

"Your life is your own."

"Then I won't choose no devil." Melandra had stamped her foot down on the wooden step so hard the ashtray had bounced.

Grandmamie gathered up the cards and tucked them back into her purse. "Maybe you can break the cycle, but every Durand woman I can think of, as far back as I can know, has been stupid about love. Sometimes I think we're cursed."

And like every other instance in Mel's life, Grandmamie had been right. If only Mel had remembered the conversation the day Terry pulled up in his red Firebird.

Rushdie spoke, yanking Mel through the decades, back to warm cramped attorney's office. "Bottomline is don't let men like that scare you, Ms. Durand. If he ain't got nothing on you, you have nothing to worry about. He's got no case."

Mel saw his Firebird parked in Grandmamie's driveway.

She saw the black dress she wore the day of her grandmother's funeral as she stepped out onto the porch to greet him.

She heard the squeal of brakes, felt the car rock on impact.

But he does have something on me, Mel thought bitterly. *He really does.*

17

L ady placed her heavy snout on King's knee. He looked away from his laptop and regarded the sad, desperate eyes. "Need a walk? Er, *un promenade?*"

She sat back on her heels and shook her head. King knew this to be *yes*.

He regarded the case file he'd been annotating. It was as good a place to pause as any. "All right. I could use a break too."

He wouldn't mind a coffee and maybe even a snack. The afternoon slump was getting to him. Usually he powered through with a short nap, but since Piper had been working at the shop today, he hadn't wanted to walk away from the office. But a short thirty minutes or so would help his productivity and carry him until five or six.

"Come on then."

King closed his laptop, locked it in his industrial desk and checked his coat pocket for his keys and wallet. Confirming he had all that he needed, he stepped out of The Crescent City Detective Agency and into the Quarter's crowded streets. He bumped shoulders immediately with a tall man holding a plastic container of booze.

He looked ready to say something to King until he turned and took in the full size of the man standing before him. Then Lady began to growl.

"You all right?" King asked with a cocked eyebrow.

"Yeah, I'm all right." He turned away to rejoin his friends.

To King, who was doing his best to remain sober these days, Carnival was a particularly trying time. It wasn't just that alcohol in the Quarter spiked, it was that the flush of open drunkenness left him feeling like the only sober guy at the party. It was a feeling he'd never enjoyed.

"I'm going to need that paczki now," King muttered to himself. "A nice powdery one with raspberry filling. What do you think?"

Lady had wandered forward to squat beside a trash can.

King had his coffee twenty minutes later and was feeling more alert. He'd even forgotten the ache in his lower back, which had been aggravating him since the weather turned cold back in November.

He stood outside the French Market, watching girls in Carnival masks haggle with a merchant about the price of a shoulder bag when Mel appeared. She stepped out of a bank with a stack of empty deposit bags in her hand, pulling the door closed behind her.

"Hey," King said, smiling. There was a certain pleasure seeing a friendly face he hadn't been expecting. He crossed the walkway to her. "Bank run?"

"I've only got Piper until two. Thought I'd handle it before she left for the agency."

King had forgotten about that. It was past 1:30 now.

"Can I walk you back?" he asked. He thought he smelled cigarettes on her hair, which was strange. King knew she didn't smoke.

"Sure." But she didn't start walking. Instead she bent to scratch Lady's ears. Her bangles rolled forward on her wrists, creating a beautiful musical melody that King deeply enjoyed.

Lady pressed her head into Mel's hand.

"*Ma grande*," Mel murmured. "*Tu es une bonne chienne, non?*"

Lady's tail thumped against King's leg.

King harrumphed. "I would be jealous if I hadn't gotten Lady for the both of us."

After Dmitri Petrov and his goons came to King's apartment and abducted them, he'd decided it was definitely time to invest in a guard dog. But Lady was becoming more pet than working dog.

King would be lying if he said he wasn't a little lonely on the nights Lady slept in Melandra's apartment. He often found himself glancing at the empty dog bed, knowing that Lady probably preferred Mel—who let her sleep in the bed.

Mel snapped her fingers and Lady fell into step beside her as they began their stroll back toward Royal Street.

While beside her, King took Mel's measure. He saw the deep purple beneath her eyes which she'd tried to hide with makeup and her dry, dehydrated lips that she kept chewing nervously.

He thought, *a husband. Why didn't you tell me?* It hurt to think they were not as close as King thought they were.

"You been sleeping okay?" King asked. He pretended to be more interested in his coffee than her.

"No. I'll be glad when Carnival is over."

She took a step to the right to let a group of teens pass.

King scratched the back of his head. "We'll get a short reprieve before St. Patrick's Day."

"I don't mind the one or two-day festivals," Mel said. "It's when they carry on for weeks like this. The Carnival and Christmas sprints are what do in my old bones."

King laughed. "If you're old, what am I?"

She shot him a warning look even though she was at least fourteen years his junior.

King spotted a tall man leaning in a doorway, a cowboy hat perched on his head. It wasn't *that* man but it was close enough to remind King what was really bothering him, buzzing like a fly in the back of his mind.

"I've been seeing a guy hanging around the shop," King said. He'd turned his chin just enough to watch her expression without giving himself away. "

Her face tightened. "Oh yeah?"

"You know him? Because he seems to know you."

Mel clasped her opposite elbow. "I know him."

"Who is he?"

"Not someone worth talking about."

Jackson Square broke open in front of them. The line from Café du Monde cut across their path, snaking around the artists selling paintings and trinkets perfectly sized to fit into one's carry-on bag. A saxophone whined out of sight.

"Is it the same guy that came into the shop? The one who was giving you trouble?" he asked. *Is it your husband? The one you lied to me about?*

He enjoyed the click of Lady's nails against the stones, even over all the other noises threatening to drown it out.

"I'll handle him," Mel said again. "You're busy enough."

"I've always got time for my friends, Mel."

Again her face tightened and King struggled to understand what he was seeing. Anger? Remorse?

Even as they crossed onto Royal Street and found a quieter street, he was none the wiser. The truth of the situation remained just beyond his reach. He grasped for it once, twice, but found only darkness.

His agency came into view.

"Is it serious?"

Mel whirled on him and now he had no doubt that it was anger on her face. "I told you I'll handle it."

Lady's ears flicked back against her head.

"Okay." King stopped in front of his door. "Message received. I'll stay out of it."

"Thank you."

"But I'll see you tonight, right?" King asked, sensing that their time together had ended.

Mel frowned. "For what?"

"RuPaul's show is on."

Her eyes pinched closed. "Actually, I'm going to bed early, if it's all the same to you. See if I can't get a few hours before the drunks really get going."

It *wasn't* all the same to him, but he wasn't going to say so. "Sure. I'll record it."

When Mel turned away, presumably to return to her shop around the corner, King called after her. "Take Lady."

When Mel looked ready to refuse, King added, "She misses you."

This earned him a small half smile. To the dog she said, "*Suivez.*"

Lady didn't have to be told twice. She took off after Mel in a happy trot.

King stood outside his door with his cooling coffee in his hand and watched them go. He didn't like the sinking feeling in his chest. He didn't like it at all.

18

Piper glanced at the wall clock and saw she had fifteen minutes left before the shop closed. There was only one shopper left, two if she counted the man behind the purple curtain getting a palm reading from Mel. With such a thin crowd, Piper thought it was safe to start her closing routine.

She couldn't break down the drawer or count out the money yet in case the big girl in the Care Bear t-shirt wanted to make a purchase, but that wouldn't take her long. There was the sweeping and glass cleaning, the restocking of shelves, and forward-facing the merchandise. She completed each task quickly and efficiently, but her mind wandered.

Piper had texted Dani as she'd promised Henry she would do—only to receive radio silence. Nada. Even after all that talk about *I'm sorry I ghosted you*—it seemed like she was doing it again.

But why? She thought the dinner had gone okay despite the initial awkwardness.

Piper put the glass cleaner under the counter and picked up her phone for the hundredth time that day. Zero messages.

She frowned. "I mean, I can't *make* her hang out with me," she muttered aloud. "She's the one who said she'd missed *me*."

She put her phone down and sighed.

Speaking to no one she added, "I've made myself *perfectly* available. If she really wanted to talk, she would've said something," she repeated. "Or maybe the dinner was just about getting some guilt off her chest for lying to me in the first place. God, why are people so difficult. Use your words people."

A polite cough interrupted Piper's rolling monologue.

Piper looked up and saw the girl in the Care Bear t-shirt holding a 12-inch Pillar of Love candle.

"Girl, *same*." The girl gave Piper a sympathetic smile and handed the candle over for purchase.

WITH THE DAY'S MONEY LOCKED IN THE SAFE TO BE deposited tomorrow, Piper turned off the lights and locked the doors. Melandra had excused herself after her last reading, walking up the stairs to her apartment with Lady on her heels.

Another woman who won't talk to me, Piper had thought, watching her go. Her pensive silences and distant looks hurt to watch only because Piper knew no amount of prying would get Mel to open up and let her in on the situation.

Piper picked up her phone and texted a number she knew by heart.

Pick me up.

A pressure formed between her ears seconds later and then popped.

Lou stepped from the shadows beside the rack of hoodies and into a beam of moonlight. It cut across her face dramatically, highlighting her lips.

"That was quick," Piper slid her phone into her pocket.

"It seemed urgent."

"No danger," Piper clarified grabbing her backpack off the floor. She stopped short of admitting she felt lonely. "For me anyway."

A sharp tug on her heart strings made her look down. Piper prided herself on the fact that she was the go-to for all her friends. When they had trouble, they called her. And Mel was dealing with something and wouldn't even talk to her about it. It hurt. It hurt in the same way it had hurt to know that King and Lou had been working with Dani behind her back.

"What do you mean?" Lou asked.

"Mel's dealing with something and won't speak up about it. You think I'm easy to talk to right?"

Lou only blinked at her. "Yes."

Piper sighed. "I mean, you don't talk much but that's not the point. Why wouldn't she tell me what's going on?"

"She hasn't told King anything either. If she had, he'd tell me to watch her."

Piper pursed her lips. "Good point."

She'd seen King come through the shop just before eight that evening. He'd stopped and said hello to Piper, asking how she was doing. Then he'd glanced at the purple curtain and asked, *she back there?*

When Piper said she was, that had been the end of it. King hadn't looked worried or afraid. He hadn't asked any questions.

"Where did you want to go?" Lou rested the cuff of her leather jacket on the glass counter. Piper appreciated that she didn't put her fingers on the glass she just cleaned.

"What are you doing tonight?" Piper asked.

"Hunting Fish."

Piper snorted. "Gonna need a pole for that?"

Lou didn't even smile.

"Okay, bad joke. But when the world finds out what a monster he is, he's going to wish he had a better last name." Piper adjusted the pack on her back. "So you're busy? No chance we can hang out?"

She could go down to Wild Cat if she wanted to. She'd drink with Henry and their friends and dance all that pent up energy off until collapsing into bed before dawn.

But she wasn't in the mood to drink and the bars were less fun during Carnival anyway. That many bodies made talking and dancing nearly impossible. And there was always that one person who hadn't put on enough deodorant, ruining it for everyone else.

Lou pushed her sunglasses up on her head. "You can come with me."

Piper's heart stuttered in her chest. "Come with *you*? To *stalk* a serial killer?"

Lou's lips quirked. "I won't be getting that close."

Piper felt the stupid grin spread across her face. "Hell *yeah* I want to go with you. You've never taken me into the field before. I wanna see what you do."

"You'll have to be quiet and you can't yell if I move us suddenly."

"Control my vocal chords. Got it." Piper snorted. "That's not the first time a woman has asked me to do so."

Lou arched an eyebrow.

A blush spread across Piper's cheeks and she averted her gaze first. "Never mind. Let's do this. How long will we follow him?"

"Maybe hours. Maybe thirty minutes." She slid her glasses back down over her eyes. "Do you need anything before we go?"

Piper tapped the pack on her shoulders. "I should dump this off at my apartment. Then I'll be ready to go. Listen." She leveled Lou with a stern look. "I've seen the cop movies.

I know stakeouts are serious business. I won't be loud or stupid."

"I trust you." Lou's lips twitched with a smile as she reached out and wrapped a hand around Piper's wrist.

LOU KNEW THERE WAS A RISK IN BRINGING PIPER ALONG. It was true she'd only planned to watch Fish from a distance tonight. She also wanted to check on Jennifer McGrath and make sure she was still alive and kicking. And Lou would be lying if she said she wasn't curious to appraise the state of Fish's hunger. The carved arm and ragged nails she'd seen earlier suggested that feeding time was near. But how long could he hold out? Apart from cutting himself, what other methods did he use to beat back the ravenous beast inside him?

Lou had to know.

But things could always go wrong on a hunt. Piper was smart and resourceful. Lou herself had been impressed by her survival instincts more than once in their short acquaintance. But tonight she was Lou's responsibility.

You're bringing her along. You keep her safe.

Lou suspected it was the weight of responsibility that caused the strange knocking in her chest after they deposited Piper's backpack on her kitchen counter.

"Oh, let me pee," Piper begged. "It'll only take a second."

Lou stood in the apartment, noting its tidiness and charm. It had high arched windows and hardwood floors. It reminded her a little Konstantine's loft in Florence's city center.

She pushed this thought away as the faucet in the adjacent room squeaked off.

"Okay," Piper said, wiping her hands on the side of her

jeans. She crossed to the door and turned the bolt, locking them inside the apartment. "I'm ready."

Lou stepped toward her, sliding one hand up the girl's back. There was a puff of surprise on Lou's cheek the moment before her grip on Piper tightened and Lou pulled them both through the dark.

Lou's boots settled on solid ground first. Piper's balance tilted, but Lou held tight until she settled on her feet. A relieved little sigh rolled past the girl's lips as Lou released her.

They looked around, trying to figure out where her compass had brought them.

Lou stepped forward, aware immediately of the large cavernous space around her. The sound of her boots on concrete echoed in a way only possible with high ceilings.

Lou took another step forward as headlights whipped around an adjacent aisle. It was followed by the recognizable *beep beep beep* of a machine backing up.

A tug on her arm made her turn. Piper pointed at a door on their right. A strip of light shone through the cracks surrounding it as well as one port window high in its face.

Lou exited first, willing to take the blunt of any danger they might intercept in the light.

Lou understood immediately why her compass had chosen the adjacent storerooms rather than this. The grocery store was brightly lit with its overbearing bulbs beaming down from above.

To her left was a dairy case full of stacked yogurts, tubs of cream cheese, butter, and plastic-wrapped cheeses lined up in their individual dispensers. On her right began the cases of milk.

Fish was in front of the milk. He had the door propped open with his hip as he read the label on a bottle of fat-free chocolate milk.

"He *is* a monster," Piper whispered into Lou's ear. "Fat *free* chocolate milk?"

Lou elbowed her slightly, crossing the aisle. Piper followed suit showing profound interest in a box of aluminum foil on the shelf at eye level. Lou realized they didn't have hand baskets or shopping carts. Lou pulled a package of napkins off the shelf and held it loosely in her fist.

Piper seemed to have the same idea. "I'll get a cart."

As soon as Piper rounded the corner and disappeared out of sight, something in Lou's chest relaxed. It was one thing to put herself so close to Fish. Even though she knew what he was, and what he'd done to at least a dozen women, she wasn't afraid of him. In fact, that self-destructive core inside her, that part that wanted to throw herself from the cliff and see if she could survive the fall, leaned toward Fish like frost-bitten hands toward a fire.

But on top of this old, familiar desire to put her hand in the flames was a new and interesting impulse.

Piper wasn't his type. She was the right age, but she was blonde. Lou didn't think Fish had ever hunted or killed a blond, based on the photos she'd seen. Still, Lou found herself wanting to keep Piper behind her.

Why did I bring her?

Because Piper had worried her, hadn't she?

The moment she'd gotten the text *pick me up*, a tug in Lou's stomach had caused a jerk of worry in her guts. Once she'd seen Piper for herself, realized it was a social call and not a cry for help, she'd still been left with Piper's sad, lonely expression.

Lou grabbed a box of plastic forks from the shelf and placed them on top of the napkins.

She replayed the last few months in her head as she trailed Fish from the dairy section into the baked goods. He plucked a box of brownie mix from the shelf and Lou recalled the cake she received from Piper last month. It was the second birthday cake Piper had given her. And what had Lou given Piper for her birthday?

Nothing.

She wasn't even sure when it was.

There was nothing she had consciously done to nurture this affection—no gift giving, certainly. Yet Piper had been doggedly kind and generous, sometimes about the simplest things.

She'd given Lou the remote when they'd watched television. They'd sat on Piper's couch watching a show about a serial killer who kills serial killers.

I feel like you'd connect with this guy, Piper had said, plopping a popcorn bowl into Lou's lap.

They had day trips: San Francisco, New York, Chicago, San Diego, London, Paris, and Kyoto.

Why had she taken Piper? Usually because the girl had made some small remark about wanting to see a landmark, a building or eat at a specific restaurant.

Do you know they have a sculpture in Millennium Park that's shaped like a bean? It's called Cloud Gate.

San Diego is supposed to have some of the best beaches.

Have you ever had New York pizza? Real New York pizza?

What's the Eiffel tower look like at night?

But she had never asked Lou to take her. She'd never expected Lou to use her power—a talent that came as easy to her as thinking. Lou had *wanted* to show her.

They'd been friends for almost seven months when Lou learned that Piper had never actually left the city of New Orleans except for twice—a spring break trip to Panama City her junior year of high school—and another vague trip, in which Piper had left out a great many details, in which Piper drove her friend Henry out-of-state to visit his sister.

If there had been a particular moment or gesture that had

created this friendship, Lou had missed it. Now it was simply here as if it always had been.

"Psst."

Lou jumped, turning away from Fish who was exiting the end of the aisle

"Whoa," Piper whispered. "Did I scare you?"

Piper searched her face as she pushed the cart to a stop beside her. "You okay?"

Lou focused on the cart. She was surprised to find it half full. A bag of potato chips, a box of breakfast pastries, two packages of cookies, and a two-liter of soda sat in the bottom of the cart.

Lou arched a brow at her.

Piper smacked her lips. "For *authenticity*. Wouldn't you be suspicious of two people following you with an *empty* cart?"

Lou put her forks and napkins in the cart beside the two-liter of soda.

"I'll push, you stalk." Piper wagged her eyebrows.

Lou took her time exiting the aisle. She pretended to read the signs as her eyes roved. She spotted the familiar button-down shirt and loafers farther up the center aisle. She started after him, working to close the distance. When she felt like he was within range, she slowed again, pretending to look at an end-cap of pink lemonade in colorful tubs featuring bright summer scenes that didn't match the winter pressing against the store windows.

Fish pushed his cart into checkout line number six, even though it was noticeably longer than both lines four and five. The cashier saw him the moment that he pulled into her line and gave him a tight smile.

Fish's spine straightened immediately, clearly pleased by the attention.

Lou turned to Piper who was reading the box of breakfast pastries. "Is it trans-fat or saturated fat that's bad for you?"

"Why don't you push the cart over to the bathrooms?" Lou nodded at the sign beside customer service. "I'll be over in a minute."

"Got it." Piper pivoted the cart in that direction.

Fish was now only two patrons behind. Lou decided to grab a magazine off the rack in the checkout line next to his and pretended to read an article about an actor's supposed plastic surgery. Lou looked at the glossy photographs without seeing them. Behind her sunglasses, she flicked her gaze toward Fish who'd finally reached the cashier.

She watched the exchange.

He was bouncing lightly on his feet as he spoke to her. Excitement? Contained joy? The cashier looked as tired as the first night Lou saw her. Her makeup hid dark circles, but not the puffiness caused by lack of sleep. As she made change, her gaze flicked up to meet Lou's.

Then it slid away.

Fish pushed his cart toward the exit and Lou crossed to the bathroom. Piper was frowning. "I've got something to show you."

"It'll have to wait," Lou told her and grabbed her wrist, pulling her into the bathrooms. "Come here."

The bathroom door hadn't closed all the way when Lou flicked off the switch. In a stall, a woman cried out in surprise, but Lou was already pulling them through the dark.

They were in the alley beside the exit. The sharp cold hit her cheeks instantly and Lou had a passing thought that they couldn't linger. Piper wasn't dressed warmly enough for an Ohio winter.

"We won't stay long," Lou whispered into her ear as Piper began to shiver.

"I'm okay."

The swoosh of automatic doors opening caught Lou's

attention. Fish appeared with his shopping cart. *He's practically running to his car*, she thought.

Once the back end of the SUV opened, he threw the sacks into the back the way she'd seen a worker throwing bags of dog food onto a pile.

She would have smiled, amused by his desperate movements, but again she felt like she was looking through an opaque glass, seeing only the reflection of herself inside. She didn't like it.

Piper tugged on Lou's sleeve, three sharp yanks and Lou turned.

She was pointing at a woman, alone with no cart, exiting from the same door Fish had. When she saw that Fish hadn't yet climbed into the driver's seat, her steps faltered. She slowed and veered off to the right. She tucked her chin down as if to hide her face.

Strange behavior, Lou thought, *for someone leaving a grocery store.*

She regarded the red hoodie and slight build and recognized the familiarity.

Fish was already backing out of his parking space and speeding in the direction of his home. Lou searched the compass within her but felt no danger. Maybe he would cut himself tonight. Maybe he'd fuck his wife a little more roughly. Lou was curious to know how he'd handle the aggression bubbling inside him.

"It's too dark to get her picture," Lou said, watching the woman climb into a red Honda and turn the key. She also drove in the direction of Fish's house.

"Good thing I got a picture when we were in the store," Piper said and gave Lou a devilish grin.

"When you sent me to stand by the bathrooms I spotted her. I saw her when I went to get the cart too, and both times she was watching Fish."

Lou frowned, thinking she'd done a pretty good job of not being too obvious.

"I've got a good one of her face."

Piper handed over her smart phone so Lou could look at the picture more closely. There was something familiar about her—her dark complexion, her features.

"I've seen her before," Lou said, frowning at the picture. "I'm pretty sure she was outside Fish's house the other night, stalking around."

"Why would another woman be stalking him?" Piper asked and Lou had the distinct impression she was asking herself, not Lou. Sure enough the answers came immediately. "Maybe she's a reporter who's on to him. Or maybe a detective. What do you think?"

Lou was kind enough not to point out that not every person sneaking around was a reporter.

"We'll find out who she is," Lou said.

"Yeah we've got recognition programs for that, don't we?" Piper's teeth were chattering.

"Come on," Lou said, and wrapped her arms around the girl. They'd done what they could tonight. "Let's get cocoa."

19

King opened the fridge and considered his dinner options. It was after eleven at night, but he was hungry. The shelves weren't entirely bare, but nothing screamed *eat me*. There were the usual suspects, half-used condiments and a half gallon of milk. There were two wrapped steaks that he'd planned to grill for dinner but had decided on take out. Then there was a pack of unopened bacon.

Beyond that, two apples, one soggy and brown, and what was left of his drunken noodles with chicken.

He decided on the noodles, vowing to do some proper grocery shopping tomorrow.

Take-out box in hand, he closed the fridge.

Piper and Lou stepped forward.

He squeezed the box so hard the lid popped off. "Christ."

Lady barked in response. The short yap came from Mel's apartment across the walkway.

"I'm fine!" King called, turning his chin toward the door. "It's just Lou."

Piper threw up her hands. "Who the hell am I?"

Since there was no follow-up bark or scratching at his door, he assumed that Mel had shushed the dog.

He regarded the two of them. "Is there not enough shadow in front of my door for you to *knock*?"

"On the balcony there is," Lou admitted, shrugging in her leather coat. King noted his tired, weary face in her reflective sunglasses. He grimaced. "We wanted to see if you were awake."

"And it's cold out there." Piper tossed an empty Styrofoam cup into King's trash.

"Where have you been?" he asked, frowning at the cup. He didn't recognize the logo stamped in red lettering across the compressed material.

Lou pushed her sunglasses up on top of her head. "Stalking Fish."

"But plot twist!" Piper pulled her phone from her pocket and pushed buttons wildly. After a moment of delighted humming, she turned the phone so King could see the screen. "Someone is already following him."

King accepted the phone, setting the carton of drunken noodles on the counter. "Are you sure?"

"Totally." Piper pointed at the face, grinning triumphantly. "She was doing what we did. But she had salsa and chips."

King looked up, frowning.

"We found him in the grocery store," Lou clarified.

Piper bounced on her heels. "We had a cart and everything. We were like real detectives. It was *so* cool."

King couldn't help but smile. Piper's enthusiasm was contagious.

"And you found her following him too?" he asked, frowning at the grainy photo. He tried to enlarge it but that made it worse.

"Yeah," Piper said, coming around to stand shoulder to shoulder with him. "She followed him in the store and then out into the parking lot. Then she got in a red Honda and followed him out of the parking lot."

"We don't know she was following him." Lou took the carton of drunken noodles and sniffed it. "We stopped tracking them in the parking lot. They could've been heading in the same direction. Or not."

King squinted at the phone. There was something familiar about the face, but King couldn't place where he'd seen it before. He forwarded himself the picture, and heard his own phone buzz on the coffee table in the other room.

"So can you do it?" Piper asked.

King looked up from the photo and found them both looking at him expectantly. He felt like he'd missed something. "Do what?"

"Can you run the photo and find out who she is?" Piper asked.

King shrugged. "I can try but I don't have access to the same databases that I did when I was active with the DEA. And since Sampson told me to back off, I've tried to stay off their servers illegally. I can call in a favor and ask someone to do it, but you know what they say. Three may keep a secret if two of them are dead."

"Right. Someone might wonder why we're looking into her." Piper bit her lip.

"Why can't you ask Konstantine?" King asked handing over the phone. "He's far better at finding people than I am. This picture is more than enough for him to get what he needs."

Lou's warm grin evaporated. She turned away, crossing to the balcony door. She gazed out at the light as if suddenly very interested in the raucous below.

Piper pocketed the phone. "Is this our case or not?"

King arched an eyebrow, hoping Piper would elaborate.

But she only shook her head and shoved the carton of noodles into his hand. "Don't let us interrupt your dinner."

King pulled a plate from the cabinet, dumped the noodles onto it, and slid the whole thing into the microwave.

So was there trouble in paradise? Were things not lovey-dovey between Konstantine and Lou? He had no idea what their relationship even looked like, or if it was officially a relationship at all. But she'd saved his life when the whole world hunted him and he'd turned up when Dmitri Petrov had hunted her.

They could be friends, Lucy's voice chided gently in his mind. *Friends protect friends.*

You haven't seen the way they look at each other, King thought. *I sure don't look at my friends that way.*

The microwave beeped and King retrieved his noodles and soda and took both to the sofa. "So you've nothing else to report on Fish?" King forked noodles into his mouth.

Lou turned from the balcony. "He's cutting himself."

"If he's cutting, he's trying to numb out."

"Is that common?" Lou asked.

His fork scraped the plate. "As a coping mechanism? Sure. Anything to stave off the craving a little longer. One guy burned his arm whenever he was trying not to kill."

"Did it work?" she asked.

King snorted before forking more noodles into his mouth. "What do you think?"

"These records smell like weed." Piper crouched down in front of the stack leaning against his speaker. "Is this where you keep your weed, because man, it's not even subtle."

"How much longer before he caves?" Lou asked.

"Some killers go years without killing. Maybe he'll slip into a dormant period."

Lou turned away effectively ending the conversation. There was something in the hard set of her shoulders that told King to drop it. He didn't take it personally. If she had a problem, she'd speak her mind. She was too much like her aunt to give him grace for long.

Piper pulled out one of the vinyl records and opened it on her lap. It was *Sam Cooke Portrait of a Legend*. She fingered the edges. She frowned at him. "Why is this one so much newer than the others?"

"It's a replacement." He scraped the last bite of noodles off his plate into his mouth. "Lou—if I gave you the name of someone, no. Shit. I don't have a name."

Lou turned toward him, clearly intrigued.

King scratched his jaw. "If I said, find the man who killed Rita Cross, would you be able to do it?"

She knew what he meant. "Yes."

"Really? That would be enough?"

"When I found Fish all I was thinking was give me someone who kills women and thinks he's getting away with it."

King couldn't hide his surprise. "Huh. That's impressive."

"Who's Rita Cross?" Lou asked.

"A woman who was murdered. Do you—" he searched for a word. "Get any *vibes* about where her killer might be?"

Konstantine be damned. If the killer was around, he deserved to answer for his crimes.

"No," Lou said.

"No what?"

"Nothing is coming up."

King took another drink of his soda, vaguely aware that it was way too late at night to be drinking this shit. "What does that mean?"

"He could be dead."

He is being dealt with. Isn't that what Konstantine promised?

Piper looked up from the record. "How does Mel seem to you?"

King thought of Mel's anger as she told him to back off earlier that day.

"She's okay."

Piper shook her head. "See, *no*. I can't be the only one who sees it. Something is getting to her. When I showed up for work the other day she was halfway to a panic attack about something, and asked me to read her cards. Spoiler, they weren't happy cards. Then that guy came in and was giving her shit."

"The guy with the feather in his hat?" King asked. "The bone choker."

"*Yes*." Piper groaned. "I don't like him. I think he's The Devil."

Lou had gone so still beside him King had to turn his head to make sure Lou was still there.

King arched a brow. "Do you mean this literally or—"

"When I read her cards, she drew The Devil. It's a person who screws with you. Gets in your head. You know, a bad person."

"Or it could mean you're lying to yourself," King said.

Piper crinkled her nose. "True. But I think in this case, it's *him*."

King thought of the way Lady had growled, her nose through the slats of his balcony.

"I've seen him around." King pushed away the plate and reached for his soda. "Do you think he's harassing her?"

"Want me to pick him up?" Lou asked.

King snorted. "Not yet, Cujo. We don't know that he's actually the problem."

"I wish she'd just talk to us," Piper said. She slipped the vinyl back into the pile and stood. "Why can't she just talk to us? We're her friends, right?"

King took a long drink and smacked his lips. "Some people like to handle their problems on their own. Mel is one of those people."

"That's stupid. We love her and —" Piper began.

"Are you trying to tell me you're *not* one of those people? Because I seem to remember you standing in the middle of the office with tears rolling down your face and you sure didn't tell me what was going on."

Piper pushed out her lower lip. "Not fair."

"She knows we're here for her," King said. "If she needs help, she'll ask."

Lou was regarding him with a cold expression that he couldn't quite read. But it made the hair on the back of his neck raise up.

That's big talk coming from you, Robert, Lucy whispered in his mind. And then, *those in the most danger don't even know how to ask.*

She's a capable woman, King thought. *Nothing is going to happen to her.*

Even to himself, he couldn't tell if he was stating a fact or a wish.

20

Mel opened her side table drawer. She shoved aside the notepads, the pens, sticky notes the half-used tube of Chapstick. She slammed the door shut and yanked open the next drawer.

Lady barked, a sharp, alerting sound.

"*Calme*," Mel hissed.

Lady's ears lay flat against her head.

King's voice rumbled from across the hallway but then nothing. Whatever he wanted, it wasn't important. But this momentary interruption allowed Mel to look up from her work and see her surroundings for the first time.

Every drawer in her kitchen and living room were pulled open. The cushions on her couch had been lifted and thrown to the floor. The pillows were strewn everywhere.

She'd searched every inch of this apartment. *Every inch.*

Her tarot cards were gone. She had a horrible feeling she knew where they were.

No, she begged. *No, I've just put them somewhere and forgotten.*

They've been in our family since 1804, Grandmamie's voice chided in her mind. *Over two hundred years and you've lost them.*

"I haven't lost them," Mel mumbled, pulling her shawl tighter around her. *And they aren't really two hundred years old.* But even as she thought this, her heart sagged in her chest.

According to Grandmamie's account, the original deck was given to her great-great-great-great-great-great-aunt Josephine Beloit by her mother Simone when Haiti won its independence. *We make our own future now*, she was supposed to have said. Who knew if it was true.

As the deck was passed from woman to woman throughout the centuries, it was updated as necessary. If a card was damaged, it was redrawn by its owner's hand. That explained the varied styles spread throughout the generations. Mel was certain that none of the cards in the current deck were original to the deck Josephine received in 1804. But she also couldn't say they weren't.

The Ace of Cups and The Fool for example, looked older than dirt to her.

Grandmamie had always insisted that it wasn't the age of the cards themselves. It was that their own spirits had imprinted on the deck and as long as it passed through their family, it didn't matter if they were touching the exact same card or not.

It's our history in the cards. It's our blood and sweat in these cards, Grandmamie used to say. *We made the magic. Don't forget that.*

"I haven't lost them," she said again and stepped out of her apartment into the hallway.

Lady moved to follow her but Mel held up her hand.

"*Restez.*"

Lady whined, the closest thing to an objection Mel had ever heard, but she obeyed. She fell back on her haunches, her ears lying flat against her head.

"I just want to look one more place."

Mel paused outside King's apartment door. She raised her fist to knock but then heard Lou's voice. She hesitated. They were working. She shouldn't bother them. And she'd already shown too much of her distress as it was. If she alerted them now that she'd misplaced her cards, they would only worry more.

They might get involved in the situation she'd worked so hard to keep them out of.

She crept away, trying to keep her footfall silent as she descended the steps into the shop. She checked the cubbies beneath the register. She checked—nonsensically—the register itself. She pulled back the purple curtain and gazed into the nook where she conducted her readings with the full air of *Melandra the Magnificent* or whatever her customers called her behind her back.

But there were only the two low benches, covered in bright Bedouin cushions and the wood table resting between. She lifted the extinguished candles as if to find something hidden beneath. She ran her hand along the cushions.

No cards. On neither her side, nor on the customer's side.

She sat down with her face in her hands and pushed back against the tears. "When did he take them?" she whispered. "When did he have the chance?"

It hardly mattered now, did it? It mattered only that Terry had managed to get his filthy hands on them in the first place.

She stepped from the nook and pulled the curtain behind her.

A ghostly face hung in the glass outside her shop door. It's skull-like face and a skeleton grin filled her with rage. Tremors shot down each arm, curling her hands into fists. Without consciously deciding to, she stormed to the door, unlocked the bolt, and pushed out into the chaotic night.

The music rose to a nauseating cacophony. The scents of

booze, piss, and fried foods hit her like a physical force, even as the cold February wind seized and tumbled her hair.

"Give them back," she hissed, letting the door fall closed behind her. "You goddamn bastard give them back!"

Terry's grin only widened. "Give what back?"

She shoved him hard. "Don't bullshit me, Terry! You took 'em. I know you took 'em from my own damn pockets. Hand them over!"

Was it when he slammed her against the building? When her hands were full of groceries? She couldn't be sure. When had she used them last? All her appointments since then had been palm readings, hadn't they? Had she brought out her cards at all?

Lights from the shop windows sparked in his eyes. They shone liquid black.

He smirked, capturing her wrists in his grip. "I don't know what you're talking about."

"You know how much those cards mean to me. *You know*."

For the first time, she felt herself on the verge of real tears. Whether she was crying from anger, loss, or perhaps both, she couldn't be sure.

His smile spread too white, revealing too many wolfish teeth. "It's a good trick, isn't it? You pick up a lot of tricks in prison."

She yanked her wrists from his grip and stormed into the throbbing crowd. She batted the drunks aside as she stepped through the streets, searching, looking for—*there*.

"Donny!" Melandra called. She waved at the uniformed officer. "Donny!"

The cop who'd been standing on the corner talking to another officer turned at the sound of his name. His black wool coat brushed his chin but didn't hide his smile.

"I need to report a theft!" She pointed at Terry. "Thief!"

A rough hand seized her upper arm. It squeezed so hard she cried out.

"Shut your mouth, woman," he said. "Shut it *now*. If you tell him a damn thing you'll never see your cards again. I'll burn every single one, you hear me? And once I'm done with that, I'll make a confession of my own. I'll tell them what you did, you hear me? I'll tell them *everything*. Then we can rot in prison together."

Melandra remembered the first time she saw Terry in Hokum's Bar and Grill down by the interstate. She'd been only fifteen at the time, but looked old enough that old man Bill Hokum let her wait tables three nights a week after school. Bill had been a good friend of Grandmamie's and she'd trusted him to keep an eye on her girl.

On Friday nights, men from the neighboring parish came into the bar and played pool in the back. One night, a new boy came in with the Henrietta crowd. Mel met his eyes instantly, as if she'd felt him enter the bar.

He'd smiled first and she hadn't returned it even though the heat in her face was enough to give her away.

Something inside her prayed that would be the end of it.

Forty minutes later, he was at the bar, placing a dollar bill on the counter. "Quarters for the jukebox, miss."

His voice was how she'd imagined it. Smooth bourbon poured into a glass like Grandmamie drank on Sunday nights after church.

She'd made change without looking higher than his mouth.

"You mute or something?" he asked, taking the quarters she'd placed where the dollar had been a minute before.

"No, she just don't talk to strangers," Bob had called from the end of the bar. "Get out of here."

And if only *that* had been the end of it.

But Terry had kept playing pool in the back with his

friends. Melandra eventually began talking and before she knew it, she was hustling half the pool halls in three parishes with him.

If only I'd honored Grandmamie's wish, Mel cursed herself. *If only I hadn't been such a damn fool.*

It was the biggest fight they'd had in her life, the night Grandmamie had demanded Melandra stay away from Terry. *Have you learned nothing from my mistakes? Nothing at all?*

The old woman had hissed. And she was an old woman now, aging for reasons Mel wouldn't understand until later.

When Grandmamie got her pancreatic cancer diagnosis and was given months to live, Mel did finally honor her request. She stopped going to the bar. She stayed with her grandmother day and night until she died just seven months later.

"Don't be a fool," Grandmamie had begged her in one of her last lucid moments.

Not two hours later Terry was in her driveway in his Firebird beckoning her to *come on now. You've had enough of all this.*

And she had. For better or worse, she had left with him. She'd never been so desperate to escape anything in her life, not since living in the small apartment with her strung out mother in Baton Rouge—those dark days before her mother overdosed and her life with Grandmamie began.

She'd used to think those early days with her mother were the darkest of her life. That was only because her time with Terry had not begun. The hustling, the drinking, the vagabond way he liked to crisscross below the Mason-Dixon line. All of it culminating in the worst moment of her life.

Will you drive? Terry had asked her.

And though it was dark and pouring rain and though she'd had a couple of drinks herself, she'd said *yes*.

Damn her, she'd said *yes*.

Terrence jerked his hand free of Melandra's arm and she

found herself in the present moment again, surrounded by pushing bodies, with only her pain left to contend with.

"Careful what you say now," Terry spat.

Donny pushed aside the last bodies between them and reached her, smiling. As soon as he saw her face, his smile faded.

"Mel, what's wrong? What's been stolen?"

Mel wrung her hands. She leaned her weight against the brick. "I—"

She turned but Terrence was gone. He'd faded into the crowd and with him any chance that she could get her cards back tonight.

She searched the crowd but didn't see him. She couldn't spot the leather hat or that single black crow feather in the sea of laughing, horrible faces. There was no hint of that wild, murderous smile.

It didn't mean he wasn't watching.

"I'm sorry," Melandra stuttered. She forced a smile. "I'm so sorry for calling you over like that, Mr. Edwards."

Donny frowned, clearly taken aback by her sudden formality. "What happened?"

Mel straightened her shoulders and released a slow breath between her teeth. "I thought someone had pickpocketed me."

She let out a laugh. It was supposed to sound relieved, bordering on nonchalant. But it sounded strained and nervous to her own ears. She forced a smile. "But I've got everything on me. So I'm very sorry to have scared you like that."

Donny was still frowning.

Another sharp laugh. "You probably think I'm one of those hysterical women that cry about everything."

"I don't think that." Donny's frown only deepened. He was searching her face. "Are you really okay?"

"I'm fine. I feel stupid for overreacting, but I'm fine."

This at least was partially true. Mel had never felt so stupid in her life. Stupid for ever having gotten involved with Terrence in the first place.

"Honestly," Mel said with an air of conspiracy. "I haven't been sleeping well this week. I think it's the noise."

Donny favored her with a polite smile. "That's all of us. *Carnival.*" He gestured at the masked faces around them. The throbbing bodies swayed, drinks spilling over from their cups and splashing on the street.

Mel nodded companionably. "I'm going to try to get some sleep now. Thank you for coming over when I called you. I'm so sorry if I scared you."

The frown was back. "You can always call on us, Mel. Always."

She nodded, making her apologies. *Stupid. Stupid, stupid woman.*

When she reached the door of Fortunes and Fixes, a hand clamped over hers, pinning it against the handle. She wasn't surprised. She'd known he'd stay close.

"You'll get your cards back when I get my money," a voice whispered in her ear.

She jerked her head back. She didn't want his breath on her.

Terrance glared down at her. "You have until Friday to pay me or I'm going to burn them. I swear to God. Just pay me and I'll leave."

"How do I know you'll really leave?" she asked. Because she was more than aware that he could stay. He could stay and haunt her for the rest of her life. What was stopping him?

His skeleton grin was back. So many teeth.

That's how he looked that night on a backroad somewhere in west Louisiana. The rain beating down on his head and shoulders as he stared down at the road, his face bright in the headlights as the windshield wipers furiously worked back and forth across the fogging glass.

Did I kill her? Mel had asked. *Did I—*

Stay in the car, he'd said.

And she had. God forgive her, she had.

He released her hand, but not his hold on her and he knew it. "I guess we'll see, won't we?"

21

King leaned back in his office chair, pressing the phone to his opposite ear. His eyes roved the sunlit office, vaguely taking in the coffee station and the red plastic chairs. Piper's laptop was still open, the way she'd left it before stepping out to grab them sandwiches. King glanced at his watch and wondered how long he would have to wait on hold.

"Here it is," Sampson said finally, the line crackled with the sound of movement. Maybe it was papers shuffling or the phone brushing the collar of Sampson's shirt. "Jeffrey Rodgers Fish. Shadyville High School, American History teacher. Sound right to you?"

"That's the one."

"I had to make three phone calls for this," Sampson said, grumpily.

"Don't give me that," King said, rubbing his nose. "I sent you the info on both the Robinson and Henley cases yesterday."

"Fair enough." Sampson smacked his lips. "To answer your question, no. He's had no prior charges but he had two comments on his work record that I think you might find interesting."

King twirled a pen between his knuckles. "I'm listening."

"Two girls at his school have made complaints about him."

The pen stopped twirling. "What kind of complaints?"

"One said he was keeping her after school to do work."

"Sounds teacherly."

"Yeah, but she claims that she didn't need to do the extra work and thought he was trying to get her alone."

"That sounds *less* teacherly."

"Her official statement called him 'creepy'. The school dismissed her claims until her mother got involved. She's a pediatrician, pillar of the community, something like that. They gave the girl an exam and she tested out of his class and into the AP course. She graduated six months later. Problem solved. The other girl had the same problem, but her family moved out of state before it was resolved."

This wasn't anything King could use for a bonafide case against Fish. Predatory behavior toward female students certainly counted as part of the behavior for murderous sociopaths, but unfortunately something as ambiguous as a student-teacher conflict wouldn't hold in court.

King scratched at his jaw. "Anything else?"

"Yes," Sampson said conspiratorially. "And *this* is more interesting."

"I'm listening."

"One night Fish was stopped by a patrol car."

"What time?"

Papers shuffled on Sampson's end again. "Just past midnight. The patrol car stopped him because he wasn't wearing a seatbelt."

"Careless," King clucked.

"When the officer got out of his patrol car, he realized the back bumper was soaked in what he first thought was mud."

King sat up in his seat. "It wasn't mud."

"Nope. The officer asked him to get out of the car, explained why he'd stopped him, and brought him to the back of the car to show him the blood."

King couldn't suppress a laugh. "What did he say to get out of this?"

"Claims he hit a deer and that it must've been the deer's blood. The cop makes him open the trunk anyway, but there's nothing in there save the tire and jack. A few reusable grocery bags. And the cop can't test the blood right there on the side of the road, so he gives him the ticket and lets him go."

"Seems lenient."

"Especially given the fact that if he'd been a black man, and not just a white guy in a button down, he probably would've been shot."

King agreed.

"But the best part," Sampson said. "Is that Fish traded in that car two weeks later."

"That is interesting. Especially if the blood wasn't from a deer and the scuff marks weren't from antlers."

"Maybe some shoes kicking out." There was a long pause "Christ. People are sick."

"Yeah, it gets into your head if you're not careful. But I admit, there's also something satisfying about it."

"Robbie." Sampson's tone was suddenly grave. "I'm worried about your mental health, buddy."

The door opened and Piper appeared with two paper-wrapped sub sandwiches in her arms. She arched her eyebrows at his expression, but he shook his head. *Nothing to worry about.*

"I told you. I've got an interest in cold cases. Keeps my mind young."

Sampson laughed. "That's what Sudoku is for."

Piper placed the sub sandwich and his change on his desk

before pulling a cold Dr. Pepper from their mini fridge. He thanked her with a wink and a thumbs up.

"Fish has the look, I admit," Sampson said. "But what have you *actually* got on the guy?"

King pulled the tab on the soda, enjoying the crack of the opening can. "We'll find out, won't we?"

The door chime rang again and a man in uniform crossed the threshold into the detective agency. His black boots thudded heavily against the wooden floor.

"Hey Donny," Piper said before taking a big bite of her sub-sandwich. "What can we do for you?"

The police officer nodded toward King. "I need to talk to him if he's got a minute."

Piper met King's gaze with her lips pursed in question.

Sampson must've heard either the chime, or Donny's voice. "You gotta go, I take it?"

"Yeah," King admitted, putting his soda on the desktop. "But thanks for calling and letting me know what you found out."

"Anytime." Sampson ended the call without saying good-bye. It was a bad habit that King had set the precedent for, so he couldn't complain.

King stood and offered his hand. "Hey Donny. How've you been?"

"Not bad," he replied blandly, barely shaking his hand.

King knew the local cop as one of the officers who commonly patrolled the French Quarter. For that reason, he was a friendly and familiar face with his ragged eyebrow scar that bisected his left brow and a small cleft lip scar from a surgery he had as a kid.

Piper pulled up one of the chairs so that Donny could sit across from King.

"Oh, it's okay," he protested. "I can't stay long."

And yet he sat down in the chair.

"What can I do for you?" King tried to discern the source of the cop's nervousness. He'd never worked with one of the street cops on a case before, nor would it make sense that he would come to King with information when good law enforcement absolutely required that the chain of command be upheld for all evidence and procedures so that they can pass a conviction in the court of law.

Maybe it was a personal inquiry. God, King hoped Donny's wife wasn't having an affair.

"It's about Melandra," Donny said.

"What?" Piper and King spoke in unison.

King shot her a look. *You can stay but be quiet.*

Piper rolled her eyes and made an impatient gesture with her hands. Fortunately, this was done behind Donny's back.

"I was patrolling last night with Ramika, and Mel called out to me. At first she looked, well, I'm not sure how to describe it. Like she was pissed but also pretty scared. She said she'd been robbed."

"By who?"

"That's the funny part." Donny shook his head. "I saw the man who was talking to her. I'd spotted her before she spotted me actually, but I was working and she was talking to this guy so I didn't think nothing of it. But then I see her coming at me and he grabs her. That's when I knew something was up. But then he sort of disappeared before I got to her."

Disappeared. King's stomach dropped. He thought of the man in the leather hat with the crow feather sticking out of one side and the bone choker stretched across his dark throat. Hadn't he disappeared on King too?

King relayed this description.

Donny sat up straighter. "Yeah, that's him. You've seen him?"

"Yeah," King said, recalling the way the man had rolled his

eyes up to meet King's from the street below. "And I've seen him pull the disappearing act."

"By the time we got to speaking, she said she hadn't been robbed and was clearly trying to smooth it over, you know? I didn't want to push it but what could I do?"

"Nothing," King said, sympathetically.

Donny licked his lips and sheepishly met King's gaze.

King leaned forward and grinned. "But you did do something, didn't you?"

"Not officially." Donny flashed a sheepish smile. "Between you and me, I might have gone across the street to the convenience store and got the security tape from Larry. I might've also got a match on the guy. I just wanted to know who the hell he was."

"And?"

"The name's Terrence Lamott. He just got out of prison two weeks ago for murder. *And* he's Melandra's husband."

King glanced at Piper and saw her reddening face and working jaw. She looked ready to explode.

Donny rubbed his forehead as if a headache was coming on. "He's on parole so he can't fuck up or he goes right back in, but that doesn't mean shit."

"People reoffend all the time."

"Anyway, Mel might not want to talk about it but I thought at least I could tell you. You live and work so close, you can keep an eye on her."

Donny stood from his seat.

King, sensing the departure mixed in with the apology, reached across the desk and offered his hand. "Thanks for telling me. I appreciate it."

Piper bounced in her seat, making her chair emit tiny desperate squeaks. Both King and Donny glanced her way.

She stopped bouncing. "Sorry."

"If that guy starts giving her any shit, call me." Donny

dragged his chair across the room to where Piper had taken it from.

"Will do."

With an apologetic smile, Donny slipped from the office out into the sunlit streets.

Piper was out of her chair before the door fully closed. "Husband. *Husband!* Did you even know she was married?"

"No," King said, absentmindedly flicking the pull tab on his soda. Because Mel had told him a different story. In her version, she was married to an abusive alcoholic for thirty years and then she'd divorced him. It had been ugly, but she had gotten a nice settlement and it had allowed her to buy her shop. The idea she'd lied—felt like she *had* to lie to *him*—formed a cold rock in the pit of his gut. "No, I didn't know."

"And he's a murderer! Who *stole* something from her!"

"You need to calm down."

"Calm down!" Piper cried. She threw up her hands. "This murderer is harassing her and stealing her shit and she's too scared to even talk to us about it. I will *not* calm down. We have to do something."

"She must have a reason for wanting us to stay out of it," King said. He wasn't sure if he was trying to reassure Piper or himself. A horrible tight sensation had formed below his solar plexus and was growing. The nerves in his arms and legs felt jittery with weakness.

Piper crossed her arms over her chest. "She's wrong. She needs us."

Think, King scolded himself. *Think. Why would she tell you to stay out of it? Embarrassment? Fear?*

"And he's a murderer," Piper muttered to herself while pacing. "Mel is married to a *murderer*. And not the good kind, like Lou. Like the bad kind of murderer."

"We don't know who he killed or why." King covered his eyes.

"What are we going to do?" Piper asked, coming up on the balls of her feet expectantly.

"Shhh. Be quiet I'm trying to think."

"Think later. *What are we going to do?*" Piper paced anxiously in front of him. "We *are* going to do something. We have to get rid of this guy. We—we have to protect her."

"Of course we'll protect her," King said.

The problem was King knew Melandra well. He understood from the start and this omission, though surprising, made sense to him. It also meant that given what he knew about Melandra, she was already protecting herself. And if she was, the question was from what...

Something must've happened. Somewhere in their shared history, something must have happened. *I have to figure out what it was.*

It would take a lot of asking. He'd have to talk to her family, his family, old friends. Cell mates and people from his time in prison—because boy don't people talk in prison. He'd have to go through the husband's records and history. This would take a while, but he had to know what happened if he was going to help Mel.

King lifted his phone, chewing his lip while he considered which call he should make first.

22

L ou was perched on a stool inside the busy ramen house when she felt the tug in her abdomen. Someone was calling for her. It didn't feel like panic or the nerve-singeing ignition of all-consuming fear. But it got her attention. She dipped her chopsticks into her warm bowl of Tonkatsu and glanced at the bustling Tokyo street beyond, trying to get a sense of where the call was coming from.

Japanese, which had always been a beautiful and melodious language to her, filled her ears. It was complete with the exception of two American tourists sharing a table near the back of the noodle shop. Their brash, loud mouths ran as their cameras and shopping bags crowded around their feet.

Another desperate pull, this one a little more urgent than the last.

She did the math in her head. It was almost noon in Tokyo, which meant that it was almost ten in New Orleans.

With a sigh, Lou shoveled as much of the food into her mouth as possible, placed a generous stack of yen beside her bowl and nodded to the chef on the other side of the counter. "*Dōmo arigatōgozaimashita.*"

Then Lou was walking toward the bathroom in the back, a room so small she couldn't fully extend her arms without brushing the tiled walls on all sides.

No matter. She only needed its momentary darkness, long enough for the shadows to overtake her, wrap her body with their power and sift her through the underbelly of the world.

A new bathroom formed around her. The smell of cooking meat and smoke was replaced with the rancid burn of alcohol. The voices were all American now and about twenty times louder than they needed to be as they fought to overcome the Beyoncé blasting through the unseen speakers. The walls vibrated.

Lou stepped out of a dark corner into the bar itself, and was greeted by a crush of bodies. Lou spotted Piper right away.

"There you are." She stepped forward, flipping one blonde pigtail over her shoulder and hooked her arm through Lou's.

"What's going on?" Lou asked.

"I'll tell you outside. I'm sweating to death in here."

Piper pulled her through the throng of bodies, aware that more than once her guns shifted beneath her leather jacket, pressing into her ribs. If the passersby felt it, they showed no sign.

Because everyone is drunk, Lou thought. *They aren't noticing anything.*

Piper raised her hand and waved to a small throng of girls near the DJ booth. One bit her lip and pouted, giving Lou a ruthless once over the moment before Piper pulled her from the bar and into the open street. It was twenty degrees cooler outside, but crowd control wasn't much better.

"Are you ditching your friends?" Lou asked.

"Sort of. I invited them out because I'm trying not to think about freaking Dani, or the fact that Mel's *husband* is a *murderer* and out of *prison* and I have an exam in two days that I don't feel remotely good about—"

"Stop," Lou said, pulling her to a halt in the middle of the street. Outside the bar, it was easier to smell the alcohol on Piper's breath. She was well on her way to drunk. "Say all that again. Slowly."

"I mean Scarlett is nice but I shouldn't be sleeping with one woman when I'm thinking about another one. That's not healthy, man. And drinking and screwing all night has never helped anyone pass an exam." She burped and pressed her fist into her chest. "That I know of."

Lou pushed her sunglasses up on her head. "Tell me about Mel and the husband."

Piper pinched the bridge of her nose. "Oh *god* that burns. Ever burped in your nose?"

"Mel," Lou insisted. "Has a husband?"

"It turns out that creepy guy I don't like is Mel's *husband*. And he just got out of prison a couple weeks ago after being in there for twenty-something years for beating his pregnant girlfriend to death. He's a cheater, woman beater, and baby killer man. A total trash human."

Lou listened carefully as Piper recounted Donny's story. As some point Lou realized that Piper hadn't texted her when she'd needed her. Unlike King, who always sent his messages like a page, Piper had relied on the fact that her simple desire to see Lou was enough to summon her.

"You didn't page me. How did you know I'd come?" Lou's reached out and steadied Piper on her feet.

"I didn't *know* you'd come. I just hoped."

"And if I hadn't?"

"I would've tried paging you, but I like knowing I can reach you like this." She placed her fingers at her temples and hummed. "I don't know when another Dmitri Petrov is gonna show up. And I'm not going to wait until I'm actually kidnapped—*again*—to make sure the alarm system still works if you know what I'm saying."

"I won't let anything like that happen again," Lou said. And she was surprised by both the admission and the swell of possessiveness that rose in her chest at the idea of someone hurting Piper.

"Back at you." Piper blushed, looking embarrassed. "But King said we can't kill the husband. Yet. He's investigating the guy or something. But I swear to God, if he put his hands on her..." Piper rolled her eyes to the sky and pretended to choke an imaginary neck. "I'll kill him."

Lou thought of Fish and the tender way his wife leaned toward him, smiling as she offered her cheek for a kiss. *No,* she thought. *Sometimes the monsters stay hidden in the dark.* "You're certain he's threatening her now?"

"Oh yeah. And *we're* going to do something about it because she's Mel. She's one of us. We're not going to let some sleaze bucket assho—" Piper bit her lip the moment her eyes fixed on something over Lou's shoulder. Piper hiccupped. "Oh shit. Play it cool."

Lou felt the girl behind her before she stepped into Lou's line of sight. The impulse to pull her gun or turn and seize the person approaching rose in her. But since Piper's expression looked somewhere between apologetic and annoyed, she suspected this would've been an overreaction.

"Hey P." A girl with curly dark hair came to stand beside Piper. "You heading out?"

"Yeah," Piper said with an apologetic smile. She hiccupped again. "My cousin Lou*ann* is in town for Carnival. I promised to show her around if she came so—"

"It's nice to meet you." The girl extended her hand. The attitude shift was palpable.

She's okay with me now that she knows I'm not a threat, Lou realized and something about the ridiculousness of it—that

this girl would find her to be competition for Piper's affec-
tions—made Lou smile.

"Nice to meet you." Lou adjusted her jacket to make sure
it stayed over her guns.

"Anyway, you were having a good time and I didn't want to
interrupt and—"

"It's fine. We're heading over to Veronica's anyway. Amy
wants to smoke. You guys can come if you want."

"No, that's not her scene," Piper said, pointing at Lou.
"We'll probably walk around the Quarter then get beignets
and coffee. She'll be out cold before midnight."

Lou said nothing.

Scarlett gave Piper a long, pitiful stare and then sighed.
"Call me later."

"Yeah, sure."

With one last lingering look, Scarlett followed her friends
up the crowded street.

"I'm going to Hell," Piper whispered.

With a tight smile, Piper waved to the departing group
one more time.

"I'm terrible. She's probably going to go home and cry
about this. I'm the one who invited her out and got her hopes
up. Why did I do that? I'm so dumb."

Lou couldn't help but grin. "She'll live."

Piper nudged her hard with an elbow. "Shut up. If Dani
would just return my freaking calls I wouldn't be here right
now. Besides you're one to talk with your Italian stallion
drama. Oh, speaking of which, King said he couldn't get
anything on that mysterious stalker. Her face didn't match
any of his data sweeps. He suggests that you ask
Konstantine."

Lou slid her glasses down on her face, hiding her
eyes.

Piper hiccupped again. "I could come with you to talk to

him. I can even do the talking. I'm feeling pretty chatty right now."

"He's in Venice."

"I've always wanted to go to Venice." Piper threw an arm around Lou's shoulder "Isn't it Carnival there too? How cool would that be to visit *actual* Venice during Carnival?"

Lou glanced up the street at the drunks leaning against buildings and laughing loudly in the streets. The smell of piss hung around them. No doubt someone was relieving themselves against a brick wall.

Piper tugged on her wrist. "Come on. Let's do it. I've got the photo on my phone and we need to know who this woman is and what she wants with Fish. And I need a distraction from a certain MIA journalist."

"You realize it's about five in the morning there," Lou said. "Konstantine will probably be in bed."

A sly smile flickered across Piper's lips. "I mean, we need to know who this woman is, so..."

With a resigned sigh, Lou pulled Piper into the deep shadow of a darkened stoop. She leaned her body against Piper's and heard the girl's throat click. But already her attention was sliding away, searching the other side of the world for her intended target.

Something fell into place and like a current inside her, the waters changed. The pull swept through her. Lou let go, giving herself over to it.

Lou had been expecting a hotel room. Or maybe a room in a villa if Vittoria was any kind of hostess.

What she *hadn't* been expecting was a large and opulent ballroom full of swelling music, writhing bodies, and full costumed regalia.

Her first thought, *it's nearly dawn* was drowned in the melancholic music of strings. She couldn't see the violins, violas or cellos, but their twined voices echoed below the cavernous ceilings and the women in busty corsets and ornate masks swayed and laughed. Men in long jackets stood speaking to one another. Pairs danced in the center.

Lou spotted Konstantine immediately. She knew it was him even with the mask.

He had one arm over the back of a velvet chair. His clothes weren't archaic or costumed like the others around him. He wore a simple black suit, perfectly cut to his body, and an open red shirt beneath. His mask was also red, covering only the top half of his face.

He was speaking to the woman beside him, a beautiful blonde with large radiant curls. Her breasts were pushed up nearly to her chin by the white corset she wore. Her costume resembled a peacock, from the long willowy feathers protruding from her shimmering mask to the cape and dress filled with those same placid eyes.

Piper stumbled beside her, seizing her arm as she righted herself. "Whoa. Look at this place!"

It was this movement that drew Konstantine's eye. The smile on his lips faltered for a moment and he touched the woman's arm, excusing himself.

The bodies in the room parted.

"Oh boy," Piper murmured, nudging Lou. "Here he comes. That's Konstantine, right?"

"Why are you giggling?"

"I don't know." Piper covered her mouth. "It's funny. Look at him."

Konstantine stopped just short of her, regarding her through the dark slits of his ruby mask. "Ciao."

Lou raised an eyebrow. "*Ciao*."

"Is that booze over there?" Piper pointed at a bar on the right side of the dance floor. A man in a black and white suit and white plaster mask was behind the bar refilling glasses. "I'm going to get a drink."

Something hard pressed into Lou's open hand. It was Piper's phone.

"5567," Piper whispered into Lou's ear. "It's the last picture I took."

"Take this," Konstantine said, reaching behind his head to untie his mask.

"Oooo, okay. Thanks." Piper tied Konstantine's mask over her face and struck a haughty pose with one hand on her hip. "How do I look?"

Konstantine nodded. If Piper saw it, she made no further reply, already making a beeline for the bar.

"Is she safe here?" Lou asked, watching her weave through the bodies. She noticed that they did not part for her the way they had for Konstantine.

"With her face covered," he replied. He shifted to the right and Lou followed his gaze. She wasn't surprised to find Stefano there, lurking in the dark. She hadn't spotted him as quickly or easily as she had Konstantine, but she'd known he would be close. Something about the man's possessiveness of Konstantine amused her. The cold look he gave her only made her smile more.

Konstantine dragged a thumb across his cheekbone and Stefano nodded once.

"What does that mean?" She mimicked him, dragging her thumb across her cheek.

"He'll look after her," Konstantine said with a half-smile. "This is neutral territory and no one should cause trouble, but just in case."

"Shame," Lou said. "I'm in the mood for a fight."

She was very aware of his body beside her. He was turned, his feet pointing toward hers, his hands clasped loosely in front of him. And his smell. It was heady. It made her think of a deep wood, an endless forest full of moonlight.

"Yes, I imagine all of this hunting and not killing is a challenge for you," he said, watching her face carefully. "Does it remind you of your days hunting Angelo?"

"Yes," she said, realizing the truth of it for the first time. "Yes, it is like that."

Silence stretched between them. She found she couldn't figure out how to start the conversation.

Just show him the picture. What's wrong with you?

"I thought you'd be in bed," she said.

"The party will continue until dawn."

She nodded as if this mattered.

"When I saw you, you already had your eyes on me," Konstantine said. Lou admitted, only to herself, that she enjoyed listening to him speak. "How did you know it was me?"

She shrugged in her leather jacket. "You forget how much time I've spent watching you."

"I'm flattered." But he didn't sound flattered. His laugh was tight and tired.

She glanced toward the white peacock who'd fallen into conversation with another woman. But her gaze slid to Lou every few seconds.

"Is that your hostess?" Lou asked. "Vittoria."

"Yes."

"Will she mind that I've crashed her party?" Lou's eyes slid instinctively to Piper. She was on the dance floor now, swaying with everyone else, pausing only long enough to take a long drink. Several feet away Stefano lurked dutifully.

"I will explain that you are with me," he said, softly. "Though I suspect she knows you can come and go as you please."

If Vittoria isn't the reason for his fatigue, it must be me, she realized.

His low voice interrupted her thoughts. "Dare I hope that you came to see me simply because you missed me?"

He was looking at her now. She felt the gaze on the side of her face.

She lifted the phone, punched in the passcode and found the app that opened Piper's photos. The last photos were actually selfies of Piper in the bar. Before that, three photos of Lady with her head on her paws. The blurred tail suggested an enthusiastic wag. It was nearly ten photos back before she found Fish's mysterious stalker.

"A woman is following Fish. She's tracking him like I am."

"*Exactly* as you are?" Konstantine asked, eyebrows rising.

"No. She's using more conventional methods. King looked into her but couldn't find anything."

Konstantine opened a text message and sent the photo of the woman to a number he punched in. Lou heard the buzz in his pocket, understanding that he'd sent it to himself.

He looked at the photo for a long time, before handing the phone back to her.

"Have I offended you?"

Lou met his gaze. "Your heart's still beating. I'm pretty sure I've shot everyone who has ever offended me."

His lips twitched with a smile. "I've only noticed that you haven't come to see me since..."

She arched an eyebrow, wondering if he was going to say it right here in the open. They were somewhat alone in their corner of the ballroom. But Lou had no doubt ears were listening.

"Since the shower," he finished.

"I've been busy." Lou shifted in her leather jacket again. She felt the guns rub against her ribs. It made her feel better knowing they were close.

"I'm also busy." His eyes traced her jaw before focusing on her lips. "And I still want you in my bed every night. You *sleep*, don't you?"

She met his eyes and an icy wind rolled through her. The

wind was of her own making, she knew it. She was steeling herself against...whatever this was. "What do you want from me?"

"You."

The ice hardened in her chest and stomach. Even her limbs grew heavy with it. She looked away first.

"I'll find this woman for you," Konstantine said, slipping his hands into his pockets. "Even if it's only an excuse to see you again."

He bowed his head, rolling his eyes up to meet hers and then backed away with one hand over his heart. She watched him go with a strange sensation in her guts. It was an ache.

Piper saw Konstantine crossing the floor and bounced over to him. She was offering the mask, her hands already behind her head, ready to untie it, but he waved her off with a kind smile.

Then Piper was bounding across the room toward Lou.

"This place is amazing! Free booze and free food. They've got a bunch of those little cakes and something that I *really* hope is sausage. Oh and the ladies! God, there's this one who is *soooo* cute. I don't know a word she's saying, but that's probably for the best, right? Talking is where I usually go wrong. Talking is the worst. That's why I'm a listener. People think it's because I'm sweet but really it's because I'm *smart*."

Lou watched Konstantine take his place beside his host again and the possessive way she leaned into him while meeting Lou's gaze made the hairs on her arm rise.

23

P iper sat up in bed and instantly regretted it. The world spun around her, falling into a tailspin. The room kaleidoscoped out of focus.

"Whoa." She fisted her sheets as if they would stop her whirling. "Man, what did I *drink*?"

Her head throbbed and instantly was made worse by the earsplitting ring tone. She groaned, fumbling for the device on her side table, desperate to end the "Fools" by Troye Siven ringtone as quickly as possible.

"Hello," she croaked. Her tongue scraped over her teeth like sandpaper. She tried to clear her throat. "Hello, hi?"

She saw the glass of water on the side table and the bottle of aspirin. A vague memory of Lou placing the glass and pills there surfaced in her mind. That would explain the fact she was still in her clothes and smelled like booze. At least Lou had removed her shoes before dumping her onto the mattress. Had she stayed the night? Piper couldn't remember.

Beside her phone, propped against the glass, was a note in Lou's simple print. Squinting Piper read, *Payback is coming.*

Even with the smiley face at the end, it wasn't a note one wanted to receive from Lou Thorne.

Payback? Payback for what? What did I do?

But then she'd remembered. She'd promised Lou she would be the one to talk to Konstantine, but at first chance, she left her alone with him in favor of the open bar.

Oops.

"Hey. Hi. It's me." Dani's voice faltered. "Were you still sleeping?"

Something in her tone encouraged Piper to check the time. She pulled the phone from her ear and squinted at the time. It was almost ten. She was supposed to be at the shop ten minutes ago.

"Oh shit." Piper threw back the covers and seized the aspirin. She tapped four out into her hand and drowned them with the water.

"If this is a bad time—" Dani began.

"No, no." Piper stumbled from the bed to the adjacent full-length mirror. Her clothes were rumpled but passable. She smelled a little like booze, but nothing some deodorant and a couple sprays of body mist wouldn't fix. Piper would wash her face, brush her teeth, grab a granola bar from the cabinet. If she was quick about it, she would only be about twenty minutes late. "What's up?"

She put the phone on speaker so that she could shoot Mel a text. *Out with Lou last night. Overslept. So sorry. See you in five.*

Piper got the thumbs up emoji for her trouble.

"I wanted to apologize for not contacting you again," Dani said, her voice echoed through the speaker phone as Piper went into the bathroom and turned on the faucet. "Something came up and I got distracted."

"It's okay," Piper said, fishing a washcloth off the shelf. "I'm glad that you called."

And to her surprise, she was.

"I was hoping that you could come by tonight for dinner at my place. I'd like a chance to explain. Again."

"I close tonight," Piper said, balancing the phone on the ledge above the sink so she could splash hot water on her face. "How do you feel about a late dinner? 10:30?"

"It's perfect," Dani said. "I'll text you my new address, okay?"

It wasn't a full minute after the call ended that Piper's phone buzzed with the text. She recognized the small neighborhood north of the Garden District. If Dani's new place was there, then she was paying at least two grand a month in rent.

"Ouch." Piper whistled, stuffing the toothbrush slathered in paste into her mouth.

When she closed Dani's text, her eye caught on a number she didn't recognize. She frowned at it, opening the text with a press of her thumb.

There was the image of the woman, Fish's stalker, staring back at her.

"Oh shit," she said, realizing what she must be looking at. Her thumb raced over the keypad. *Konstantine?*

A moment later, *sì, piper.*

Piper spit into the sink. *You better not have installed any tracker crap on my phone dude.*

Or what? What was she going to do if he had? Ask Lou to kill him?

She sighed and added, *Just use the photo to find the chick, k?*
I have only the photo.

"Lies," Piper grumbled, scooping water into her mouth from the running faucet. Of course she couldn't say anything. She'd given Lou the phone to begin with and it wasn't like Konstantine was supposed to memorize it with his eyes or something. But the idea of a crime lord, even one who was supposedly on their side didn't leave her feeling particularly secure.

May I ask you a question?

Piper spit into the sink. To her reflection she said, "See. This is how it starts."

About?

Our mutual friend

She reread the text several times. With each pass, a dropping sensation intensified in her stomach. She knew she was on a precipice here and that it would be so easy to cross over to the other side, a darker, more dangerous side.

"Damn," she murmured and typed her reply. *You can ask, but I reserve the right to not answer.*

To her reflection she said, "She better not kill me for this."

WHEN PIPER LOCKED UP THE SHOP AT TEN MINUTES AFTER close that night, she expected to see Mel's husband lurking in the streets outside. But she saw no sign of him. Still she lingered at the entrance until she saw Mel ascend the stairs, Lady on her heels, and disappear into her apartment. Only then did she take off through the Quarter, maneuvering through the bodies that stood between her and the St. Charles Avenue streetcar stop.

She tracked her progress on her phone, the little blue dot of her position moving as she moved, until she found herself in front of a pink stucco building with old French windows. In the foyer, there were four buttons. Piper mashed the button beside Dani's name.

"Hello?" A voice cracked through the speaker.

Piper leaned toward the com. "It's me."

The door buzzed and Piper was allowed to pass through the locked inner door. The door on the far right opened and

Dani stepped out into the hall, one hand still resting on the door itself as if she might change her mind and shut it at any minute.

God, she's beautiful.

In a wine-colored turtleneck and tight jeans, her dark complexion seemed to glow.

"Hi." She chewed her lower lip. "Come on in."

Something about Dani reminded Piper of the night before, of the woman in the peacock outfit who'd been a bit handsy with Konstantine. She'd been curious about the beautiful, busty blonde, especially since all the eyes in the room seemed to track her and Konstantine. But Piper was admittedly distracted by the pretty drunk girl in a cat mask who kept whispering super sexy Italian in her ear.

Piper stepped inside the apartment and slipped her shoes off, leaving them by the door. She just assumed since Dani was in socks herself that this was the protocol.

But Dani shook her head. "You don't have to do that."

"It's okay." The shoes were already off. Piper wasn't going to put them back on.

One quick visual inspection of the apartment told Piper she wouldn't have been comfortable wearing the shoes anyway. It was immaculate with twelve-foot ceilings and the rounded French windows that Piper had admired from the outside. It was an open floor plan so the dining area, kitchen, and living room were all laid bare. There were two doors off a short hallway but they were open too. The walls were a cheerful yellow. The ceilings and trim were creamy white.

Something rubbed against her leg and Piper looked down to find a fluffy Russian blue cat blinking large gold eyes up at her.

"That's Octavia," Dani said, stepping forward with a bottle of wine and two glasses. "I call her Tavi. You're not allergic are you?"

"A bit, but she's fine." Piper frowned at the wine. "I don't want to drink tonight. I had a bit too much last night, if you know what I mean."

Dani put the wine glasses down on the counter and smiled. But the smile was tight. "Did you go out for Carnival?"

"In *Venice*." Piper couldn't help but say it. "I didn't even need a passport. We were only there for like an hour but still. Being friends with Lou has its benefits."

Dani was nodding, but Piper had the distinct feeling that she wasn't hearing what Piper said.

Dani filled her glass of wine to the top. "She was here this morning. She was the one who told me I'd better call you. I was in the shower and she just opened the door and—" A small, nervous laugh escaped her. "She scared the hell out of me."

"Wait, what? Lou got in your shower?"

Payback is coming—is that what she'd meant by that? That she was going to force me to talk to Dani because I forced her to talk to Konstantine? Vicious!

Piper pouted. "If you only called me because Lou made you—"

"No." Dani brought the wine to her lips but didn't drink it. She still held the bottle in the other hand. "No, I wanted to talk to you. She just gave me the little push I needed. I'm just saying that yes, Lou is a good friend to you."

By popping into your shower and making demands? Piper wondered.

Piper rubbed her forehead, feeling a headache blooming behind her skull again. She tried to remember the last time she took a dose of aspirin. "I hope she sees it that way."

Dani's brow furrowed. "What do you mean?"

"Uh, I offered some love advice to her beau that wasn't really mine to give."

Hopefully it won't backfire on my ass.

Konstantine had promised not to say a word and Piper had suggested that Lou's reluctance to accept Konstantine's devotion was probably because Lou had lost the only man she ever loved when she was a child. Even if he hadn't been Paolo Konstantine, brother to the man who pulled the trigger, even if she hadn't been Louie Thorne, executioner to hundreds of men just like him—there was that simple fact. It was true Lou only felt in control when she had a gun in her hand and she didn't attach to people because she understood how easy it was for them to disappear. Especially men like Konstantine.

Didn't you almost die just, like, a year ago? she'd asked. *Do you think she's forgotten that?*

Konstantine had conceded the point.

More than once during their text session, Piper had thought, *I'm texting one of the world's most dangerous men. Ruler of the underground. This guy probably tortures people on a Saturday. Life is so weird.*

Dani smirked.

"What?"

"It doesn't matter." Dani drank half her wine in one go. Then she said, "I wanted to apologize. Again."

Piper refrained from tapping her fingers on the glass tabletop. "For?"

"When we had dinner the other night, I know I gave you the impression that I wouldn't disappear again and then I did just that. I ghosted you *again*. I'm sorry."

Dani searched her face and Piper realized she was waiting for a reaction. But Piper, perhaps from having such an exciting night before, then a long day at the shop, felt mostly tired.

"It's okay," she said.

Dani grimaced. "Don't do that."

"What?"

"Don't just forgive me like that."

Piper laughed. "It's easy when you don't really care."

Dani flinched.

"I didn't mean I don't care about you. I'm just tired and I have a headache and I'm worried about—" *Mel mostly, but also Lou.* "—my people. I'm sure that if you ghosted me you had a good reason, right?"

There. Piper had left it wide open for Dani to explain herself. Piper waited.

It was clear by the way Dani wrung the wine glass in her hand, the way she put the bottle down on the table, the way she chewed her lower lip, staring at her hands. All of it signaled that she was working up to it—whatever it was—and Piper knew well enough to hold the space.

I wish I had three more aspirin though. Italian booze was no joke. Her head was killing her.

"I didn't call you back because I was in the hospital."

"So you're sick?" *Oh god, cancer? Something worse?* Piper's mind raced.

"Not that kind of hospital." Dani chewed her lip. "I was at the Crescent City Psych Hospital."

So I did trigger an episode, like you thought I would.

"I've checked myself in a few times this year, just a few days here and there—when the episodes get really bad." She licked her lips again, then pulled on her ear. "It's a good thing the hospital has Wi-Fi, right? Otherwise, I probably would've lost my job by now."

The nervous laugh that escaped Dani set Piper's teeth on edge.

Once she dared a glance up, finally meeting Piper's eyes, Dani grimaced harder. "Don't look at me that way. That's exactly why I didn't call you. I didn't want you to see me as this pathetic, broken little doll."

"I don't see—" Piper began but Piper didn't get very far.

The words fell from Dani's lips hot and fast. "I wake up in the middle of the night screaming because I think someone is in my bedroom. I couldn't even stay one night in my old apartment because all I could see is *oh, this is where he tortured me. Oh here is where they tied me to a chair and punched me in the stomach a million times. Here is where he pulled out a fistful of my hair. Here is where they*—"

She covered her face and began to cry.

Piper stood and slid her arms around Dani's waist.

"It's okay," she whispered into her ear. She placed a kiss on the top of her ear, then her temple. "It's okay."

"Terrible things happen to people all the time. I don't know why I can't get past this."

"Maybe because you were almost beaten to death for information you didn't even have and then the psychopath cut off your finger? I don't think anyone could just *get past* that. You're putting too much pressure on yourself."

Dani didn't seem to hear her. "I didn't want you to see me this way. But I also didn't want you to think I didn't care about you. I'm so weak. I thought adversity made you stronger."

"Hey. Don't say that." Piper pulled back, cupping Dani's cheeks in her hands. "Listen, I think it's important to point out that you were strong before all this bullshit happened. Shit like this doesn't make women stronger. It makes everything *harder*. You don't have anything to prove to me. Or the world."

Dani's eyes were bright with unshed tears. Her lip trembled. "You must think—"

"I think you're an amazing, smart, courageous woman who had a really fucked up experience. And you survived and it's going to take some time to heal. Maybe you'll never heal completely and that's okay."

"But you're surrounded by strong women. Lou—"

Piper laughed, a tight bewildered sound. "We can't compare ourselves to *Lou*." *And it isn't like that girl hasn't got her own problems.* "And I've *never* been through something like what you've been through."

Dani cried softly into Piper's shoulder and Piper held her. There was nothing else to be done. After the sobs died to a quiet mewling, Piper spoke. "What happened to you, *happened*. Period. You don't have to justify your pain to anyone, okay? Not me or anyone else. I'm going to say this a million times until you believe me."

Dani pulled back and dabbed at her eyes. "I'm sorry. I stayed away so you wouldn't see me fall apart and I'm falling apart anyway."

Piper pushed the hair back from Dani's face. "I'd rather see you fall apart than not see you at all."

Dani laughed, a sad, desperate little sound that could be interpreted a hundred ways. "You don't mean that."

Piper grabbed both sides of her face, forcing Dani to look her in the eyes. "I mean it. Okay? I mean it."

Dani looked around her apartment as if seeing it for the first time. "Are you hungry? Will you stay the night?"

Piper smiled, unwilling to point out that these two questions were entirely unrelated. "Yes."

24

As Melandra's spoon stirred cream into her coffee, her eyes fixed on some point in the distant past. Her bare kitchen wall served as the screen for the theater of her mind. The table creaked under the press of her elbows as she adjusted herself, unable to get comfortable.

The apartment, she realized, was the antithesis of the trailer she'd shared with Terry all those years ago. It had been narrow, stuffed with furniture that had come from the Salvation Army, mostly browns and yellows with tears at their seams. And no matter how hard she'd cleaned its windows, it seemed not enough light had ever filled those small rooms.

She'd spent nearly six years working first shift in a small manufacturing plant to pay for it. On the weekends, she wandered the rooms of that old trailer, doing her best to keep the little place clean. As she scrubbed toilets and showers and packed up all their clothes to be taken down to the coin-operated laundromat at the other end of the trailer park.

On most days, her Grandmamie's voice had haunted her.

Us Durand women are both blessed and cursed, Melandra. You hear me? Blessed with the sight but also blind in the heart. We're

destined for bad men, every one of us, and if you fool enough to go an'
have a girl child of your own, she gonna be as blind as the rest of us.

Now, decades later in her beautiful, airy apartment full of
light, Mel still remembered feeding quarters into the slot,
adding the powdered soap to the machine, and thinking that
Grandmamie had been right. Mel had been blinded. By
Terry's easy smile. By the way he'd lower his voice and
whisper directly into her ear all the things she needed to hear.
How he'd lean his hip into her hip and her whole body would
soften.

A damn fool, Mel thought, bringing her coffee to her lips.
But at least I didn't have a baby girl.

When Terry was arrested, and his body was slammed onto
the floor of their little trailer so hard the whole place shook,
she'd been ashamed of how relieved she felt. How could she
be *relieved* to see her husband cuffed and dragged from the
room?

She looked over the rim of her coffee mug to the three
cards spread before her on her kitchen table. They echoed
the long ago spread laid out by her dead grandmother's
crooked fingers.

Then it had been The Devil, Justice, Death.

Now it was The Devil, The Wheel of Fortune, and Death.

It was The Wheel of Fortune she fixed her eyes on, a card
she's laid off to one side. The problem with the wheel was
that she couldn't be sure if it was turning for or against her.
Change for the best, change for the worst. It could go
either way.

If it was turning for the worst—what of it? Didn't Mel
know, in her heart, that she had it coming? However this
shook out, with her dead or in prison, she had it coming.

She had it coming because of what happened in
November 1982.

It had been flurrying on and off all day, in that way it did sometimes in Louisiana. No real snow would come of it, but it was enough to make the roads slick and the face and knuckles cold.

By the time they'd left the bar at two in the morning, it had given over to rain. Terry had been in a good mood. He'd won the pool games he'd played, and hadn't gotten caught cheating. Then he'd drank away half his winnings to celebrate.

"You drive," he'd told her as they stumbled down the steps into the gravel lot.

Mel hadn't wanted to. She'd drank two beers herself and though she wasn't drunk she was tipsy enough to know it was a bad idea.

He threw her the keys to the Firebird and missed. They hit the gravel at her feet.

"We should call a cab."

"I ain't leaving my car here." He'd unzipped his pants and began pissing on a bush beside the bar door. "Drive or I will."

She'd bent and fished the keys out of the gravel despite the sense of pending dread filling her.

I'd known, she thought. *I'd known something would happen and I drove anyway.*

She'd put the key in the ignition, turned it, and pulled out of the lot onto the dark country road. She'd driven slowly, but it hadn't mattered. She'd gotten tired, as she always did with a few drinks in her. The soft sound of rain splashing against the windshield hadn't helped.

Her eyes had closed only for a moment. Then the car hit something, hard. She slammed on the brakes, skidding to a stop in the middle of the road. Each swipe of the wiper blades had revealed the rain falling in her headlights and the bend in the road ahead.

Her first thought—*if I'd slept for even ten seconds longer, we would've slammed right into those trees.*

Her second thought—*what did I hit?*

Terry'd come awake beside her, jolting up in his seat. "What the hell happened?"

"I hit something."

Mel craned in her seat, looking behind her. A lump lay in the middle of the dark road. The red taillights gave it a demonic glow. But it had the unmistakable shape of a human body. A small woman? A child?

"Oh god," she whispered. "Oh my god, I hit somebody."

He'd turned in his seat, looking back over his shoulder into the dark. "Stay here."

He pushed open the passenger side door.

Mel'd begun opening her door when Terry had grabbed her arm hard, yanking her back into the seat. "Stay here I said."

First he went to the front of the car, stood in the headlights and inspected the damage while rain pelted his face. He rubbed something with his hand and swore. Then he'd walked to the back of the car, bent down over the unmoving form.

That's when she put her face in her hands and began to cry.

He'd gotten back in the car, dragging a hand down his face. "Drive."

She'd looked around, searching the darkness for help, or a witness. She'd seen a light through the trees.

"We can go to that house and call for help."

He'd grabbed the back of her hair and pulled hard enough to bring startled tears to her eyes. "*Drive* or I'll pull you out and I'll drive."

And God forgive her, she had driven away from the scene without having to be told twice.

"It was an animal," he'd whispered. "You hear me. It was an animal."

"It wasn't! It—"

He'd slapped her and that was the end of it.

The next day he took five hundred dollars from her account and the car went into the shop. That was the last they ever spoke of it until he went to prison.

"If I pay him off, he'll just come back. If I go to the police, he'll run. Or he might tell them what happened."

Or maybe he won't give me a chance to confess at all, Mel thought. *He's never liked not getting his way.*

She reached past the three cards and lifted the revolver resting there. She noted its weight in her hand, the finality of it.

Lady placed her head on Mel's leg. A long, mournful whine escaped the dog. Mel cupped one ear with her hand but her eyes remained fixed on the gun.

"There, now. Everything's gonna be all right."

25

Konstantine woke the moment he felt the weight beside him. He instinctually reached for his gun before the familiar scent washed over him. He relaxed. Turning only his head, he saw the outline of her body.

Lou lay on her back, her eyes closed, her lips slightly parted. Her dark lashes rested on her cheeks. For a long while he only looked at her, watching her chest rise and fall. She was dreaming and he longed to know what she dreamt of. Killers prowling the night? Drug dealers? His dead brother Angelo with his gun? Her father or mother? Her aunt?

Him?

The familiar stab of rejection shot through him. He ached to reach out and touch her but to do so would break the spell. Maybe he would never see her again.

Maybe the girl, Piper, had been wrong.

She comes to see you. She's not doing that with anybody else, man.

No. She hadn't joined another man's bed. His constant canvassing of the internet for photos, video clips, or any other trace of her existence, *was* in the name of protecting her anonymity, but he did look for other men.

There had been a few, before they'd begun—whatever it was they had now.

But she wasn't sleeping in anyone else's bed, braless. She wasn't taking showers with them or wearing their black sweats. And most importantly, she went to no one else—save the old detective in New Orleans—when she needed help.

It was more than that.

She chooses me when she dreams, he thought, watching her breathe beside him. *What are dreams but our deepest desires?*

Don't rush her, man. She's like a cat. She's going to love you on her terms.

That at least, Konstantine had agreed with. The girl, despite her American slang, had seemed very wise in her text messages. It contrasted with her sweet, angelic face. She looked like a child when standing next to Lou.

He recalled the way the girl had looked, laughing, hanging off of Lou's shoulder in the ballroom. What a contrast. Lou, somber and imperial. The girl blond, smiling, and infused with girlish radiance. Proserpina in her two forms.

Konstantine traced the line of her jaw with his gaze, down her throat to the small hollow there. He longed to touch it with his lips.

A sound over his right shoulder caught his ear. He turned and saw Vittoria in the doorway. She beckoned him forward.

As silently as he could, he slipped from the bed, pausing to regard her once more.

He pulled the door closed behind him.

Vittoria was in a red dressing gown. Her face had been wiped of its makeup and she looked her age now.

"*Mi stavi guardando??*" Konstantine asked as she settled into a leather chair. *Were you watching me?*

"I have cameras everywhere in this house."

"I know." Konstantine had wired into her system before ever agreeing to stay at her villa.

"Clever boy." Vittoria grinned. "Imagine my surprise when a woman appeared in your bed. Does that happen often?"

"Why are you speaking in English?" Konstantine asked and settled into the leather armchair across from her.

"I need to practice," she purred, turning her glass in the light. She flicked her eyes up to meet his. "You didn't answer my question."

"Don't worry about her," Konstantine said.

"I worry about everything that happens in my home. In my city. Italy. The world. To be a woman in this business you have to worry twice as much as the men," she said with a playful pout. "How lucky you were to be born with a dick, *fratello*."

Konstantine didn't rise to this bait.

"If she can appear and disappear like in the rumors, I wonder what else may be true." Vittoria rose from her seat and crossed to Konstantine. She sat down on his lap, perching on his knee. "*L'hai scopata?*"

Konstantine frowned up at her. "*Greggia.*"

She laughed. Then in English, "If you haven't, you certainly want to. I see it in your eyes. Do you own her then? Have you made her love you? Is that why she seeks you out in the night like some *vampira?*"

"She doesn't love me." Despite the sinking in his chest he felt he'd spoken the truth.

Vittoria clucked her tongue. "A shame. With Fernando Martinelli as a father you should be better at this."

LOU WOKE WHEN THE DOOR CREAKED SHUT. THE SMALL sound pulled her straight from her dreams. She couldn't remember what she'd been dreaming of—something about a car sinking through red waters and a monster that waited outside its windows to snap her up.

Lou sat up, taking inventory of the room. She was in a high, four-post bed. On the right were floor-to-ceiling shutters, latched tight. Dim light squeezed through the slats, cascading over the uneven tiled floor. Against the far wall, an armoire twice her size sagged.

She didn't recognize the room or its furniture. But she knew the smell that lingered on the pillows around her, on the sheets.

Voices carried from somewhere outside the room and she saw the light under the door. She slid from the high bed, feeling her bare feet press into the cold tiled floor.

At the door, she grabbed the handle and turned it ever so slightly. She held her breath as if they might somehow dampen the sound.

Fortunately, the door did not creak and through the crack she could see the large expanse of a living room. A soft fire crackled against the far wall. Framing the fire were two armchairs facing one another.

Even without the white peacock costume, Lou recognized the woman immediately. She sat sprawled on one of the leather armchairs with a glass of wine in hand. Then she rose, crossed the room and sat on Konstantine's lap.

The movement obscured her view of his face, of his reaction to her. But she saw what he didn't do—push her off, move her away, demand that she stop.

Why should he? she asked herself. *If this is what is required to make a business deal, why stop now?*

Yet there was an intense heat building in her face.

She backed away from the door the way one moves away from the sparking wick of a stick of dynamite. Then through the darkness, she was gone.

26

After failing to sleep in her own bed, Lou put on jeans, her guns, and her leather jacket. She grabbed her mirrored sunglasses off the counter and stepped into her linen closet once more.

This really was the only way to deal with a restless night.

The scent of cedar swelled around her and she pressed her back against the wooden wall.

Through the dark she searched for her target—Fish. And like anyone, Fish had his usual haunts. He went to work at the high school. He favored the grocery near his house. He worked in the garage and took his son to the park.

But Lou's compass didn't direct her to any of these destinations.

When the dark opened around her, she was in the forest. Pine sap stuck to her fingers as she clung to the tree. Her boots settled on dried needles. Clouds moving across the sky dappled the moonlight, causing the shadows to sway and swell like water across the ground.

For a horrible heartbeat, Lou thought Fish might be behind her. Ready for her.

But then she heard a grunt, a small muffled cry.

The clouds moved and moonlight spilled over Jeffrey Fish's hunched body.

There was no victim. No struggle as she had feared. It was only Jeffrey on his knees, pants down.

She moved closer silently, careful not to betray her approach with a snapping twig or shifting rock. His erection was in his hand as he furiously pumped it up and down. Sweat stood out on his brow as his eyes rolled closed.

Lou could smell the death from here. It wasn't unlike passing roadkill on a hot summer day, mixed with the scent of overturned earth. She didn't need to look into the grave to know what she would see. By the smell of the corpse, she didn't think it was the grocer, who she'd checked on just that afternoon.

She suspected it was someone else. Someone killed recently.

Rage welled within her. She drew her gun before she knew what she was doing.

Shoot him. Shoot him and kick his corpse into this grave and be done with all this bullshit. Broken systems and stupid rules that no one plays by. End it. End it now.

No! This was Aunt Lucy's cry. *Think of the families. Think of the families who'll never know what happened. Who will lie awake at night and pray for news, any news, to get past the horrible limbo of uncertainty.*

Gritting her teeth, Lou raised her boot and kicked out. Fish cried out, falling forward into the grave.

By the time Fish managed to spit the soil from his mouth and begin screaming, Lou was already gone.

KING WOKE WHEN HIS BEDROOM LIGHT CLICKED ON. LOU

stood over his bed scowling at him. He squinted up at her, his heart rocketing in his chest.

"What?"

"He's killed again," she said. The coldness in her voice echoed through his bones.

King sat up, scrubbing at his eyes. "Who?"

"Fish killed someone."

"How?"

"I wasn't there," Lou said in that same flat tone. "I suspect he tortured her then fucked her like the others. He was certainly masturbating over her grave—"

"Christ."

"I want to take him now. I'll keep him somewhere until you can build your case."

King looked at her. Again, her face betrayed nothing. It was better to listen to her voice, which at least, gave a hint of the fury raging inside her.

"We can't take him to court if you do that. Him missing with only complicate the case."

She rolled her shoulders in her jacket. It was the first real threat of aggression he'd seen from her. "He *killed* someone and we didn't *stop* him."

King glanced at the urn on side table. *What do I tell her? Reason with her. She's smart.*

"Fine. Then let's expose him. I'll take them to the grave where he was jerking off. With his DNA, that might be enough to get the conviction."

"But not enough to tie him to the other cases."

"That's what the photos are for."

"We can't use the photos without a warrant to obtain them lawfully. And we can't get that if we don't have a reason to go into his house. They'll want to know how we know about the grave. We'd have to fabricate witnesses that we don't have or who might lose their cool during cross interrogation. The system requires—"

"Your system is broken," Lou said and here her face contorted. As much as it frightened King to see it, in a way, it was a relief. When he had no idea what she was thinking in that dark mind of hers, he found it all the more difficult to respond.

"I know you're frustrated. I am too. I didn't want any more women to die either," he said, trying to wipe at his dry, tacky mouth. "But we don't have enough to convict. Not a white, high school teacher from suburbia. At the very least we need the DNA."

"*Go* to the grave and *get* it."

King pinched his eyes shut. He wasn't awake enough for this. What time was it? It was just past midnight. He'd barely gotten a single REM cycle before she'd showed up. Now he was likely to spend the night tossing, turning, and likely blaming himself for a murder they might have prevented if they'd been quicker.

He pinched the bridge of his nose. "It's not that easy. I'm not even an agent anymore. I'm not sanctioned by any agency. I can't just show up in someone's jurisdiction and point a finger at Fish and say he did it."

His ears popped and he opened his eyes.

Lou was gone.

Groaning, he fell back against his pillow. He reached out and found the edge of the urn with his fingers. "I'm doing the best I can," he whispered.

Yes, but is it enough?

27

D ani watched Piper reach into her bag and pull out several items. "You have your toothbrush with you. That's convenient."

"Never know when you're going to need to brush your teeth." She hoped her smile looked easy and not the least bit guilty. She didn't want to mention that she'd packed yesterday in case she went home with Scarlett. In addition to the collapsible travel toothbrush, her small tin box included a small bottle of face wash, deodorant, hair ties, and clean underwear.

Piper hadn't packed pajamas, but she could sleep in her t-shirt and boxers. The only problem was, as she stood in the doorway to Dani's bedroom with her face scrubbed and teeth brushed, she wasn't sure where she was supposed to sleep.

She watched Dani pull back one side of the sheets and lift a pillow.

"Am I sleeping on the couch or—?" Piper asked. *Don't shuffle awkwardly. You look stupid.*

To Piper's relief, Dani was visibly disappointed. "Oh. You can if you want to."

Piper couldn't suppress her grin. "Or I could sleep here."

She grabbed the other side of the sheets and turned them down.

Dani's cheeks reddened. "Do you want a glass of water? I like to have a glass of water."

"Sure." Piper slipped into the bed and pulled the sheets over her lap. She arranged and rearranged them trying to decide where they lay best.

Stop it, she chided herself. *Nothing's going to happen. You don't need to look sexy in her bed.*

She'd thought they were heading in that direction with their make-out sessions in the stockroom, before Dmitri almost killed them, of course.

Dani reappeared with the waters and a sheepish shy smile on her face. "I hope that no ice is okay."

"It's great. Thanks."

Dani handed the glass over. "You know, I was so nervous about you coming over, but now that you're here I feel so much better. I feel saf—"

The closet door opened and Lou stepped into the room.

Dani yelped in surprise, dropping her water glass.

Lou stopped where she stood, one hand on the handle.

"Christ, Lou!" Piper threw back the covers. "Warn us!"

Dani's hand was over her heart as she stared down at the water on the hardwood floor. "I'm going to get a towel."

She stumbled from the room, out of sight.

"Was I interrupting something?" Lou frowned at the water.

"No. I mean, yes. But not *that*. Man, she's got PTSD from Dmitri, you can't just pop into her bedroom at night like that."

"She's never minded before."

Piper's brows shot up. "Excuse me?"

Dani reappeared and gave Lou an apologetic smile. "I'm

sorry I screamed. Usually I feel the ear-pop thing when you show up. Obviously I wasn't paying attention."

Piper swallowed. "Would you say you can count on one hand the number of times you've had chats in darkened bedrooms? I'm just curious."

Dani blotted at the water on the floor. "I wasn't counting."

Piper sucked her teeth. "On one hand or two would you say?"

Dani refolded the towel. "We only talk about work. Except yesterday when she told me I should give you a call. That was a first."

Two people can play at this game, Piper thought.

She raised her chin defiantly. "Yeah, well, *I've* been texting Konstantine."

"He's probably scraped your phone of all its data and is tracking you now."

Piper placed a hand on her hip. "You don't know that."

Dani stood with the soaked rag in her hand. "You wouldn't be here if it wasn't important. What happened?"

"Fish killed a woman."

Piper sank onto the bed. "Oh shit, the grocer?"

"No. It was someone else. The corpse was...fresh, but not that fresh."

Piper glanced at Dani. When they told her that Dani had been helping them verify details of the case, Piper had imagined that meant Google searches or well-placed calls. She hadn't realized that Dani was so thoroughly entangled in the entire process.

The jealousy made her throat tight. The problem was, she couldn't be sure what she was jealous about. Lou and Dani's working relationship. Or was she feeling left out again?

"So we know nothing about this woman," Piper said, determined to be part of this.

"We don't know it was a woman," Dani said.

"The corpse was wearing a blue floral top," Lou offered. "And we know Fish hunts women."

"What did King say?"

Piper scoffed. "How do you know that she's even spoken to King about it?"

"He's worried about jurisdiction."

Dani frowned. "If the bodies are found, won't that activate jurisdiction?"

"First someone has to discover them."

Piper placed her hands on her hip. "Should I just go make coffee? Or am I included in this conversation?"

They both looked at her. Lou frowned. "Of course you're included."

Dani patted the bed beside her. "Come here. We'll hatch our plan together."

Something about her sweet voice or the way she tilted her chin down ever so slightly when she called Piper closer was enough to soothe that ache in her chest.

Piper settled onto the bed beside Dani. Dani fished a pair of glasses out of her side table and slipped them on.

She caught Piper's eyes. "What? Why are you looking at me like that?"

"I've never seen you in glasses. It's hot. You look like Lois Lane."

"Thanks." Dani blushed. She flicked her eyes up to meet Lou's. "So we need someone to find the bodies. Then what?"

28

King pulled the tab on his diet soda and listened to it crack and fizz. With the long week behind him, he settled into his red leather couch and groped for the remote. He hadn't decided what he wanted to do for dinner yet. The grocery shopping hadn't happened as he'd hoped.

He'd pushed to have the last bit of work done before leaving the office at six that evening, hoping for a weekend of no paperwork.

Piper's check was written, tucked into an envelope and slid under her apartment door. He'd wrapped up four outstanding cases, closing out their invoices. He emailed his other clients and gave them updates.

The frantic, high energy of Carnival hadn't helped. All that frivolity in the Quarter seemed to permeate his skin like humidity. He needed this quiet weekend to recharge, even if true rejuvenation wouldn't be possible until after the festivities.

He enjoyed the feeling tremendously. Organization, order, progression grounded his life in a way that few other things could. He still remembered his arrival in New Orleans and those first boozy, restless months. Now he understood how ridiculous the notion had been—that he would simply pass a quiet retirement in a city like New Orleans.

Whether or not he'd known it at the time, he'd come to the city to drink himself to death.

He'd told himself that it was to relax and enjoy the lively atmosphere. He was half convinced it was for the food and for the bars. That should've been his first warning sign. He could've chosen a golf community in Florida or even a beach house in North Carolina. But no, he'd chosen one of the most crime ridden cities in the US.

Why would he do that unless he was secretly hoping to either work or get himself into trouble?

King glanced at the bouquet of flowers on his coffee table. A rich spray of orange, yellow and pink blossoms rested in the green glass vase. A card stuck up from its center, perched on its plastic pedestal.

Thanks for everything. Until next time – Beth

His eyes slid to the urn sitting beside it. "Oh come on. It's not like that."

Beth McMiller was the assistant DA. The flowers were a thank you for the critical evidence King provided in an attempted murder case. It was only footage from a laundromat across the street from the crime scene.

Immediately King felt foolish to be explaining—to an urn —why he received flowers from another woman, but the lack of reply was worse. The feelings that welled up and overtook him were much *worse*.

Lucy didn't give a damn about who was or wasn't sending him flowers because Lucy was dead.

Lucy was dead.

And though he'd been living with this reality for over a

year, it hit him again. A horse kick to the chest and he folded over, putting his head in his hands.

He began to cry.

I just miss her, he thought. *It's fine to cry. I just miss her.*

So he let himself cry while the television rambled on about gas prices, political scandals, and an earthquake in Ecuador that left over a hundred people dead. He cried because he missed Lucy's face, her voice and the brief, beautiful summer they'd had together. But he cried harder about what he couldn't remember, and the years they hadn't had.

He wasn't sure how long he went on like this, letting the sweet, heady scent of the flowers perfume this dark, secret moment. He probably would've gone on most of the night like that if he hadn't heard the word *graves*.

He looked up, sniffling. The television screen blurred through his tears.

He blinked and dabbed at his eyes. He mashed the volume button on the control, turning it up louder.

"This is the second grave discovered in the area today. Both contained the bodies of young women between the ages of eighteen and thirty."

A young male reporter with a large mole beside his left eye continued to stare solemnly into the camera lens.

"The body found here in Ridgeway Park was nearly three miles from the nearest road. The grave was discovered when a resident birder left the trail in search of an oriole. The birder's dog discovered a disturbed patch of earth. Within moments, the witness realized just what his dog was digging up."

The camera angle widened and for a moment King saw the patch of road, and the police cars parking in a long line between two barricades.

When the camera swept forward one more time, King's

breath hitched. He sat forward, moving toward the edge of his seat.

On the side of the road, beside the news van, King saw a woman that looked suspiciously like Dani speaking to another reporter. In fact, he was so certain that's who it was, he would've put $500 on red.

I wonder how Dani got all the way to Ohio, he thought bitterly. *Way to force my hand, kid.*

And Fish's hand. Without a doubt, King knew the discovery of not one but two graves would incite Fish to react. King just wasn't sure what that reaction would be.

If Fish was the vainglorious type, he might turn himself in, confess to the crimes, and bask in the limelight of a highly publicized trial. If he was more desperate, hungrier, he might instead go on a killing spree. If he felt as though he had little time left to slake that dark desire within him, he would use his final free hours to gorge himself on his favorite prey. Or similarly, he might disappear or lay low in hopes that he could continue to hunt once the danger had passed. Many killers had dormant periods. There was no reason to think that Fish wouldn't see that as a viable option for himself.

Whatever happened next, the fact remained that Lou had changed the rules of the game and King had better prepare for it.

He stood and crossed the living room to his cell phone, which lay connected to its charger. He pulled the cord out of the phone and entered his passcode. He hoped Lou would be quick about answering his page.

But before he could type in her number, the phone rang in his hand.

He hesitated, thumb hovering over the green acceptance button flashing on his screen. He didn't recognize the scrolling number. While it could be a telemarketer, it could also be someone important. He decided to take the gamble and answered the call before it could go to voicemail.

"King, speaking."

"Robert King," a man said.

"Yeah, that's me."

"It's assistant deputy Dayton Richardson with the Baton Rouge PD. I was told to call you about the inquiry you made earlier this week."

King took the phone over to his armchair beside the record player and sank into it. "I'm listening."

He let his fingers trail absently over the worn covers of his records while the man spoke. He listened for a long time, only interjecting a clarifying question when necessary. When the call ended, he sat back in the chair.

The news had moved onto a commercial for auto insurance. King only vaguely noted this, his mind turning over all that he'd just learned about Melandra and her husband.

He stood, punching in the first of many numbers into his phone. "So much for a quiet weekend."

29

L ou stood in her apartment, staring out at the setting sun. Her plain white t-shirt and Konstantine's sweats hung loosely from her body as she sipped her coffee. It didn't matter if it was seven at night. It was morning somewhere. Maybe not in St. Louis, New Orleans, or Italy, but somewhere and coffee drinking was really just a signal for her brain to start its day.

After a very long night in Ohio, she'd fallen into bed around noon and had slept for six straight hours.

The Mississippi River blazed in her eyes as she sipped the warm coffee, rotating her shoulders to relax them the best she could.

She was only halfway through her coffee when her watch buzzed. She took another sip. When it buzzed a second time, she wasn't surprised. She expected King to be livid about the graves. By now, the story would have broken on most of the news channels.

Except it wasn't King's number on the screen. It was Florence.

Konstantine.

Her stomach turned. The coffee turned bitter on her tongue and suddenly the brilliant orange blaze she'd been enjoying just a moment before, burned too bright.

She put her coffee on the counter and picked up the Browning pistol. She walked halfway toward the closet before turning back and grabbing the coffee. She cradled it against her chest as she pulled the linen closet door closed. Two heartbeats and she'd crossed an ocean.

Rough tile formed under her bare feet. A winter breeze slid along her skin. She was in Konstantine's apartment. The sight of him in his tight jeans and a black turtleneck hardened something inside her, as if she were preparing for a physical blow.

He poured himself a glass of wine. He spoke with barely a glance at her. "Can I offer you a glass of prosecco?"

She lifted her coffee. "I'm all set."

He came into the living room, holding his wine glass in his right hand. He regarded her for a long moment and under the weight of that stare she felt the itch inside her grow. She didn't want to stay. In fact, she half-turned, stepping toward the shadows from where she came, but then Konstantine spoke.

"I know who your stalker is."

She stopped, turning back.

He settled behind his desk and turned on the lamp. His wet hair shone in the light. It had been pushed back from his forehead, framing a beautiful square face that he'd shaved. But it was his green eyes she kept looking at.

"Her name is Diana Dennard."

He turned his computer toward her so that she could see the photographs on the screen. Two photographs sat enlarged side-by-side. The photo on the right was the woman Lou recognized. Thirty-something with round blue eyes and blond hair. The photo on the left was her as a child, crooked teeth, and a shy smile. An abundance of freckles sprayed across her sun-kissed nose.

"I believe I know why King recognized her."

"Why?"

"She was in the news," he said. "Her parents reported her missing in 1995. They were convinced she was kidnapped after school. There were witnesses saying a man in a blue Acura pulled up to the sidewalk and that she got into the car with him. She was gone for nine weeks."

Nine weeks is a long time, Lou thought. *A lot can happen in nine weeks.*

"When she came home, she said she'd run away. That seems to be the end of it."

"So why is she following Fish?" Lou asked, unable to hide her curiosity. She placed her coffee on the desk and perched on its edge.

"I've tracked her movements and can tell she's been in the area for over a year. Before Ohio, she was in Pennsylvania."

None of this told Lou why the woman had an interest in Fish.

"Is she police or something?"

"No. Even in the deep organizations, I found no mention of her. She uses aliases for her purchases. I know of at least four that I can track purchases to in the last twelve months. She should be more careful. She could go to prison for a long time given how many credit card scams she's run."

He was watching her face expectantly. Maybe he was expecting payment for this work.

"Anything else?" she asked.

He sat back in his chair and brought the prosecco to his lips. "No."

A natural lull filled the space between them. Lou found it unbearable. She stood and took her coffee with her.

"Do you want me to keep digging?" he asked.

"Yes. Thank you," she said and stepped toward the shadows.

"Why did you leave?" he asked. "When you saw us together?"

Lou froze halfway across the room.

"Vittoria had a camera in my bedroom. She has cameras in all the rooms, actually. I knew this before I visited. I'm not surprised. But I recorded her footage anyway, just to see for myself."

Lou eased her shoulders away from her ear and turned back. "It sounds like you don't trust each other."

"That is how it is with my family." He met her gaze over the rim of his wine glass. In the shadow, his green eyes looked nearly black. "I cannot even trust my own sister."

She felt her stomach clench. She knew by the smile on his face that her body had betrayed her.

He sat the glass down and laced his fingers behind his head. "Yes, Vittoria is another of Fernando Martinelli's bastards. There are many more than you know, not just those you've disposed of. But Vittoria is the only other one who is, as you say, still in the family business."

Lou suddenly couldn't decide what to do with her coffee cup. She lifted it, looked at it, considered where she might put it down.

"Why do you look disappointed that she is my sister?" Konstantine asked.

Lou shrugged. "It would have been easier."

"What would have been easier?"

"If you were fucking another woman. It would be easier for me."

He sat upright in his chair. For a long time he only regarded her with his unflinching gaze. Then he shook his head as if to rid himself of an unpleasant thought. He said, "I hate disappointing you, but this one you'll have to live with. I have no intention of having other lovers."

"*Lovers*." Lou snorts.

"Girlfriends. Women. Whatever you want to call them."

"Even if it meant I'd actually fuck you?"

His eyebrows raised.

"You have to understand that since I was a child, I've been this way."

She tapped the Browning impatiently against her thigh. "Principled?"

He looked up through his eyelashes at her. "When I want something, nothing less will do. I would rather work harder for the thing I want than to substitute for something that cannot compare."

The shadows around her softened. It would be so easy to give herself over to them, to slip through the dark without so much as a goodbye.

"Will you speak to her?"

Lou stilled. "What do I possibly have to say to Vittoria?"

"Diana Dennard," he said. "Will you ask her why she's following Fish?"

"If I get the chance."

He rose from the desk, leaving the prosecco behind. He crossed to her slowly as one might approach an animal ready to run.

"What are you doing?" she asked.

He laughed softly. "I was going to ask you to come closer, but I know better. I'll come to you."

He stopped just short of her, aligning his body with hers so that their hips were only centimeters apart. His lips grazed the side of her face.

"I missed you," he whispered. "I was sad to find you'd gone when I returned to the bed."

"You didn't seem sad," she said, thinking of the way

Vittoria had draped herself over him. It hadn't seemed sisterly in Lou's opinion.

"Vittoria can be boorish and immature, but she isn't stupid. She won't make an enemy out of you just to entertain herself. Her survival instincts are far too high. Besides I believe she is like your Piper."

"Piper," she corrected. He'd pronounced it like *Pepper*. "What do you mean?"

"*Lesbica*." His eyes traced the side of her neck. "She prefers women to men. Perhaps *I* should be the one who is worried."

"You're assuming I'd hurt someone for you."

"You made a good example of Nico."

He leaned forward until she could feel the heat of his body wafting toward her. He smelled like the prosecco and some sort of earthy soap.

"I missed you," he said again and the back of his hand brushed hers. It was part question, part invitation.

When she didn't immediately move away, he clasped her hand and pulled her to him.

He bent his head and kissed her neck. First it was the barest brush. Another question. He moved up her throat to her jaw to her lips. He kissed more deeply when she didn't refuse him. She enjoyed the taste of wine on his lips.

"I am sure you've just woken up." He put his chin on her shoulder. "But I'm exhausted."

"I'll let you sleep," she said and took a step back.

"Stay."

She wanted to count the vertebrae in his lower back, trace them with her fingertips. But she realized she was still holding her coffee and the Browning pistol.

"Stay until I fall asleep?" he asked, as if already sensing some concession must be made.

She held up the gun and the coffee. "I'm bringing these."

30

Mel pulled back the purple curtain and stepped into the shop. It was cooler in the store than it had been in the tiny space with its burning candles and heady incense. The woman whose cards Melandra had just read, sniffed twice as she stepped around her.

"Take care now," Melandra said. It wasn't meant to be a menacing remark and yet the woman had burst into fresh tears, exiting the shop as one would flee a fire.

Piper looked up from behind the register and arched a brow. "That bad, huh?"

"Her husband is cheating on her."

Piper pouted her lips. "Ouch."

"With her sister."

"God, why do you tell them stuff like that?" Piper laid down the pen she'd been using to furiously scrawl at their ongoing to-do list.

"I didn't. I only told her that things weren't going well at home."

Melandra hadn't had the heart to tell that woman a lot of

things. That not only was her husband cheating on her with her sister, but that her sister was pregnant with his child. That would be what hurt her most, as it had been clear to Melandra's inner eye that the woman had longed to have children of her own, and after years of trying and failing had not been able to carry a child to term.

What would happen to them once the child was born? Melandra could only wonder.

Mel braced herself for a question she'd been expecting. But it didn't come. She'd done her best to hide the fact that her cards were gone. She'd scheduled only palm readings for the walk-ins, letting Piper do the card readings. For those who'd insisted on cards, she'd used an old deck that she'd kept on display for customers.

If Piper had noticed the display cards were gone, she hadn't said anything.

You should be used to hiding things and keeping secrets, she chided herself. *Aren't you full of them?*

Piper tapped her pen against the notepad. "All I've got left to do is clean the front door glass and call the Hamway distributor again about the masks. They still haven't come."

"I'll do it," Melandra said. Her bangles jingled as she reached for the pad and pen, plucking them from Piper's grip. "You can go. Don't you have a test tomorrow?"

"Yeah, but it's online. As long as I finish it by midnight, I'm good." She pulled her cell phone from her pocket and read the time. "I've got 26 hours to take it. Plenty of time."

"Maybe you want to study," she suggested.

Get out of here. Melandra's stomach knotted as she noticed the time. *He's going to walk through that door any minute now.*

"Mel." Piper's voice was low and strained. "If you were in trouble, would you tell me?"

Melandra searched the girl's face. "No."

A surprised laugh squeaked out of her. "At least you're honest."

Melandra forced her own smile but it felt false on her face. The cheek muscles were too tight. They resisted.

"I know you think I'm just a kid."

"Who said that?

"I'm trying to say," Piper flicked her eyes up to Mel's. "I love you, okay? And if you needed something, *anything*, I'm here for you. And so is King. And Lou."

Mel understood then, with perfectly clarity that Piper knew about Terrence. Maybe she didn't know who he was or what he wanted, but she sensed the danger. Likely it wasn't only Piper but King and Lou who knew as well. If they knew, that meant she didn't have much time to resolve this on her own. They would step in and she couldn't have that.

This was her burden. Hers alone.

Melandra placed a hand on Piper's shoulder. "Don't you worry about me."

A shaky breath escaped the girl, but the deep worry darkening her face didn't recede.

"Go home," Melandra said finally, removing her hand. She took the pen and notepad. "I'll handle the rest."

At first Melandra thought she was going to resist, put up a fight, demand to stay until the shop was locked up or maybe escort Melandra up the stairs to her apartment door.

Instead she grabbed her phone. She bent and seized her backpack from the floor and hefted it onto one shoulder.

She frowned at Mel. "I'll check in tomorrow."

"Good luck on your test." Melandra followed her to the door.

Piper stepped out into the night. The smell of fried food from the convenience store across the street greeted them. It instilled a craving for egg rolls and orange chicken in Mel's gut. Add to it a nice side of white rice.

The icy wind gusted, pulling tears from Piper's eyes. "Night."

Melandra locked the door behind her and followed her as far as the picture windows allowed. When she was out of sight, Melandra stood in the dim shop, considering her options. She wasn't going to clean the front door glass or call the distributor. Not tonight.

The phone rang.

Her heart skipped a beat in her chest and her stomach twisted. The sudden urge to empty her bowels filled her. She looked down at the ancient cordless phone beside the register as if it were a beast come to life. Each trill echoed louder and longer, until it made her think of a rabbit Grandmamie had once killed.

We gotta eat, the old woman had said. It had screamed as she'd pulled it from its wired hutch.

Melandra answered on the fourth ring. "Madame Melandra's Fortunes and Fixes."

"Do you have my money?" he asked in lieu of saying hello. Terrence had always been an impatient man.

"And if I don't?"

"Don't fuck with me, woman. I will go to the police and tell them the truth. I'll tell them what you did."

"Maybe I want to go to prison." What was meant to be a joke, came out remarkably calm. *I meant that*, she realized, surprised. *At least in prison, I'd know I was paying for what I did. Then this guilt wouldn't be able to grow inside me like a cancer, poisoning all my days. And he wouldn't be controlling me anymore.*

Terrence laughed but there was no humor in it. It was an irritated, bitter sound, punctuated by a sucking of teeth. "Only a dumb bitch would say that. Clearly you ain't ever been in prison."

Melandra said nothing.

"Listen to me," he began. "Either you bring me what I ask

for, or I'm going to come to that shop and take it, you hear me? I'm tired of playing around."

She pulled once on the locked door then mounted the stairs to her apartment as he ranted.

She found it dark and quiet. Lady was with King tonight. She'd insisted that King take her, suspecting this very moment would come.

Terrence laughed and Mel heard the real pleasure in it. "Oh yes, I'm going to enjoy reeducating you, woman. You know, I learned a few tricks in prison, too. I know how to do more than just slap a bitch around now. You wanna find out what I learned?"

Melandra's eyes fell on the duffle bag on the kitchen table. It was little more than a shadowed outline in the pale moonlight filtering through her kitchen window. She turned on the light and crossed to the table.

"After I beat you so bad you can't walk. I'll leave you one good eye so you can see me burn every one of your grandmamie's damn cards."

Melandra opened the bag. At the very bottom were the bricks. They filled one half of the bag. On top of that lie a coil of rope as thick as Melandra's wrist. Lastly, the revolver she'd had since '78 sat tucked into a loop of rope. She counted the divots marking each chamber.

What would Terrence do when he realized the duffle had no money?

On the table beside the duffle were her instructions to King, including the power of attorney for him to dissolve and reallocate her assets per her instructions.

King was a good man. He would do what she asked of him. She'd done her best to apologize for this burden. She was sorry to ask King for this last favor, but she didn't have anyone else in the city that she trusted.

"You hear this?" Terrence asked. The sound of ripping

paper crackled through the line. "That's them cards right there. You hear it?"

"I have the money," she said in what she thought was a convincing panic.

In truth, she felt almost nothing. It was funny how her mind had blanked, shut down in the face of his threats. Had it always been this way when he'd tormented her? Or was this a new development? She couldn't recall.

"I'll bring the money down to the canal," she said. "There's a little plaza by the Julia Station. Be there in twenty minutes."

"I'll be there in fifteen," he said fiercely. "And if you don't have my money I'll be turning what's left of you over to the police."

She lifted the gun from the bag and felt the weight of it in her hand. The metal was strangely warm, as if alive. It was ready. And so was she.

"I'm on my way," she whispered as her hand tightened on the revolver.

"Good." She heard Terry's smile through the phone. "I'll be waiting."

31

P iper brought the two mugs of coffee over to the sofa and sat down beside Dani. She placed one of the steaming mugs into Dani's hands.

Dani barely managed a *thank you* before Piper returned to the subject at hand. "I'm just saying there's a lot that can go wrong."

"Yes," Dani said, before bringing the mug to her lips and blowing.

She chewed her lip nervously. "Lou has many, many talents but she doesn't really specialize in trying to keep the bad guys alive, you know?"

"I know," Dani said again, following Piper with her gaze.

Piper was pacing her living room again, unaware that she was doing so. "What if he stabs her or shoots her or something because she's trying not to hurt him?"

"I'm pretty sure she's been stabbed and shot before," Dani offered, doing her best to keep her voice level, steady in order to balance out Piper's obvious concerns.

Piper huffed. "Yeah, I guess she's kinda indestructible.

No. See *that's* what we start thinking and then *BAM* she's going to get seriously hurt. Maybe even die. That's how the universe is. It doesn't want you getting too cozy, thinking you know things."

"Will you sit down beside me?" Dani asked.

Piper stopped pacing. She crossed to the sofa with her coffee mug and sat down beside her once again.

Dani placed a hand on her knee. "We did everything we could. All we have to do right now is wait."

"Oh god, then there's Mel!" Piper exclaimed. She put her coffee on the table and began pacing again. "What are we going to do about her murderous husband? That guy is just as much of a monster as the dudes Lou hunts. No wonder she was so calm when that dirty cop pointed a gun at her."

Or when Dmitri Petrov's men threatened to shoot her in the head. Piper had caught herself from saying these lasts thoughts aloud at least, realizing that Dani didn't want to be reminded of Petrov.

"King's working on that." Dani said from her place on the sofa. "Piper? You're doing it again."

Piper stopped pacing. "Sorry."

"Come sit down."

Piper sank onto the sofa for a third time and sighed. "Sorry. I'm sure me freaking out isn't helping your PTSD. I'm just so worried about everyone and I feel like I'm not doing enough."

Dani reached across the sofa and put her hand on top of Piper's.

A cool chill skittered across Piper's skin. She licked her lips compulsively. After several beats of agonizing silence, Dani broke it first.

"This is better," Dani said, placing her mug on the coffee table and turning toward Piper.

Piper settled against her sofa cushions. "Me sitting and shutting the hell up?"

"No." Dani cocked her head playfully. "Freaking out. *Together*. It's better than doing it alone."

Piper's heart swelled in her chest. It seemed to double then triple in size.

"Piper," Dani began, glancing first at her hands before flicking her eyes up to meet Piper's. Then she laced their fingers together. "Can I kiss you?"

Piper only managed to swallow against the knot in her throat. "For real?"

"No ulterior motives. No secrets. Just kiss you."

I think it's the only thing I've wanted for like fourteen months, Piper thought.

Instead she shrugged. "It might be cool."

Dani mimicked her. "Yeah. Cool."

"Really cool."

"Absolutely cool."

"Would you mind if I just—"

"Pleas—"

Piper was across the sofa before permission fully passed Dani's lips. She kissed her once, twice, and somewhere between the third and fourth kisses the flurry of lips devolved into one, long continuous make-out session.

Piper pulled back, breathless. "Should I keep going?"

"Yes." Dani's kisses fanned across Piper's cheek to her neck and down to her collarbone. "Assuming that's what you want."

"I like this. This is nice." Piper swooned, heat flooding her head.

She pushed Dani onto the flat of her back on her sofa and bent to kiss her again. But she hesitated. "Wait, is this too much too soon? Aren't you—"

A deep blush had filled Dani's cheeks. She came up onto

her elbows, trying to snare Piper's lips. "I'm okay. I'm really, *really* okay."

"Are you sure? I don't want to trigger—"

"Piper!" Dani exclaimed, grabbing the girl's shirt and pulling her back down. "Shut up and kiss me."

32

L ou waited until Konstantine's breath slowed to a steady rhythm. He lay on his back, his face turned toward her. His eyes were closed and moonlight collected in his dark lashes as his chest rose like a cresting ocean wave. The woodsy scent she'd come to associate with him—amber and sandalwood—surrounded her. It was on his clothes and hair, of course. But also on the pillows and sheets.

On her.

She couldn't explain why she'd agreed to stay, or why she'd propped her back against the headboard and drank her warm coffee until he'd drifted off to sleep. She couldn't explain why it was sweet—the fact he slept so well beside her.

He trusts you, her father's voice said in her mind. *Do you trust him?*

That was the question. And why did trusting him matter? It was more important that she trusted herself. She knew there was nothing he could do to her that would break her.

That should be enough.

With her eyes, she traced the light cutting across his

cheek, down to his lips. They rested slightly open with a hint of teeth between them. She wanted to kiss him.

Hell, if she was being honest with herself, she wanted to do a lot more than kiss him.

She knew herself well enough to know she wouldn't disappear once they'd crossed that final threshold, as she had with every other man in her sexual history. She would keep fucking him. And if she did...

Then what?

She leaned toward his lips, moving in to seal that mouth with her own when a shocking jerk reverberated through her body. It was like catching a fishhook in her navel. It yanked hard through her abdomen, sending electric sparks up her spine.

Her back arched with a sharp inhale.

Konstantine's eyes opened instantly. "What's wrong?"

Her eyes pinched closed. Lou searched the darkness. Her compass whirled wildly trying to fix on a space and time. The frantic, desperate pull was unquestionably urgent.

Who? her mind begged. *Where?*

Piper? No.

King?

"Louie," Konstantine whispered. His cold hands touched her burning face. "What's wrong?"

The compass latched onto its target at last.

"It's Fish." She pried open her eyes. "I have to go."

"Take me with you," he said, still cupping her face.

She managed to get the coffee cup back to the nightstand, surprised she hadn't spilled its contents all over them both.

"No," she said. "Call King."

Konstantine's irritation was clear. She'd scared him. "And tell him what?"

"Fish is hurting her. We need to move now."

"Where are they?"

"At her house."

"How can you know that?" Konstantine was on his feet. He bent to remove his phone from its charger.

How could she explain it to him? That once she'd been in a place, knew its smell, its taste, she could recognize it as well as a face she'd seen before. And even if she could articulate the experience for him, now wasn't the time. The darkness pulled at her skin, her body, her face like a torrential river. Its current was hellbent on carrying her to where she needed to be.

"He's at McGrath's house." She turned her head, glancing at him from the side of her eye to make sure he was listening. "Tell him."

Then she let the darkness take her.

She opened her eyes and found herself in a kitchen, holding the Browning pistol she'd taken with her to Konstantine's.

Outdated checked tile ran from wall to wall. The kitchen looked ransacked. The cabinets stood open. A stack of pots had been half-pulled from their resting place and thrown across the floor. A drawer had been yanked from its track. Forks, spoons and butter knives were strewn like confetti. They sparkled in the moonlight pouring through a kitchen window. Sugar packets littered the counter and floor. Two chairs had been turned on their sides.

It was the blood that stopped Lou in her tracks.

A large splash lay on the tile, soaking through a few of the sugar packets. It had turned half of the white paper a dark red. Then a trail began. It dripped toward the living room. Lou followed it to the base of some stairs.

A woman screamed. The sound echoed through Lou's spine, sparking electricity through her arms to her fingertips. Two shadows swept over the white walls above. Lou took the stairs two or three at a time. The blood had soaked into the carpet at the top of the stairs. A new trail formed from this landing into the bedroom at the end of the hall. Lou placed a hand on the bannister, listening for a moment to make sure she knew where the sounds of struggle were coming from.

Definitely from the bedroom straight ahead. The door itself confirmed this.

It hung at an angle, with splinters jutting from the busted handle. McGrath must have locked herself in the bedroom to buy time. Fish must have busted through the door shortly after.

A lamp flew past the open door and shattered against the wall. Ceramic shards and lightbulb glass rained down on the carpet.

Then Fish was there.

He rounded the bed, hair in disarray. His chest was heaving like a wild dog's and his body hunched as if in hunger. He was *snarling*. The sight of him like that—more beast than man—stunned Lou.

Perhaps because it was so different from the drug lackeys she so often hunted. Different from the fools like Walker who went quietly, ignorantly, to their own deaths. She'd seen this level of maniacal animalism only a few times—in Dmitri Petrov most recently, as he demanded that she account for the murder of his son. Before that, it had been Nico who'd wanted Konstantine's complete and utter destruction for inheriting the wealth and power he'd believed belonged to him.

But those outbursts, those demands for retribution had made sense to her.

Fish's made no sense. Logically, McGrath owed him nothing. She had never wronged or hurt him. How could he look at her as if he *deserved* her life? As if he *deserved* her pain?

When he rounded the bed out of her sight, Jennifer screamed.

The fear in the cry cut through Lou's confusion and sharpened her awareness to this single moment in time. She pulled her gun and pointed it. She remained hidden in the hallway but her shot was clear. All she had to do was pull the trigger and spill his brains all over the wall.

Take him alive. We need him alive. We need him—

"Fuck." Lou lowered the gun and rushed into the bedroom.

Jennifer stood in one corner, her arms out as if bracing herself against both walls. Her chest heaved. Her eyes were wide and frightened. An overturned lamp gave her face a severe, ghostly appearance.

Her eyes flicked from Fish to Lou's only a second before Lou seized him.

She grabbed a fistful of his hair and pulled him back through the dark.

Not to La Loon—though *oh* how she longed to do it—but instead to the kitchen, putting distance between the murderer and his target.

The jarring outdated kitchen tile reappeared. Her bare feet squeaked against the floor as she released Fish, shoving him forward into the cabinets. A butter knife shifted underfoot.

He hit the edge of the counter hard. All the air left him in a surprised *oomph.* When he turned, he lost his balance. His black sneakers slid on the sugar packets. His arms pinwheeled as he struggled to right himself, kicking one of the pots into a corner.

His struggle to right himself gave Lou time to slip the gun into her waistband and free her hands.

Once he was able to right himself again, he saw her for the first time. His eyes roved her body, taking in oversized sweats and t-shirt. Her bare feet and disheveled hair.

Lou expected the usual questions. *Who are you? How did I get here?*

Instead, Fish charged her.

She sidestepped him easily and when she did, brought her elbow down hard on his shoulder.

He screamed and hit the far wall with the full force of his momentum. Pushing off the wall, he grabbed an overturned chair and hurled it at her. She ducked, feeling it pass over her head, stirring a slight breeze before crashing behind her. He lifted the second chair and this one didn't sail past as cleanly. One of its legs clipped her shoulder, spinning the chair off in a new direction. It hit the counter and broke off a leg. Both pieces clattered to the floor.

Fish used the moment to charge again, hoping to catch her in the squatting position. But before he reached her, Lou sidestepped into the shadow created by the kitchen table.

The world disappeared and reappeared, offering her a more secure position in the doorway between the living room and kitchen.

He only looked for her for a moment. Then he was at the drawers, ripping them open, tossing contents on the floor. When he didn't find what he wanted, he moved on to the next drawer.

What does he think is happening? she wondered. Then, *he's not thinking. He's gone feral with...what? His hunger? His need to feed or cause pain? What?*

And he wasn't the only one. Lou felt that part of herself—the ravenous, insatiable part, burning with a longing, a deep ache throbbing through her entire core. She wanted to pull her gun. She wanted to shoot him and see his head knock back as if punched the second before his brains sprayed out behind him in a delicious final release.

She wanted his blood on her hands, on her lips. She

wanted to see his anger turn to fear as she hurt him—slowly, deliberately.

He might think that he can return to McGrath, that he can finish this game, but Lou had no intention of letting him out of this kitchen.

Lou stepped into the light, giving him a target.

He snarled, fresh fury overtaking his face.

With his newfound knife, he slashed at her. She folded her elbow deflecting the blow, but his immediate reverse thrust caught her upper arm. Fresh hot pain cut cold across her flesh.

It burned, igniting an indignation that bordered on humorous.

Lou pushed this away, focusing on the glinting blade coming toward her. He'd folded it against his arm.

He struck at her throat, but missed and nicked the collarbone.

Blood soaked the collar of her shirt.

She lifted Fish off his feet by the front of his shirt and slammed him into the kitchen table. It didn't crumple as she thought it might. The wood only creaked, miraculously withstanding the blow. She drove her elbow into his forearm with such force that the knife dropped from his hand and clattered to the floor.

He howled, groping for her hair. He managed a fistful and yanked hard. Lou saw stars, but more than that, a rage unfurled inside her. She *hated* having her hair pulled. She hated it worse than a punch to the jaw or ear. She hated it worse than being stabbed or kicked in the guts.

Before she fully articulated the rage, or understood why it had been so immediate and all encompassing, she'd pulled her gun and pressed it under Fish's chin.

Lou's scalp burned. She pushed the gun into Fish's chin

harder until a small sound of panic escaped him. His hands trembled on either side of his head.

That hungry hand inside her writhed. It opened and closed within her, desperate.

We need him. We need him. We need—

Lou screamed, a berserker's battle cry and brought her gun across Fish's jaw hard, rendering him unconscious.

The man went limp on the table.

Red and blue lights splashed across the bare kitchen wall.

Lou checked on Fish once more before crossing the living room to the window. There were the police, and no surprise, a news van. It must've been Dani's doing. But across the street was a shadowed figure, lingering under the tree as Lou herself had done weeks before.

"Are you okay?" Lou called out to Jennifer.

"Yeah," she replied weakly. "Is it over?"

"The police are here. Come let them in."

As soon as Jennifer's steps resounded on the stairs, Lou was across the street, standing under the thick darkness cast by the old tree's limbs.

"Quite the spectacle," Lou said into the woman's ears.

The woman jumped, turning toward Lou's voice.

She took one look at Lou and whistled. "You look like shit."

Lou glanced down at the ruined shirt.

"Are you responsible for this circus?" she gestured toward the house. "It's a pretty quick response for the police *and* the media."

The front door opened and police crowded in, pushing past Jennifer who held open the door. She was shaken and unharmed. Lou felt—*relief.*

The news crew crowded the porch, ready and eager for the goriest of details.

"Why were you watching him?" Lou asked.

"For the same reason I suspect you were," she said, staring at Lou again. "How did you get here so fast? Were you sleeping inside the house?"

"We should have coffee and talk about it."

"Why should I meet you for coffee when you can't even answer the questions I've already asked?"

"You could try asking better questions," Lou replied.

Diana snorted, pushing the hood back from her face. She took an unflinching appraisal of Lou's appearance. "Maybe you'll want to clean up first. You look like Carrie had a slumber party and it went *all* wrong."

Lou touched her throat and found it was still bleeding.

Diana glanced at the house again, at the police crawling over it like ants. The yellow tape was going up. The news crews were pushed back. Jennifer, with her hands wrapped around her body in the perfect mimicry of a victim, answered an officer's questions.

"Yes to coffee. Only I'm not going to tell you where. Let's see if you'll just turn up like you keep doing. Don't keep me waiting."

Diana started down the sidewalk. She didn't walk to one of the cars parked on the street, nor to one of the houses. Instead, she hopped over the low stone wall and disappeared into the adjacent field.

Lou watched her go.

She stood in the shadows a long time. Long after Fish was dragged from the house in handcuffs. Long after McGrath was wrapped in a blanket and tucked into the back of an ambulance for safekeeping.

She stood there until the hunger inside felt manageable again.

Only then did she peer through the darkness, directing her inner eye to hunt for Diana Dennard.

33

Lou stopped at her apartment long enough to clean and patch her wounds. After throwing away the ruined white t-shirt, she changed into jeans, a black t-shirt, her boots and glasses. At the last second, she decided to put on her father's vest under her shirt.

It wasn't an entirely rational decision. Would Dennard really try to kill her in the open? She didn't think so. Yet Lou knew it was best to trust her instincts even when they didn't make sense.

So the vest went on.

Her compass delivered her to the edge of a parking lot.

The lot was unpaved, gravel shifting under her boots. It had only six or seven cars, lined up along the front of the Susie-Q's All Night Diner. It looked like an old-fashioned airstream camper, but longer, with a proper door and windows.

Diana Dennard was sitting in the booth that aligned with the second window on the right.

Lou crossed the lot and pulled open the door. Showtunes

featuring a lot of brass greeted her. Diana saw her immediately.

"How did you do it?" She looked at her watch, as Lou slid into the opposite bench.

Lou raised her eyebrows, signaling a desire for clarification.

"How did you know where I was? This is some deep state shit. Are you FBI? CIA?" She held the steaming coffee mug with both hands. "You've got access to the city's cameras or something?"

"Does this place have cameras?" Lou asked. She didn't see any.

"So you don't work for anyone?"

"I don't work for anyone."

It was true enough. No one wrote her a paycheck. Though she did work with people, didn't she? That fact was becoming more and more clear to her.

"You're like me then," she said, almost in disbelief. She scoffed, looking away toward the window. When she caught sight of her reflection, the loose blond ponytail and dark circles under the eyes, she scowled. "I was wondering how many of us there might be. Vigilantes, prowling the night, finishing off the assholes of the world."

Vigilante. It wasn't the first time that Lou had heard the word but she'd never used it in conjunction with herself. And it had never occurred to her that there might be other women like her, out there hunting killers.

As she watched Diana turn her mug in her hand nervously, she realized, perhaps arrogantly, that it never occurred to her that another woman would be up for the job. Not an ordinary woman anyway—one who was bound to a time and place. Would Lou have pursued Martinelli if she hadn't had her abilities?

Yes. But she might not have gotten as far.

She'd learned to fight and shoot, but she knew what her real advantage was.

"Were you pursuing Fish for personal reasons?" Lou asked, aware that Dennard didn't want to look her in the eyes. It unnerved people to see their own faces reflected back in her glasses. She often wore them to mess with King for that very reason.

But now, she removed her glasses, folded them and placed them on the table.

Yet the woman stared into her coffee. "No. I knew what he was and that Jennifer was in danger. That's her name, right? I found it in a tax record from two years ago."

Lou didn't want this to be an endless conversation, and she loathed small talk. "Do you hunt these men because of what happened to you in 1995?"

Diana's eyes flicked up to Lou's. "You really want the story?"

Lou said nothing.

Diana opened her mouth to reply but the waitress appeared in her old-fashioned white apron with a menu under her arm. "You keep multiplying. Can I get you something?"

"Coffee," Lou said, refusing the menu.

Tense silence hung between them as the waitress left and returned with a coffee mug and coffee pot. They watched the cup fill.

"Cream or sugar?"

"No."

Then they were alone again.

"Poor little Diana Dennard's origin story. It seems unfair that you know who I am and what I do and I don't even know your name." Diana flicked her large blue eyes up to Lou's. "If Fish didn't hurt you, why hunt him?"

She scoffed. "Fish is a *breed*. You understand that, right? A *species*. Men like him think they can prey on women and get away with it. Someone needs to change their mind about that."

"What happened in the nine weeks you were missing?"

Diana pushed her own coffee mug away. "Give me your name and I'll tell you."

"Lou."

"Lou what?"

Lou arched an eyebrow. "Just Lou."

Diana smiled. But before the expression had a chance to fully settle onto Lou's face, it hardened again. "One of my father's friends rolled up to my school one day, telling me that my dad wanted me to ride home with him."

Lou's stomach clenched.

"So I get in his car. I put on my seat belt. I listen to him because I know my dad loves this guy and trusts him. Even though I wanted to walk home with my friend and I knew we were going the wrong way, I still stayed, quiet and obedient like the good little girl I was raised to be. That's how they get you. They count on the fact we've all been raised to be good little girls."

Lou lifted the coffee to her lips. It didn't hide her furious, working jaw.

"Anyway, this so-called *family friend*, locked me in a sound-proof shed for nine weeks." Diana squinted. "I don't really need to describe what happened in the shed, do I?"

"No."

Diana's cheeks had reddened and her jaw was tight. It was several minutes before she spoke again.

"When I escaped, I knew better than to tell my father what his *friend* had done to me. He wasn't going to turn him in. Adults don't listen to kids and even at twelve I understood that. So when I got home, I told them I'd run away. When the *family friend* came over to congratulate my father on my safe and sound return, I *smiled* at the bastard."

"How?" Lou couldn't imagine smiling at Martinelli.

"I wanted him to think he won because I had plans. I'd spent nine *long* weeks making these plans. I wasn't going to screw them up."

Lou drank her coffee and said nothing.

Diana, emboldened by the silence leaned forward over the table.

"One night I went to his house where he lived with his perfect family. I rang the doorbell. When he answered, I told him I thought I'd left something in the shed. Would he come out and check for me? You should've seen the excitement on his fucking face. It was disgusting. So I went to the shed with my father's pistol and I waited for him. He came in. He shut the door behind him. Then he said something I'll never forget. He said, 'I knew you'd be back.' He already had half an erection pushing through the front of his fucking khakis. He still had that erection after I shot him."

They both fell silent as the waitress approached again.

"Thirsty weren't you?" The waitress smiled at Lou.

"Thanks." Lou accepted the top-off, forcing her lips to mimic the smile.

Dennard waited until she was out of earshot before speaking again. "I've been hunting bastards like him ever since. Serial rapists, women killers, abusers. Anything to do with children and women really. I happened upon Fish because—" She seemed to catch herself here.

"How do you find out about them?" Lou asked hoping to coax her into talking more.

And Lou was curious how she managed to find the men. She didn't think this woman had an inner compass that responded to *take me to a serial killer*.

"I have an internet forum where women can report offenses anonymously. A lot of them report offenses that the cops have dismissed. I came here because a woman reported her sister missing. Because the sister had a history of drug use, the cops said she was probably just holed up in a drug den somewhere, but the sister insisted it wasn't true. She'd been sober for two years."

She paused to take a sip of her coffee.

"So I came to town to check it out, interview witnesses and all that jazz. I found out that the last time she was seen was at a coffee shop and *who* followed her out of that coffee shop three weeks ago?"

"Fish."

Diana smirked. "I'm well versed in stalker behavior. I should be an expert by now after doing this for twenty years. And it looks like I was right. I'm glad I stuck around even though I didn't catch him before he hurt the sister. I have a feeling she's in one of the graves they found the other day."

Lou said nothing.

"Did you have anything to do with that story breaking open by chance?"

Lou lifted the warm mug to her lips.

Diana shrugged. "I'm disappointed that you let him get arrested though. What happens if he's released? All he needs is the sympathy of some judge calling him 'a good family man' or a 'man with values' or some shit like that. It happens all the damn time."

Lou didn't like hearing her fears voiced back to her.

She pushed her coffee cup away. "Do you always give them over to the authorities?"

"No."

"Maybe you're not FBI then." Diana grinned. "And what will you do if he goes free? You have a protocol for that?"

"I'll handle it," Lou said and wasn't sure why she suddenly felt so defensive. It had been something about the comment regarding the broken system. It wasn't that she disagreed. After all, the system created men like Senator Ryanson and

DEA agent Chad Brasso—two men directly responsible for her father's own death. But it also created men like King. Surely this woman knew that it wasn't so easy to tell the bad guys from the good guys.

"And how do you *handle* it, Lou?" Diana spun her coffee cup anxiously between her palms. "Do you work alone or with a team?"

Lou didn't answer.

Diana held up her hands, palm out in surrender. "All right, all right. You're not interested in sharing trade secrets. But I'll admit I'm very interested in you. I was at the house tonight. Don't look so surprised. I was camping out wondering when Fish was gonna make his move. They always do eventually. So imagine my surprise when he pulled up, went inside, started up on her, and then *BAM*. You were in the house! *What?* I didn't even see you come in. How did you get in?"

Lou recalled the destroyed kitchen. The glass, broken chairs, and those ridiculous sugar packets thrown about like Carnival confetti. But it was the blood on the floor that made her temperature boil.

"If you were there, why didn't you help her?"

Diana leaned back against the booth and shrugged. "I didn't want to step in prematurely."

Hot anger ripped through Lou. "What?"

"Situations like that make women strong. Jennifer will always feel more powerful, more capable now because of what she went through. I wasn't going to let him kill her, but I also didn't want to rob her of the fight."

Lou's fingers itched for her gun. Her desire to pull the Browning and put a bullet between this woman's eyes was immediate—and it frightened her. She'd never wanted to shoot a woman before.

Diana spoke, unaware of the emotions rolling through

Lou. "Women are strong, so much stronger than anyone gives them credit for. We are *survivors*. Every single woman you've ever met has survived something. But many of them forget it. I just want them to remember what they are."

She is crazy, Lou thought. *More than a little crazy.*

Look who's talking, a voice chided.

Diana scoffed. "I suppose you view yourself as some kind of white knight. You ride in and save the damsels before even a hair on their pretty little heads falls out of place. But women don't need to be saved. They need to pick up the sword."

Lou didn't identify with the label *white knight*. When she'd hunted Angelo and his brothers, it had never been about saving anyone. She'd simply wanted the men who murdered her father to pay.

But how could she explain that to Dennard?

"I don't think women need to be tested to prove they're strong," Lou said.

Dennard wrinkled her nose. "How feminist of you."

A sudden jerk hooked through Lou's navel. White hot heat rippled through her core, climbing up her throat. She knew instantly who was in danger and how little time she had.

Mel.

The surprise of it must've shown on Lou's face because Diana stiffened.

"What?" she asked, glancing behind her as if expecting a monster to appear.

"I have to go." Lou slid out of the booth, grabbing her sunglasses off the table. She finished the coffee in a single go.

"Another damsel in distress?" Diana gave Lou a look that couldn't exactly be described as friendly.

Lou threw a $5 bill on the table for her coffee.

"Until next time then, *Lou*." Dennard sat back, stretching her arms along the top of the booth.

Lou had no time to worry about what such a malicious smile meant. *Mel* had no time at all.

So without a goodbye, she stepped out of the diner and into the night.

DIANA WAITED UNTIL LOU DISAPPEARED INTO THE TREES surrounding the diner's parking lot before taking Lou's empty coffee mug, and the $5 bill and slipping them both into her bag.

34

With the duffle hanging heavy at her side, Mel limped from the streetcar stop into the station. Because of the hour, it wasn't crowded. A group of teenagers stood together smoking, laughing too loudly at a joke a red-headed boy made, complete with pantomime. A girl with a laugh like a horse's high whinny overtook all the others.

Mel's arm ached by the time she reached the end of the station platform and stepped out into the adjacent plaza. A water fountain equipped with lights changed the water from red to blue to green and there, against a concrete wall overlooking the Mississippi River, stood Terrence. His head was bent as if in prayer as he cupped a hand around his cigarette.

She switched the bag to the other arm and limped forward. She closed the distance until there was only twenty feet between them.

He turned at the sound of her approach. His eyes slid from her face down to the bag in her hand. He frowned. "That sure looks heavy. You better not have given me a hundred grand in dollar bills."

The wind blew in off the water and pushed her hair back from her face. It pulled water from Mel's eyes and iced her cheeks.

"Where are my cards?" she asked, dropping the bag at her feet.

He slipped his hands into his pockets, and stepped forward. This moved his face into the light of the adjacent streetlamp, adding an orange glow to his cheekbones and chin. It also added fire to his eyes.

"I think I'm going to hang on to them," he said, looking at her from under the brim of his hat.

"You said—"

"I know what I said. But if I'd known you would've parted with your money so easily, I would've asked for more."

Mel's anger rose inside her, uncurling like a viper in her guts.

"So here's what we're gonna do," he said, taking another easy stride forward. "You pay me, you get a *few* cards. Pay me more, you get more. Maybe you'll get all your cards back in, oh...twenty years."

She clenched her teeth, gathering what was left of her sanity. *Don't lose it now. See this through.*

"Think of it as alimony."

"My cards—"

"You shouldn't have lost them if they meant so damn much to you."

Mel bent down toward the large duffel at her feet. She unzipped it and looked inside. Her hand hovered over something.

"You won't ever stop torturing me, will you?" she asked softly.

"Why would I stop when I enjoy it so much?"

She exhaled slowly and slid her hand into the bag. "That's what I thought."

Mel stood and pointed the gun at her husband. She cocked the revolver, saw the loaded chamber slide into place.

Terry stilled. Every muscle in his body tensed like a stag sensing danger. His mouth parted ever so slightly in surprise.

"Don't look so shocked, Terry," Mel said, adjusting her grip on the gun. "You've given me little choice haven't you?"

Terrence's face twitched almost as if he were working to keep a snarl suppressed. When he spoke, his voice bore the false geniality that she'd always despised.

"You ain't gonna shoot me. Shooting a man is different than clipping one with a car and leaving him to die."

"Is it?" she asked without inflection. "I'm sure it's all the same in the eyes of God."

Terrence must've realized she meant to do it, really meant to put a bullet in his heart and be done with him. His eyes widened. His hand began to lift, extending toward her. A *no* formed on his lips.

But it was too late.

Mel pulled the trigger.

35

Good police work meant following the rules. But King understood that in order for the right thing to happen, sometimes lying was necessary.

As soon as he terminated the call with Konstantine, who had more than a little irritation in his voice King noted distantly, he decided now was one of those times. Lying was suddenly *very* necessary.

"Christ." He threw back his covers and hobbled across the room to a dresser drawer. He lifted a stack of sweaters and found the two burner phones he kept hidden there.

He dialed the non-emergency line in Fish's county. That was the only way he could be sure to get the police.

"Knox County Police can I?"

"Yes, hello!" he added as much panic to his voice as he could manage. "There's a man attacking a woman. Right inside her house! I can see it from the street."

"Where are you located, sir?"

King rattled off McGrath's address. "I'm out here walking Lady—" He glanced at the dog sitting erect in her oversized bed, watching him with alert eyes. "—and oh god!

He's chasing her! Please send someone! He's going to kill her!"

King hung up the phone. King hoped that would be enough to get someone to the house. He knew ending the call so quickly might make it seem like a prank.

"How did I do?" he asked Lady. The dog rose from her bed and walked toward him expectantly. "No, it's okay. I know I said your name, but I wasn't calling you. You can go back to bed."

She turned several circles on her large cushion before settling down again.

King went to his own bed with the burner phone still in his fist.

His original plan had been to call the Ohio Bureau of Criminal Investigation and say that he'd taken up investigating cold cases in his retirement. One such cold case had led him to Jeffery Fish. He'd hoped to already have that evidence in place when he approached the OBI but this would never work now. His anonymous tip was the best he could do.

Please go to the house, he thought. *Please. If you don't, Lou is definitely going to kill him.*

His feet rested on the little rug beside his bed. His socks sank into the white shag. The roar of Carnival raged outside.

What else can I do? He massaged his forehead. *Damn it, Lou.* She must've known blowing his cover like this would incite Fish to act like this. He racked his brain. *What else can I do?*

The good news was that now Fish had openly attacked the woman, they should be able to obtain a warrant to search his home. This assumed he was captured at the scene and Jennifer McGrath lived to tell the tale. If Jennifer was able to give a statement claiming Fish had been stalking her for the weeks leading up to the attack, it would give a judge enough probable cause to issue the warrant.

King groaned and dragged his hand down his face. He fell back against the bed and tried to consider his options for pinning Fish to the mat. Minutes bled into each other. His mind wandered. He was almost asleep again when his ears popped.

"Get up," Lou said.

King jumped, making the bed creak. Lady yipped.

His hand went instinctively to his chest. "Shit."

"Mel' s in trouble. We have to go. *Now*."

"What?" But King pushed off the bed and stumbled to the dresser. He grabbed a shirt out of the top drawer and searched for a pair of jeans to pull over his boxers. "How do you know she's in trouble?"

Lou twirled her finger in the air. He understood this meant compass had told her.

No doubt it had also told her about McGrath's close call with Fish.

"Do you think it's Terrence?" he asked, forcing his second leg into the jeans.

"It won't matter if you don't *hurry up*."

"Okay, *okay*." He wanted to ask her about McGrath and Fish and learn how the situation played out. But apparently now was not the time.

"Did the girl make it?" King asked.

"Yes and they arrested Fish." Lou scratched Lady behind the ears.

King slipped the burner phone and his cell phone in his pocket, just in case he had to make more calls tonight.

"Ready?" Lou asked.

"*Pas bouger*," King said to the dog and Lady whined.

"Sorry girl," Lou said as her hand fixed on King's arm. "We'll be back."

The darkness gathered around them.

What the—? King's mind sputtered.

Had it ever done that before? Lou had always stepped through the shadows—as Lucy had—and passed through them like a thin gossamer curtain to wherever lay on the other side.

But this, whatever had just happened, had been almost like she'd called the shadows *to* her.

The darkness pooling in the corners of his bedroom and beneath his bed and seemed to stretch toward them, overtaking her.

You're imagining shit, he warned himself. *You're tired, you're up past your bedtime, and you haven't slept properly since Carnival started up. Get ahold of yourself.*

But he couldn't shake the image of the darkness cutting across her pale face. She hadn't moved. She hadn't moved but the shadows had. He was sure of it.

Pressure doubled, tripled in his head, squeezing it in the imaginary vice he detested so much. The floor, which was no longer a floor at all, dropped out from underneath him. His stomach dropped with it. For a moment, his old claustrophobia reared inside him.

He was squeezed, twisted. This continued until the moment when he felt he might fall into complete panic— what a hell of a time to have a panic attack—then the world, finally, *blessedly*, opened up.

Sidewalk sprang up under his feet, jarring him forward. Lou held fast to his arm, unmoved by his momentum. She held him in place until he righted himself.

"God, I hate that," he said. He clasped the back of his neck.

Lou wasn't looking at him. Her eyes were searching the plaza. King realized they stood under an overhang, in the dark of a pavilion. During the day this was the seating area of the Living La Vida Lobster Bar and Grill. King noted the absurd plastic Lobster looming above the tables.

"What's he saying to her?" Lou asked, pressing one shoulder into a pillar.

King squinted across the pavilion, focusing on the man in the leather hat with the crow feather protruding from his cap. They were too far from the pair to hear the conversation. King noted only the low drone of their voices.

"What do you think is in that bag?" King asked. "It looks too heavy to be a payoff. See how she's leaning?"

"What do you want to do?" Lou's shoulders tensed under her leather jacket.

King knew what she was going to say before she even asked.

"Can I—?"

"No," King said, thinking of the first conversation he'd had that evening, before the story of Fish had broken.

"There are no families in this case," Lou said. "No one needs to know what happened so they can sleep at night. Melandra will know what happened. Isn't she the only one who matters?"

I found the camera footage, the cop had explained. *You can see everything.*

"I need the guy alive for other reasons."

Lou looked at him through her damned mirrored sunglasses. How the hell did she even see through them at night?

"I'll explain later. But for now, don't kill him," King said.

Lou was obviously disappointed. Her shoulders slumped.

King couldn't worry about that. "I'll call the police and tell them where we are."

He had an uneasy feeling about that duffle bag, finding that his gaze kept sliding from the husband to the bag. King hoped he was wrong.

He removed his cell phone from his pocket and dialed 911 for the second time that night. There was no need for the burner. He'd hoped his clout and reputation in the city would actually help them now.

"911, what's your emergency?"

Mel pulled a gun.

"Shit," Lou and King said in unison.

"Go," King said and the shadows overtook Lou before he'd even finished pronouncing the word. "Go, go, go!"

This time he was sure of it—that the darkness had in fact moved *toward* her, enveloping her and blotting out the orange lanterns circling the riverwalk and pavilion. She hadn't stepped back into it as he'd often seen her do.

She'd called the darkness. Had she even noticed?

"Hello? 911, what's your emergency?" a woman said.

"Yes, hello—" King began, moving toward the tables. A cat hissed and ran out from underneath. It bolted toward the restaurant and the cluster of trash cans to the left of the door. Once it was safe between two cans, it looked back at King over its shoulder appraisingly.

"I want to report an armed robbery in progress. I'm in the Julia Station plaza. My name is Robert King."

"We have a car in the area, Mr. King," the responder said blandly. "We can get someone to you quickly. Are you in a safe place?"

King opened his mouth to answer. That was when the shot rang out.

Lou stepped from the shadows of the closed pavilion with its discarded napkins and crumpled receipts tumbling in the icy winter breeze rolling off the river. When the world reformed around her, she was standing between Mel and her husband.

It hadn't been the exact spot she was aiming for, but the shadows must have been thickest where their bodies' shadows overlapped on the stone. And she certainly hadn't meant to turn her back on the man, who Lou understood in her core, was dangerous.

But that's where she found herself nonetheless.

Lou had only a millisecond to note Mel's gasp of surprise, register her widening eyes. It seemed like the gun jerked at the last second, rolling slightly away from its target.

Then the whip crack of a gunshot rang out.

And Lou knew something was terribly wrong. *Terribly* wrong.

The force that slammed through her body staggered her.

A hot-cold sensation ran through from her head to her toes. It began as ice water, rolling down her spine and the back of her legs. Her flesh tingled.

Then the water suddenly heated, filling her with a feverish, hot sensation that seemed to stand the hairs on her neck and arms on end.

There was a moment of blissful ignorance before the pain came. It bloomed bright and biting at the base of her throat.

She reached up to touch her neck, half believing that she wouldn't find it there. But her fingers found flesh. Blood pumped against her hand.

A wave of dizziness crashed over her, and her knees buckled.

"Oh god. Oh god. Oh god."

Lou wasn't sure who was speaking but she wanted them to shut up. The pounding in her head had escalated to a tumultuous thunder that obliterated all thought with its battle drumbeat.

She couldn't think. She barely saw the cold pavilion stone under her palms. The blood was dripping from her throat onto the stones beneath her, soaking her hand.

The black pool spread out beneath her. It was like a lake

opening up just for her. If she wasn't careful, she would fall right through—maybe to La Loon.

Or maybe to a darker, wilder place.

"Lou." A hand touched her back. A white-hot hand that made her feel weak all over. She wanted to knock it away. She thought she might have shrugged but she wasn't sure. Her arms were losing feeling, tingling the way they do when waking from sleep. And they were no longer obeying her commands.

"Lou!"

The greedy hands turned her over, rolling her onto her back. She stared up at the industrial gray sky, smoky white clouds full of diffused orange light slid by, uninterested in her petty drama.

It was King staring down at her. "Fuck. Lou! Lou can you hear me? No, she'll choke. Roll her. Lou?"

"Stop shouting," she said, or tried to say. Her throat couldn't quite find enough air to force into her lungs. The pain radiating through her right shoulder was unbearable.

"Give me your shawl," King said. "*Give it* to me!"

"I'm *trying!*"

Something rough pressed against Lou's throat, intensifying the pain. Someone was screaming. Distantly, she wondered if it was her own voice.

"I'm sorry," King said. "But we've got to compress this. You're losing blood too fast."

His shadowed face only darkened, giving a hint of features she no longer recognized.

I'm going to black out, she realized. *Any minute now I'm going to lose consciousness and—*

Someone was tugging at her chest. The familiar ripping sound of Velcro crackled in her ear. She reached out to stop the rough hands from finishing their work.

"I have to take them. I'm sorry. You can't go to the

hospital with these on. And you're *going* to the hospital, you hear me?"

The vest fell away and suddenly her chest expanded, finally able to pull in a full breath. It wasn't smooth and she didn't like that whistle-wet sound in her ears. But without the vest and shoulder holster she did find it easier to breathe.

Still, exhaustion pressed against her brain. The warmth promised sleep. A blessed, relaxing release if only she—

Someone shook her until her eyes opened. "Lou, listen to me! The police are here. You have to go. New Orleans General Hospital, do you hear me? New Orleans General! *Go! Now!*"

Red and blue lights danced across his face. The strange strobing effect intensified her dizziness and the dreamlike quality that had been pulled over the world.

"*New Orleans General.* Now!"

Come on, she told herself. Come on. *Who is in control here?*

Drawing deep on her reserves she reached out for the darkness around her. *Come on*, she begged. *I can do this.*

She coughed to clear her throat and instantly regretted it. The pain spiked in a way that made her scream again—and now she was sure it was *her* screaming. Such a strange sound. Had she ever screamed like this before?

Before she could answer her own curiosity, she was falling, falling through the black.

KING STARED AT THE BLOOD ON THE PAVING STONES WHERE Lou had been just a moment before. His heart was racing. The blood was on his sleeves, on his hands. He wondered if it was maybe on his face as well.

It's too much, he thought. *Oh god, it's too much blood.*

Had the bullet cut her carotid? He couldn't be sure. It'd been hard to see the wound clearly in the dark. The hole, before he'd covered it with his hands, had looked a little low for that. Maybe it had only torn through the shoulder. But he could be wrong. God help him, he could be *wrong*.

Please let it be the shoulder and not the neck, he begged. He wasn't sure if he was praying to a god—any god—or Lucy herself.

Not the neck. Not the neck. Let it be the shoulder. Not the neck, not the—

Because if it was her carotid, she was dead.

Mel was crying softly beside him. On her hands and knees, she rocked back and forth beside the duffle bag.

"Check him and make sure he's alive," King said, pointing at the unconscious husband.

After the gun had gone off, and the husband had been distracted by Lou's sudden materialization from nowhere, King had taken the opportunity to throw a right hook across the man's jaw, dropping him before he got the bright idea to run for it.

He'd hit the ground like a sack of bricks.

But King had had no chance to evaluate his handiwork because Lou had collapsed, making a strange noise he'd never heard before. *Like an animal dying, like an animal dying...*

Then he'd seen the blood. *So much blood.*

"Mel," King said. He squeezed the woman's knee hard enough to bruise. "See if he's still alive. Before the police get down here."

King heard car doors shut and the low voices of the police boots crossing the station. He stood and grabbed the duffle bag without fanfare. He bent and grabbed the gun without pausing his stride. At the edge of the pavilion, he threw the bag over the rail into the water. It splashed, sinking into the black water below. Next King emptied the bullets from Mel's revolver and tossed them into the canal, followed by the revolver itself. Then his own burner phone, because why not take care of all of it at once?

He ran over to the Living La Vida Loca Lobster shack. The cat, thinking he was back for another go at his tail, hissed and scuttled farther into the dark.

"Sorry," he muttered, already imagining what Lou must think of having her weapons thrown away. He shoved Lou's gun and vest into the trash bin. "You can look for them later."

If she lives.

She's going to live.

On the left side of the shack was a fountain that shot spraying water into the sky.

He plunged his hands into the icy water. He rubbed them vigorously, trying to wash Lou's blood from his hands and sleeves.

King could do nothing about the pool of blood left on the pavilion. Hopefully, they would not ask.

That was here when I arrived, King practiced in his mind. *Who knows what this asshole did before we showed up...maybe he hurt someone. He looks like a dangerous guy.*

When King returned to Mel she was still on her knees, crying.

Please let Lou make it to the hospital King begged as the flashlights swept the pavilion, fixing on the three of them at long last. He waved to get the officers' attention. "We are over here!"

"I killed her. Oh my god, I killed her." Mel wailed at his feet, her face still buried in her hands. King reached down and pulled her to standing.

"Lord in heaven, I—"

"Shut up," he said. "Let me do the talking."

36

L ou fell against the brick wall, coughing. Blood sputtered down her chin. It was a disgusting feeling, but it was hard to care much about it in the face of the unbearable pain shooting through her bones. Every time the weight in her head shifted forward or back, a new explosion of pain ricocheted through her, threatening to knock her unconscious with its ferocity.

Why am I at the grocery store? She'd been aiming for New Orleans General Hospital like King had instructed. But here she was, sliding slowly down the brick wall. Her leather jacket scraped along the face, no doubt scuffing the black hide.

Who gives a fuck? Who gives a fuck about your stupid jacket? her mind asked. *You're dying.*

And she was. She could feel it. She was too cold. Way too cold for even a February night. Her teeth chattered and face felt frozen.

Then the wall ended and she fell forward, suddenly unable to support her weight.

On her knees, she looked around. *Anybody,* she thought. *I'll take anybody.*

Only it wasn't the parking lot of the Ohio grocery store. She was looking into the back of an ambulance. Its doors were open with a pristine white bed waiting inside. It was lit with the bright fluorescents overhead as if showcased for her.

Come on in, it said. *Come on in and lay down.*

She wanted to. Her body felt so weak and exhausted. Her heart raced in her chest, in her head. She just wanted to lie down. And here was a bed.

She tried to stand but before she even got a knee out from under her, hands grabbed her shoulders.

"I'm sorry, Miss, but you can't be back here," someone said.

She screamed as the hand brushed her wound. Mel's soaked headscarf fell from her throat to the pavement beneath her. Blood sprang forth, the stream renewed.

"Whoa, *fuck*. Bernie! Bernie! Get your ass out here!"

Those relentless hands moved her and she screamed again.

"I'm sorry," the voice said. "I'm so sorry but I have to touch you."

Just let me lie down, she begged as the white bed swam in and out of her vision. *Just let me lie down.*

And that was the last thing she remembered.

For a long time there was only darkness. Cold, indifferent darkness. That was okay. Because for Lou, in a way, the darkness was as familiar as a childhood bedroom.

She walked around in it, feeling as one always does when they return home after a long time away. There was something here, waiting for her. It had been waiting patiently for a long time. But it would have to be patient for a little while longer. For now, she needed to rest.

While she slept, she dreamed.

She dreamed of La Loon.

She stood on the banks of Blood Lake, listening to the water gently lap at the shore.

In the water was every man she'd ever brought to the dumping ground. Hundreds of them, almost shoulder to shoulder, covered the lake's patina. They floated face down in the water. Their clothes billowed around them with the air trapped inside, ballooning the fabric. They almost looked like cheap blowup dolls.

It didn't matter that Lou had seen many of these men devoured or torn apart by the creature that ruled this world. They were whole now.

None of this had to make sense, she understood. This was metaphoric. She was trying to understand the message. That was all.

So she counted the bodies. She noted how they lay, sprawled face down in the water.

She thought, *it's because the lake is hungry too. It consumes what it can from our world because it is so hungry. It's hungry like me. It's hungry like everyone.*

She thought, *and like everyone, it has to eat.*

She watched the bodies float until a slow gentle breathing filled her ears. She reached out and placed a hand on the beast's reptilian head.

It was Jabbers. Her scaled skull felt cool under Lou's fingers. She traced the familiar ridges with her fingers. It cooed under her hand.

It dragged its steaming white tongue up her arm. It smelled the blood dried to her shoulder and neck.

"You can eat me," Lou said to the beast. "I think I'm dead now, too."

KONSTANTINE WOKE TO HIS PHONE RINGING.

On the third ring he realized it wasn't his business phone. It was his private line.

He threw back the covers and grabbed the phone.

"Hello?" he asked in English, knowing of only a few who might call this number.

"Hey. It's Robert King." It was the New Orleans detective. "I'm at New Orleans General Hospital and after this I need to get back to the police station, so I've got to make this quick."

King spoke rapidly, relaying what needed to be done.

"The Julia Station plaza. Yes," Konstantine confirmed. "Yes, I'll take care of it."

"There's more," King said. "It's Lou."

Konstantine listened, doing his best to understand the detective carefully despite the thunderous pounding of his heart.

When the detective was finished, Konstantine took a slow, deep breath. "I'll come right away."

37

M el shifted in the plastic chair, trying to ease the cramp in her lower back. These chairs were a special kind of torture. Mel was certain they were manufactured in a factory specifically for interrogation rooms like this one.

"Just a while longer now," Mr. Rushdie said beside her. He'd been feeding her this platitude since eight that morning when they'd first arrived to give their statements. That was over six hours ago.

"Is that right?" she asked without expecting an answer.

The man rubbed his humped back and sighed. "You'll be back in your own bed before the night is through. I promise. Can I get you anything to drink?"

Mel shook her head. She didn't believe they'd let her leave so easily. Terry would have no choice but to rat her out. The photographs might be long gone, but the fact was, she wanted to confess. She wanted this to be over. It wasn't living, what she'd been doing all these years. It couldn't go on like this.

If they gave her the chance to confess, she would. It was all she wanted to do.

It was the only thing that was *left* to do really. She couldn't mention shooting Lou without exposing her identity, but she could confess to the hit and run.

And she was going to do it—she really was. If someone would just come back into the room and take her damn statement.

Then I can die with a clear conscience.

She rubbed her face one more time, groaning into her palms.

"Just a while longer," Mr. Rushdie said placidly beside her. "Just a while now."

That's how these interrogation rooms work. They leave you in here so long you go crazy. You'll confess to anything just to get out of here.

"Now when they come back," Mr. Rushdie said for the fourteenth time. "You gonna let me do the talking, all right? We're gonna—"

The door opened and a large black man in a buttoned-up white shirt stepped into the room. His hair was cropped close to his head. In his arm was a stack of folders. His sleeves were rolled up past the elbows and his holsters could've been mistaken for suspenders at a glance.

King came in behind him, pushing a small television on top of a metal cart. Below it was the oldest VHS she'd ever seen.

King looked worse for wear. It wasn't only the dark, puffy circles under his eyes or the new gray growth that had sprouted on his jaw overnight. It was also his stride. He hadn't seen his bed yet and it showed.

"I'm sorry to keep you waiting, Ms. Durand. It took us longer to find a TV cart than we anticipated. And nineteen people were injured in a shootout in the Quarter, so everyone has been running around like headless chickens." The officer went to the other side of the table. He extended his hand.

"I'm Dick White. Robbie here has told me only good things about you—"

"Sir, let me stop you there." Mel held up her hands. She couldn't bear compliments in the face of the confession she was about to make. "I need to get some things off my chest. I—"

A hand clamped down on her shoulder. The fingers dug into the flesh of her collarbone with such sudden ferocity that she almost cried out. The words dried up in her mouth.

"Dick's been working *real* hard on this, Mel. We had to go back forty years for these tapes," King said, bending his face down to look into Mel's eyes. "I think you should listen to what he has to say before interrupting him."

"No need to rough her up," Dick said with an uneasy laugh. "We aren't going to play good cop bad cop here."

Forty years? Did that mean Dick already knew about the hit and run? Did they already have evidence of her crime?

Mel searched King's wide eyes and took the hint. "You go first."

"You'll get to say your piece," Mr. White promised, settling into the plastic chair opposite her. To King he said, "Plug that in over here. There's the socket."

King pulled the cart over into the corner and wedged the plug into the wall. He angled it so that Mel and her attorney had a clear view.

"Good," Mr. White said, rubbing his nose. "I hardly know where to begin! We've got so much to cover. You've had an exciting night, Ms. Durand. We're glad you're all right."

Mel followed King's suspicious movements with her eyes. She knew something was going on here, but she hadn't gotten a handle on it yet.

"Where is Terrence now?" Mel asked, thinking this was the safest entry point into the conversation.

"He's over in county in a holding cell." White turned to King. "You want to give her the rundown or do I?"

"After you," King said to the man with a smile that could almost be taken for joviality. To Mel, King arched his eyebrows. It seemed to her that this meant, *keep your mouth shut and listen. It'll be better for both of us.*

Mr. White shuffled his folders until fixing on one from the middle of the file. He opened it, reviewing the top page.

"We've got your statement from last night—" Mr. White began.

"And it's absolutely clear that Mr. Williams is guilty of extortion," Mr. Rushdie inserted.

"Yes, it is," the officer agreed.

"But that doesn't excuse my behavior," Mel said.

"Melandra—" Mr. Rushdie moved to drown out her words with his own. "I would advise you not to—"

"Listen to your lawyer," King interjected with a pointed look, seemingly unaware that he himself was interrupting the man.

Mr. White looked from Mel to King to the lawyer. He arched a brow. "Should I continue or do y'all need to talk about something?"

"Please, continue," Mel said, doing her best to gather her reserve.

"Terrence Williams *has* been charged with extortion as well as intimidation, harassment, and theft of property. This violates his parole, of course. We also have Robbie's testimony and Piper's and also Donny's—who you approached in the street one night, if you recall. We also have some footage from the convenience store across the street that shows him shoving you against the wall outside your shop."

King's jaw flexed.

"When we got the warrant to search his apartment we found your cards, which we believe he was holding ransom in exchange for money in addition to the violence he was inflicting on you."

"Are they okay? My cards?" Mel asked, sitting up in her seat. It's unbearable stiffness was temporarily forgotten.

King pulled a black bundle from his coat pocket and pressed it into her hands. "Piper says they're all there except the Devil card."

She began to cry. Someone rubbed her shoulders.

"Is it irreplaceable?" King asked.

Mel lifted her face. "No. I can replace it."

It was about time for her to add her own card to the deck anyway. Every woman over the generations had had to do the same. It felt right that The Devil should be hers.

"Extortion carries a twenty-year sentence, even without the parole violation and the extra charges laid against him," King said. "You'll never see him again."

"Assuming you will testify," Mr. White said.

"Of course I'll testify," Mel said. That was the least she could do. Hell, she was ready to testify against herself.

"Now, don't make any promises yet," Mr. Rushdie said. "My client—"

"I'll testify," Mel said. "Can I testify even if I'm jail?"

Detective White laughed. "Why would you be in jail?"

Mel was certain that even if she'd somehow passed a statute of limitations for the hit-in-run, even if no one had ever come forward for it or made the crime known and therefore she could receive no punishment—at the very least she would get attempted murder. She'd put bricks and rope into a duffle bag for Christ's sake. She'd taken them down to a river with a gun.

It was true that she'd only intended to scare the hell out of Terry and not actually kill him, but that hardly mattered now. She'd *fired* the gun. Someone *was* shot.

"In the plaza—" Mel began.

"Ah, yes. King is the one that hit him, not you."

"The blood—" she tried again.

"What blood?" Detective White asked. He looked to King. "You break the man's nose or something?"

"My client is tired," Mr. Rushdie interjected. "We've been here all day and—"

King leaned in and whispered in Mel's ear. "There was no duffle, no gun, no bricks, and no rope. And if you're wondering, there are no tapes from the plaza security cameras either."

Mel searched his eyes. "*What?*"

"I spoke to a friend. He's more Lou's friend than mine, but he took care of the footage. There's nothing to pin on you." Then aloud, loud enough for the squabbling White and Rushdie to hear. "We have more than enough to convict Terry for extortion."

You could not say anything, her mind suggested. *You can go back to your life, to your shop. You don't have to give everything up.*

"No," Mel said, wiping at her face. "No, I have to say something."

Both Rushdie and King looked stricken.

King held up his hand and it filled Mel with sudden anger. *No.* She would not be deterred, damn it. She was sick of living with the guilt of that night. Of closing her eyes and seeing the rain pelting the window of Terry's red Firebird. Of seeing her Grandmamie's stricken and anguished face when Terry pulled up in the driveaway.

Don't be a fool.

"Please let me show you something," King said, going around the table to the TV cart. He pressed eject on the machine, looked at the tape and put it into the VCR once more. Then as if he didn't believe she could keep her mouth shut he said, "Just give me one minute to show you one last thing, and if you still have something to say, I'll be the first to hear you out. I promise."

He lifted the remote from the cart and pressed the buttons until the television flickered on.

King rewound the tape, explaining as he went. "In May of '81, Dustin Malone submitted a complaint to the County Commissioner, to the State Patrol, to the mayor—hell, he complained to just about anyone that listened that they needed to add speed signs and a speed trap to his road. He said that twice cars had been racing by too fast and had clipped his farm dogs. There had been three crashes where drag-racing kids ended up dying. Because nobody listened to him, he installed these cameras on the edge of his property. He recorded the road for sixteen months, hoping to gather enough evidence to take the State to court over it."

Mel's heart knocked in her throat.

"I don't see how this is relevant—" Mr. Rushdie began beside her.

King stopped the tape watched for a second, rewound it, played it again. "Here we go."

Two seconds...three... and Mel's chest was so tight she couldn't draw a breath. She started, physically *jumped* in her chair when the red Firebird rolled into the frame from the right side of the screen.

Mel leaned forward, searching both sides of the road for the man. *Where is the man? He must be—*

There was no man.

A fox, low to the ground, shot out from the trees away from Malone's property line and into the road. Its lithe body was momentarily lit by the headlights of the approaching Firebird. The fox hesitated, sinking back onto its heels but it was too late. The tires struck the animal on its right side, rolling it under the car and onto the pavement. It tumbled to a stop in the glow of red taillights.

The car screeched to a halt.

The passenger door opened and a much younger—the way she often still saw him in her dreams—man stepped out into the rain. He went to the front of the car, bent down and inspected the grill. Then he went to the back of the car and saw the fox. He nudged it with his foot.

King bent close to Mel's ear and whispered. "You didn't hurt anyone, Mel. He lied to you so he could control you. You hear me? The bastard *lied*. Then he bragged to his jail buddies about it."

"But I saw..." *I didn't kill anyone. I didn't kill anyone.*

"You might have been drunk or scared or tired. Or maybe it was late, I don't know. But you didn't hit anyone. You *didn't*. He *lied* to you," King whispered.

She covered her face with her hands and began to sob.

Forty years of regret...over something that didn't happen. *Forty years, forty years, forty damn years*—

Her first emotion was raw, raging anger.

Goddamn you, Terry! Goddamn you and your lies!

But she couldn't sustain the anger in the face of such blessed relief. The relief and anger rolled through her.

Her sobs shook her whole body. Strong hands found her back, pressing gently into them. It was King, she knew.

"I can't believe you were going to shoot him and shove him into the canal," King whispered to her. A surprised little laugh escaped him. "I have to admit that surprised me."

"I wasn't," she admitted. She knew she wouldn't have been able to follow through actually taking his life. "I thought if I scared him bad enough he'd leave me the hell alone. The gun only went off because Lou surprised me."

It was over. It was really over. This ordeal with Terry, these forty plus years of torment, they were really, *truly* over.

She began to cry harder.

"You're all right," King said. He kissed the top of her

head. He rubbed her shoulders. "You're all right. You're going to be just fine."

"I'm sorry I lied to you," she said. "I told you I was divorced and—"

"I know," King interrupted, squeezing her shoulder. "It's okay. I'm not mad. It hurt, thinking there was some reason you didn't trust me, but I'm not mad."

"I trust you," she said, sniffling.

And a warm smile broke out on his face. "Good. I trust you, too."

But part of her couldn't believe she could be so totally exonerated.

There was still Lou.

Mel had shot the girl. She had watched her bleed all over the pavilion, the blood bubbling up between her lips as she screamed.

Mel lifted her face from her hands and sniffed. She dragged her nose over her sleeve, trying to clean herself up. *Oh god, Lou.* "How is she?"

38

L ou understood that she was dreaming. Or maybe she was dead. She suspected that both may be the same: dead and dreaming. It was the awareness that one clung to despite the way the world warped around a feverish mind.

Lou was in her parents' house—or rather, it was the house they'd had when they were still alive. She stood just inside the front door, overlooking the pristine living room with its fluffed cushions and vacuuming marks in the carpet as if her mother had just finished her daily pass. She noted the way the light slanted through its large bay window. It was early afternoon, perhaps even the time when she would have just come home from school.

Lou crossed the living room, half expecting to find her mother any moment, knowing the woman would click her tongue at Lou's leather boots, jacket, and the mirrored sunglasses poised on her face.

All the blood...

But her mother wasn't in the living room.

Lou passed the bathroom on the first floor, noting

distantly that this was the tub she'd disappeared from all those years ago when her parents began to take her condition seriously. But now it was dry, empty, awash in light.

She regarded it from the corner of her eye, noting how much smaller it seemed, and kept walking.

Her heart flopped in her chest when she did find her mother. She stood in the kitchen, by the stove, dragging a wooden spoon through a pot of something red.

"You're late. Your father is outside waiting for you," she said.

Lou had forgotten how high her mother's voice was. Nasal. Indignant.

Affection welled in her chest for this long dead woman. It surprised her. Her mother had never been particularly kind or patient. She had not been a loving mother. The closest Lou had gotten to tasting that experience was the day after she'd disappeared, when she was delivered safely to her mother's arms.

She'd gotten a long, lingering hug then. But that was the extent of Courtney Thorne's love before Martinelli's men shot her.

She won't even look at me.

But then she did. And Lou was stunned by their resemblance. She always thought she looked like her father and she did, but now it was undeniable that she had Courtney's features too. It was the hard mouth and eyes, the sharp cheekbones, and the build of her body. Though her mother had always bleached her hair and Lou's was dark like her father's.

"Wash your hands. Dinner's almost ready."

Lou didn't wash her hands. Instead she backed away from the kitchen and the woman tending the stove. She strode through the dining room to the doors that would let her out onto the patio.

Time skipped.

She neither opened the doors nor stepped outside.

One minute she was at the glass, looking out at the mani-cured lawn, at the clusters of daylilies and cone flowers and then she was outside. She stood beside the pool, looking down into the dancing crystalline water.

The shine was too bright.

Because this is a dream her mind reminded her. *This is how it is in dreams.*

The old gate creaked and Lou turned half expecting to see Angelo Martinelli again, bursting through the fence with a gun and an all-encompassing desire to end their lives.

But it was her father. He was in a white t-shirt and jeans —his favorite weekend outfit. His dark hair had fallen forward into his eyes as he whistled the tune *Louie* by the Kingsmen.

He was also young, no older than Konstantine. He grinned, his smile catching sunlight. "Lou-blue! I've been looking for you."

The love she'd felt for her mother paled compared to what she felt for him. It had been a drop of blood in an ocean. This was the ocean itself.

She wrapped her arms around his waist.

It's a dream, just a dream, a dream her mind reminded her.

She didn't care. It felt real enough.

A large hand pressed into her back. He planted a kiss on her forehead. Even how he smelled—though there was some-thing different about it—took her back.

"Come here," he said, motioning her toward the water.

She dug in her heels. "You'll push me in and I'll wake up."

"No I won't." He laughed and it startled her to see that she had his smile, as rare as it was for her to show it.

"We don't have a lot of time. Come on," he said.

He crossed to the glass patio table adjacent the pool and

sat in a red and white striped beach chair. He pulled something from his pocket.

It was a folded piece of paper that he began to unfold with his large, tanned fingers.

"It's not just *who*," he said. "It's when. The *when* is very important. Do you understand? Too soon and it will be worse. Too late and then more damage is done. Timing is everything."

He spread the page flat on the table.

Lou didn't see anything on the page. "It's blank."

Her father laughed as if she'd made a joke.

"I know it's a lot to take in, but it's about balance. You couldn't have saved Christine because it wasn't the right *when*."

"Who's Christine?"

Her father's finger went down the page, stopping at a name. "Like this one. You won't be able to stop this one either, but it's okay. It's not your job to save everyone Loublue."

Lou stared hard at the paper, now convinced there were names of people that she couldn't see. Dark shapes began to form on the paper, squiggly shadows, but nothing legible formed.

"I'm showing you this because I don't want you to beat yourself up about it. You're doing everything you're supposed to do."

He placed a heavy hand on her shoulder, squeezed her hard enough to feel it through the leather jacket. She didn't give a shit about names on some paper. She wanted to soak in every second with him.

He smiled. "I'm so proud of you. Do you know that? I want you to know how proud I am of the amazing woman you've become."

"I've missed you."

"I miss you too." His smile brightened. "But we'll see each other again soon. Until then, don't forget Lou-blue. I'm proud of you."

She had only a moment to appreciate the beauty of his face in the lazy summer afternoon before night fell.

It was as if someone had snapped their fingers and sunshine was replaced by moonlight. The pool was lit from the lights within. It glowed, ethereal with steam rising from its surface.

Her father was gone. A woman stood on the first step of the pool. The water rippled from her knees out toward the deep end of the pool. Her long skirt trailed the surface of the pool.

"I've come to take you back," Lucy said without turning. "You can't stay here. If you stay any longer, that might be the end of it. And there's still so much you can do. You're only getting started."

"Take me where?" Lou asked. She was trying to remember what her father had said, what he'd been doing the moment before. But already it was a memory slipping away from her. The tighter she tried to hold onto it, the faster it bled through her fingers.

"You can trust him, you know," Lucy said and then she did turn, casting Lou a mischievous look over her shoulder. She thought Lucy was talking about her father at first. Then she said, "It might help you to know that he'll outlive you."

Lou left her seat at the table and went to the pool. She stepped down onto the first step beside her aunt.

"Konstantine?"

Lucy regarded the shimmering water. Lou couldn't be sure, but it seemed like the lights inside the pool were getting brighter.

"They'll all outlive you. You won't see anyone else you love die. You've done enough of that."

Lou thought the water in her boots would chill her feet. But instead it seemed that warmth filled them, spreading up her legs into her groin, abdomen, and climbing.

"Even King?" Lou asked. "Because he's pretty old."

Lucy's smile was beautiful, radiant. She was healthy again, whole, looking the way Lou remembered her best. "Even King."

Of course King could drop dead tomorrow, or live another fifteen years.

Lucy turned and gave Lou a look full of so much sadness. She reached up and touched Lou's face, the hand cool.

The lights in the pool brightened more, causing Lou to squint her eyes against it.

"Love them while you can," her aunt said and Lou clamped her hand over hers to prevent her from disappearing.

When I open my eyes she'll be gone, she knew. *When I open my eyes—*

"Are you ready?" Lucy asked.

Lou didn't have to answer.

Her eyes opened.

She had only one moment of blessed ignorance before the pain made itself know. In this moment, she noted the hospital bed and the shape of her body tucked neatly under the blankets piled on top of her.

She noted the dark, silent television hanging from the wall above. She noted the bathroom, the hint of a toilet shining in the dark behind the partially ajar door.

Konstantine was in the doorway, speaking to a man in a white coat.

"She's awake," a man said and Lou's eyes tracked the noise.

It was Stefano, who stood by her bedside.

Both the doctor and Konstantine stopped talking and turned.

That was when the pain came—almost as if summoned by their gazes alone.

Lou groaned, trying to sit up, as if she could escape it by adjusting herself.

"Easy, easy," someone said.

"It hurts," she groaned and felt like a stupid, petulant child. "It *hurts*."

"Hold on. Here we go."

In the periphery of her eyes she saw a thumb mashing a little button several times.

"This will help."

Warmth spread through Lou's arm and into her chest.

"Welcome back!" the doctor said, perhaps too enthusiastically. "We almost lost you there!"

"Mel—" Lou began.

Konstantine shook his head and raised his brows. "Let the doctor tell you what happened and then we can...catch up, *amore mio*. Quickly though?"

The doctor released a nervous laugh. "Of course. As you know you were shot. The bullet grazed your collarbone and tore through the muscles there. The stitches will have to stay in for a while, and you'll definitely have restricted movement on your right side for, well, possibly forever. We can try PT to regain most of it back, but I suspect you'll discover some nerve damage once you begin moving it again."

Lou looked down at her shoulder and saw her arm was taped to her side and chest.

"You're incredibly lucky," the doctor went on. "Had the bullet been centimeters closer to your neck, it would've severed your carotid and you would be dead. If it had been any lower, it could've shattered your collarbone and punctured your lung. Even a centimeter lower and I wouldn't have been able to dig the fragments out of your lungs. Someone up there must be looking out for you."

Lou thought of Lucy standing in the pool, her dress floating on top of the water.

"How long until she is healed?" Konstantine asked.

"Six months is the soonest for full use of the shoulder," the doctor said.

Konstantine's gaze lingered on the doctor's face.

The doctor seemed to take the hint. "I'm sure you want to speak to your wife. So if you'll excuse me. But, uh, if you need more morphine—" He put a small remote control into her hand. "Don't hesitate to push this button."

Konstantine nodded toward the door and Stefano followed the doctor out, shutting the door behind him.

Konstantine pulled the empty chair up to the side of her bed and sank into it. He looked suddenly very, *very* tired.

"Wife?" Lou asked, leveling him with a stare.

"Only family is allowed to access medical information and make decisions on your behalf."

"Couldn't you just hack into their systems?" It hurt to talk. Not only because her neck throbbed but because her mouth was incredibly dry.

"I wanted to be in the room with you." He placed his face in his hands.

Lou closed her eyes. The morphine was pressing at the edges of her brain, making her eyes heavy. She wanted to go back to sleep.

Konstantine's deep voice drew her to consciousness again.

"Do you know how painfully *slow* an airplane ride feels when the woman you love is dying?"

"I've never been in love with a woman. And I don't fly."

His lips twitched. He settled against the back of the chair and sighed. "Would you like to know about Fish or the shop-keeper first?"

"She has a name."

"I know," he said. "But it is difficult for me to say."

"Melandra."

"Yes, but I meant without cursing *it*. She nearly killed you."

"It was an accident."

"Which is why she is alive and well. King needed only a little help making sure that there was no evidence against her."

Something in Lou's chest relaxed. It was either relief, or the morphine was working nicely.

Konstantine continued, unaware.

"Fish has been arrested and charged for murder. He confessed after two days of interrogation. King called this normal saying he is a megomanaic."

"Megalomaniac." Lou's tongue raked over her dry lips. "Can I have some water?"

Konstantine called out in Italian and Stephano's face appeared in the hospital door.

"*Acqua, per favore.*"

Stefano disappeared again.

"He loves to do your bidding," Lou said.

Konstantine's lips quirked. "For a very high price."

"How high?" Lou asked. "Because I can fetch water too."

Each sarcastic quip seemed to loosen Konstantine's shoulders, forcing them back down away from his ears.

"His case is going to court and the families now have a chance at peace. King says this was your objective. So, congratulations." Konstantine adjusted the watch on his wrist. "What happened with the woman?"

"Diana?"

"Yes."

"She told me that she's a hunter like me."

"Is she?" Konstantine rubbed his chin. "This isn't surprising. I can't imagine you are the only woman like this in the world. She must be jealous of your gifts."

"She doesn't know about them."

"I would keep it that way."

Lou tried to find the best position for her head but no matter how she turned it, she was uncomfortable. "What about Mel's husband?"

"In prison and the divorce is in process."

The door slid open and Stefano appeared with the Styrofoam cup of water. He delivered it to Konstantine.

Konstantine scooted his chair closer to the bed, angling the straw so Lou could drink.

She scowled at him.

"If you try to hold it yourself you may drop it."

With a stifled cry, she leaned forward and accepted the water.

"You look like you are in a lot of pain. I see it in your eyes."

"You're observant," she murmured between drinks.

He frowned. "Is there anything I can get you? Is there anything you want?"

Lou snorted. "I want to fuck you."

Definitely the drugs talking, she thought distantly.

Stefano exited the room with his eyebrows raised and closed the door behind him.

"I recommend we wait until you are healed."

"You're no fun. Maybe I like the pain."

He cocked his head. "You could have done it before. I made that perfectly clear."

"I didn't want you to fall in love with me."

He laughed. "I love how honest you are when you're high."

She leaned back with a grimace. It was very hard to get comfortable and she'd begun to itch. Nowhere specific but all over. Her scalp. Her chest. Her flesh crawled.

"It's too late, you know," he said after trying to help her adjust the pillows. "I'm already in love with you."

"Don't." She scowled. This was not helping her discomfort. "People in love want to get married, they want kids. I don't want any of that."

"Would you believe me if I said I only want to love you. I'm not asking for anything else."

Lou said nothing.

"Is it really so hard to believe? Or do you think you're incapable of love?" he asked, unable to let it go.

"People like me—like Fish—we don't love."

He frowned. "You are not like the men you kill, *amore mio*. You loved your father, your mother, your aunt. You love your friends."

Lou grimaced, she was scratching at her chest with the unbound hand. "Maybe not my mother."

He sat back and crossed one knee over the other. "If you don't love me, that's fine. But that doesn't mean you *can't* love."

Love them while you can. They'll outlive you.

Lou closed her eyes. It was impossible to keep them open anymore. She tried to remember what Lucy was wearing in the dream, but it was fading, and fading fast. Had her feet been in the water? Had it been nighttime? Was the pool lit from within? Lou thought so.

"You scared me," Konstantine whispered.

"I'll keep scaring you," she said, without opening her eyes.

"I'm sure you will."

39

K ing lifted the paczki from its brown pastry box, delighting in the way the dough gave softly under his touch. When he bit into it, warm raspberry jelly oozed out onto his tongue, and powdered sugar coated his lips. He was in heaven. He moaned with happiness.

Piper snorted beside him, leaning over the black wrought-iron railing. "That good, huh?"

"You want to split one?" Dani asked, looking up from the box.

King wanted to object and claim the entire dozen for his own, but that hardly seemed like appropriate Fat Tuesday spirit. And he hadn't bought the donuts. Mel had.

The four of them were waiting on the balcony, watching the crowds jostle below in anticipation of the upcoming parade.

"Yeah, I'll split one," Piper said, grinning at her. "You pick."

Dani tucked her hair behind her ear. "They all look so good."

"Yes they do," Mel agreed, crossing and uncrossing her

legs from her chair. She readjusted the rectangular card on her clipboard. It was The Devil, in progress. Most of the lean man's face was hidden beneath a tipped hat, but Mel had given him a ghost of a smile.

"It's coming along," Piper said, peering over Mel's shoulder. "It's going to be cool as hell when you add color."

"Cool as hell," Dani snorted finally selecting a paczki from the box. "Was that an intentional pun?"

Dani was about to bite into her selected paczki when she frowned, leaning over the balcony. "Someone's here."

Everyone turned.

A black car rolled up to the curb. The driver's side door opened first and Konstantine stepped out into the throng of people, politely excusing himself as he pushed through. The doors on either side of the backseat opened and two men stepped out onto the street.

They formed a buffer of space around the passenger side door, but it was Konstantine who opened it.

Piper choked on her bite. "Shit, it's Lou."

"I'll get her," Mel said, rising from her seat.

But Piper, red faced, was waving her back down. She was through the doors and out of sight before anyone could object.

"That's a Maserati," Dani said and whistled.

Mel barely looked up from the card as she bent closer to the add another line to the devil's hat.

Konstantine and Lou had disappeared beneath the balcony. Then the two men climbed into the front seat and drove it away.

Mel pulled back, frowning at the card. "Give me one of those," she said, motioning for the donut box.

King pushed the box toward her, only after taking a second donut for himself.

"Look who it is!" Piper called, throwing open the balcony

door so that Lou could step through. "Our indestructible heroine!"

The color was back in her face, which pleased King. The last time he'd seen her, she'd been white as a ghost. Her arm was still wrapped tight to her body and her leather jacket was draped over that shoulder. But she was up and moving.

"When I saw you get out of a car I thought you'd lost your powers," Piper said.

Konstantine pulled out a chair for Lou. "There wasn't an easier way to transport us both here without hurting her."

"My shoulder is...tender." Lou pushed her sunglasses up on her head with her good hand before accepting the chair.

"So no piggybacking for a while," King sucked the raspberry jelly off his fingers. "I hope you'll rest."

Lou shot him a warning look.

"That was a nice car you rolled up in," Piper said, and King caught the tonal shift.

"Thank you." Konstantine replied, simply unaware.

"Is it yours or...?" she searched.

"While I am in the city, yes."

Piper pursed her lips. "Cool, cool."

Dani grabbed her hand tenderly and pulled Piper close. "Finish this."

Piper reluctantly took the half-eaten paczki and stuffed it into her mouth. She gave Dani a suspicious look.

A handful of purple beads flew through the air past their balcony.

"Damn, we forgot beads!" Piper cried. "Be right back."

Lou looked very placid in her seat, watching the crowds below.

King couldn't tell if it was the pain in her shoulder that was subduing her or if something else was on her mind.

Then he remembered something. "I forgot to tell you. We

got an ID on the woman whose body you found in the woods
—the one we hadn't been expecting."

Lou turned toward him finally, leveling him with her gaze.

"Her name was Christine Haslett."

Lou started as if slapped.

King frowned. "You know her?"

"Did you ever say that name to me before?"

"No."

"Maybe in the hospital while you were visiting me? Maybe
someone else said it?"

King shifted his weight. "No, I don't think so. Why?"

Her scowl deepened. "It doesn't matter."

"By the sound of it, Christine was an impulse kill. She'd
been walking home from a friend's house when he picked her
up. He'd never met her and didn't have any connections to
her. It's the kind of murder he would've never gotten caught
for. But thanks to you breaking this wide open, her family will
get closure. Did you see the families on the news?"

Lou had seen the story break while she was in the
hospital. She'd had little else to do in the days before she was
allowed to go home. Konstantine had read to her and when he'd
gotten tired they'd turned on the television. A tearful woman
had stood at a podium and had given her statement to the press.
*I'll never get my baby girl back, but it helps my heart to know that this
monster will pay for what he's done. There's still justice in this world.*

Lou had felt something as she watched each mother,
father, sister, brother come to the microphone and say their
piece about Jeffrey Fish. The photographs taken from his
home had let them know which of the missing girls to
account for even though not all of their graves had been
found.

Lou also knew there was a strong possibility that Fish had not photographed all of his kills. So she might occupy her painful, sleepless nights directing her compass to those unmarked graves. She'd take Dani along. Maybe Piper. Together they would figure out how to let the police know about the graves.

"I saw the news," Lou said.

"I told you closure is important," King said. His attempt at solemnity was dampened by the powder on his lips and raspberry jelly on his face. "You should be proud of yourself for making that possible."

Will they really get closure? Lou wondered. She thought of her father and her mother whose deaths had been unexpected. She thought of Aunt Lucy, whose death had been expected. In either case, there had been no closure.

Not really.

But she let King speak his mind, aware that he was assessing her the way her father used to. She'd scared him. She understood that. Seeing her bleed out on the pavilion's stones had shaken him and part of his mind was still wrapping around the idea that she was still here.

They'll all outlive you, Lucy had said.

"And when I die?" Lou asked, turning toward him. "How will you find closure then?"

"Who's gonna die?" Piper squeaked. "Not you! I told you. You're indestructible, man."

She felt Konstantine shift in her periphery. Until that moment, he'd been politely engaging Melandra in conversation, asking about Carnival and its role in the city as well complimenting the tarot card she sketched.

He punctuated his sentences with affectionate scratches behind Lady's ears, whose tail thumped against the balcony's wooden planks.

Lou knew better. When she'd ask *and when I die?* his hand had faltered. His back had stiffened.

Lou pretended not to notice, keeping her eyes trained on King.

"I'm seventy-one years old," King said, wiping jelly from the corner of his lips. "I should be asking you that question."

"Do the men in your family die in their seventies?" Lou asked with a smile. She was doing her best to keep her tone light, teasing. But her shoulder had begun to throb again, shooting up the side of her neck into her skull.

"My dad kicked off at 86. His dad went at 82. So I've probably got ten to fifteen years if I take care of myself."

"As long as we keep the gun out of Mel's hands you should be fine," Piper said around a mouthful of donut, sugar falling from her lips.

"No need." Mel covered her face with her hands. "I'll never touch another gun as long as I live."

Piper scoffed. "Never say never. That's how fate gets you."

"How do you feel?" Melandra asked Lou, settling down in the empty chair beside her. She pulled her clipboard to her chest and grimaced as if she were the one in pain.

Lou forced a smile for her benefit. "You're not the first person to shoot me. Not even the tenth."

"You almost died."

"Often," Lou said turning up the wattage on her smile. "Don't worry about it. It's not bad."

"I think she likes it," Piper said, pointing a donut at Lou's mouth, forcing Lou to open up and take a bite. "If she doesn't almost die once a week, she's bored to tears."

Piper took a bite of donut herself.

"You know," she said around her mouthful. "While you're resting we should do something fun. Like for spring break we should do a road trip."

"A road trip!" Dani cried, kneeling down on Lady's other

side. She now had two admirers and her thumping tail suggested that was just fine.

"I've never been on a road trip," Lou admitted.

Dani and Piper gave each other big, excited grins. "We're doing this."

"We need a playlist."

"And snacks."

"I have the car," Dani said. "And gas money."

"We'll split that. What do you think about Clearwater? Miami?"

"Las Vegas? Or the PCH?"

"Whoa. Go big or go home. I love it." Piper chewed her lip, thinking. "But how much time can we actually get off work?"

"Lou could just—"

"No, we have to drive! That's the point!"

"I just meant one way—"

Lou's shoulder seized up, and she squeezed her eyes closed against it.

Then Konstantine was there with a glass of water and two large pain pills. "I think it's time for these," he said, pressing them into her hand.

She took them both, tipping back the water glass until it was empty. When she handed the glass over, she caught Mel's fraught gaze.

Melandra reached her hand across the table, palm up in question. "Please forgive me."

Lou hesitated, regarding the half-finished devil on the clipboard. He bore a striking resemblance to Mel's ex-husband. At last she took the woman's smooth, dry hand. "There's nothing to forgive."

"No way!" Piper scoffed. "Doritos are *way* better than Pringles."

"Are you kidding me?" Dani rolled her eyes. "Next you'll

be telling me Reese's Pieces are better than M&Ms."

Piper squealed. "*Way* better."

"I *am* sorry," Mel said, pushing her hair back from her face. "*So*, so sorry."

"I'm sorry too," Lou said with a mischievous smile.

Mel's gaze darkened. "For what?"

"For what I'm going to do to your ex-husband the first chance I get."

EPILOGUE

Terrence Williams lay in his cell staring at the ceiling. Someone had scratched *suck my big white dick* into the concrete and drew a crude phallus beside it that looked nothing like, in Terry's opinion, an actual dick. A balloon animal, maybe.

When the nights were long like this and sleep wouldn't come, he liked to count the ways he was going to hurt Melandra Durand. It was his favorite game. He imagined tying her up and pulling all her fingernails off one by one with rusty pliers. He imagined holding her head under water in a shit-filled toilet. He imagined branding his name into her tits with a red-hot poker.

All the bitch had to do was give him what she owed him.

Why had that turned out to be so hard?

The pressure between his ears rose suddenly, the way they did in elevators that went up into high buildings. He shook his head to clear it.

When he opened his eyes again, there she was. The devil herself.

"I wondered when I might be seeing you," he said. He sat up on his elbows and regarded the young woman. She wasn't really a woman. He understood that. But she was pretty to look at all the same.

"Sorry to keep you waiting," she said from the shadows.

It was hard to hear her over the ruckus of the prison. All hours of the night people carried on, hooting and hollering, singing, screaming, or laughing.

She stepped forward just enough that her mouth and lips were lit by the lights outside his cell.

"I have a question for you," she said, and now he could see her eyes too. He'd half-expected to see them full of hellfire, but they were a soft brown like his momma's eyes. Like his little girl Alexis's eyes.

"What's that?" he asked.

"Why did you lie to Mel?"

He laughed. "*When?* I lied to that dumb bitch every day of her life."

"The night she hit the fox. Why did you tell her she'd killed someone?"

Again, Terrence thought of all the ways he wanted to hurt Melly. After pulling off her nails, he wanted to cut her ears, not all at once, but in little slices. Then maybe he would slit the cartilage between her nostrils, giving her one large one instead of two small breathing holes. Oh yes, he could do quite a bit to her face, he thought.

"I like hurting her," he said, rolling his eyes up to Lou's. "Sometimes it feels good. Hurting somebody."

He thought she might disappear then, leave him on his mattress with the ruckus of this concrete jungle, and only his mad thoughts to console him through the night.

But a wicked smile spread across her lips and Terry worried for the first time that maybe he'd said the wrong thing.

"I know what you mean," she said.

Then her hands were on him, pulling him into the waiting dark.

Did you enjoy this book? You can make a BIG difference.

I don't have the same power as big New York publishers who can buy full spread ads in magazines and you won't see my covers on the side of a bus anytime soon, but what I *do* have are wonderful readers like you.

And honest reviews from readers garner more attention for my books and help my career more than anything else I could possibly do—and I can't get a review without you! So if you would be so kind, I'd be very grateful if you would post a review for this book.

It only takes a minute or so of your time and yet you can't imagine how much it helps me. It can be as short as you like, and whether positive or negative, it really does help. I appreciate it so much and so do the readers looking for their next favorite read.

If you would be so kind, please find your preferred retailer here and leave a review for this book today.

With gratitude,

Kory

GET YOUR THREE FREE STORIES TODAY

Thank you so much for reading *Carnival*. I hope you're enjoying Louie's story. If you'd like more, I have a free, exclusive Lou Thorne story for you. Meet Louie early in her hunting days, when she pursues Benito Martinelli, the son of her enemy. This was the man her father arrested—and the reason her parents were killed months later.

You can only read this story for free by signing up for my newsletter. If you would like this story, you can get your copy by visiting www.korymshrum.com/lounewsletteroffer

I will also send you free stories from the other series that I write. If you've signed up for my newsletter already, no need to sign up again. You should have already received this story from me. Check your email and make sure it wasn't marked as spam! Can't find it? → Email me at kory@korymshrum.com and I'll take care of it.

As to the newsletter itself, I send out 2-3 a month and host a monthly giveaway exclusive to my subscribers. The prizes are usually signed books or other freebies that I think you'll enjoy. I also share information about my current projects, and personal anecdotes (like pictures of my dog). If you want these free stories and access to the exclusive give-aways, you can sign up for the newsletter at ➜ www.korymshrum.com/lounewsletteroffer

If this is not your cup of tea (I love tea), you can follow me on Facebook at www.facebook.com/korymshrum in order to be notified of my new releases.

ACKNOWLEDGMENTS

It seems we've done it again! Another book is here and I can finally resume bathing and eating and all those things I tend to neglect when I have a deadline. But before I turn on the shower, let me show my appreciation for all those who helped bring this book to life.

First and foremost, to you dear reader. You're four books into the series and you keep reading, so you must find something enjoyable here. Thank you so much. Thank you for reading my work, and sharing my work with your friends and family. You write lovely letters of encouragement and support and you, most importantly, post reviews so that other readers like you can discover and enjoy the series too. Thank you so much for all that you do and I hope you continue writing stories you love for a long time to come.

Thanks to Kimberly Benedicto, my lovely wife. I appreciate every attempt you made to keep me fed while I wrote and wrote and wrote. Thank you also for being Carnival's first reader. And your kind (blunt) criticisms. *Read: Why the hell would she do that?*

Thank you to my critique group The Four Horsemen of

the Bookocalypse! To Monica La Porta for her help with the Italian in particular (any remaining errors are my own!). To Angela Roquet for her thoughtful encouragement and Katherine Pendleton for reminding me to breathe when I start to panic.

Thank you to Christian Bentulan for another gorgeous cover. And Diana Hutchings for patiently answering all my questions about bullet wounds and severed arteries. Merci infiniment à Léa Tiralac for her help with the French dog commands.

Thanks to my assistant Alexandra Amor for formatting the book and for helping me prepare for its release, as well as keeping the show running behind scenes while I worked.

All my love to my street team. You guys continue to surprise me. You are always so excited about my work and spread the news far and wide. Thank you for being my biggest (and most appreciated) fans.

Last but not least, shout out to any typos who made it this far. You've survived three editing rounds, a formal copy-edit, five beta readers/critiquers, and 172 proofreaders. I'm truly impressed by your tenacity. Teach me your ways.

ABOUT THE AUTHOR

Kory M. Shrum is author of the bestselling *Shadows in the Water* and *Dying for a Living* series. She has loved books and words all her life. She reads almost every genre you can think of, but when she writes, she writes science fiction, fantasy, and thrillers, or often something that's all of the above. She has no idea why.

She can usually be found under thick blankets with snacks. The kettle is almost always on.

When she's not eating, reading, writing, or being a stay-at-home dog mom, she loves to plan her next travel adventure.

She lives in Michigan with her equally bookish wife, Kim, and their rescue pug, Charlemagne.

She'd love to hear from you!
www.korymshrum.com

ALSO BY KORY M. SHRUM

Dying for a Living series (complete)

Dying for a Living

Dying by the Hour

Dying for Her: A Companion Novel

Dying Light

Worth Dying For

Dying Breath

Dying Day

Shadows in the Water: Lou Thorne Thrillers (ongoing)

Shadows in the Water

Under the Bones

Danse Macabre

Carnival

Design Your Destiny Castle Cove series (ongoing)

Welcome to Castle Cove

Night Tide

Learn more about Kory's work at: www.korymshrum.com